D1035865

IRELAND

From the Act of Union · 1800
to the Death of Parnell · 1891

*Seventy-seven novels and collections
of shorter stories by twenty-two*
Irish and Anglo-Irish novelists

selected by

PROFESSOR ROBERT LEE WOLFF
Harvard University

A GARLAND SERIES

Tales
by the O'Hara Family

SECOND SERIES

The Nowlans
Peter of the Castle

John Banim

in three volumes
Volume II

Garland Publishing, Inc., New York & London
1978

For a complete list of the titles in this series,
see the final pages of Volume III.

This facsimile has been made from a copy in
the Yale University Library (In.B225.826t).

The volumes in this series are printed on acid-free,
250-year-life paper.

Library of Congress Cataloging in Publication Data

Banim, John, 1798–1842.
Tales, second series.

(Ireland, from the Act of Union, 1800,
to the death of Parnell, 1891)
Peter of the castle has also been attributed
to John and Michael Banim. Cf. Lib. of the world's best
literature, ed. by C. D. Warner.
Reprint of the 1826 ed. published by H. Colburn,
London; with new introd.
Includes bibliographical references.
CONTENTS: v. 1–3. The Nowlans,
and Peter of the castle.
1. Ireland—Fiction. I. Banim, Michael, 1796–1874,
joint author. II. Title: The Nowlans, and Peter of the
castle. III. Series.
PZ3.B225Tal   1978   [PR4057.B2]   823'.7   78-15993
ISBN 0-8240-3467-8

Printed in the United States of America

TALES

BY

THE O'HARA FAMILY.

SECOND SERIES.

COMPRISING

THE NOWLANS, AND PETER OF THE CASTLE.

——" Farewell the plumed troop and the big wars."
OTHELLO.

IN THREE VOLUMES.

VOL. II.

LONDON:

HENRY COLBURN, NEW BURLINGTON STREET.
1826.

LONDON
PRINTED BY S. AND R. BENTLEY, DORSET-STREET.

THE NOWLANS.

(CONTINUED.)

THE NOWLANS.

CHAPTER I.

JOHN NOWLAN *did* go home the next morning; but, after the final chances of the night, he might as well have staid where he was.

Riding very hard from the mean public-house where he had left Horrogan, he soon gained Long-hall. As he entered, the servants were in confusion. He enquired the cause, and learned that Mr. Long had retired to bed rather ill. Mr. Frank was also in his chamber, yet unacquainted, at Miss Letty's instance, with his uncle's accident; and she remained up in the drawing-room. Thither John hastened, agitated with all the occurrences of the day, and of the previous evening, excited with the magistrate's bumpers, fired and unsettled in his

feelings, though imagining himself fixed in a
great resolution; vehement, but without a plan.
As he sprang up the stairs, John vaguely apprehended that he sought this interview for the
purpose of at once breaking his dangerous fet-
ters; of at once telling Letty that he should
leave in the morning, and bidding her something like an eternal farewell.   When he burst,
rather abruptly, into the drawing-room, he did
not know that his features, manner, and whole
appearance, betrayed an irregular energy, the
natural effect of his fluttering state of nerve.
But Letty, roused by his entrance from her
sad reverie at the fire, saw what he could not
see ; saw the strange sparkling of eye, and the
briskness of mien and motion which bespoke a
panting purpose; and her catching of breath,
as he appeared, and her sudden rising from
her chair, showed how much she was startled.
" A thousand pardons, Miss Letty," John began, out of breath; " but you know I must be
alarmed at your uncle's sudden illness, and
very anxious to hear your opinion of it."

" You are very good, Mr. Nowlan ;" her
head cast down, as she pulled round her a
large shawl to hide the half-disposition of her
dress for bed; but, however the illness must

afflict us, I have hopes, as it is, unhappily, rather a constitutional one, that no serious danger now threatens my dear uncle."

"Thank God," said John; and there was a long pause; he standing with one hand rested on a table, she leaning against the mantelpiece; while the loud breathing of both audibly echoed through the stilled room. Suddenly he spoke again—" And good night, then, Miss Letty; *good-b'ye*, indeed; and remember me, as you know I wish to be remembered, to Mr. Long, in the morning." He advanced a step, his hand extended; she turned, fixed her glance on his now pale face and streaming eyes; grew pale in her turn, again looked away, and asked, "Why is this, Mr. Nowlan? do I rightly understand that you leave us in the morning? and if so, why in such speed?"

"I must go home to-morrow morning," he answered, speaking very slowly.

"Indeed? that is sudden and strange too," resuming her seat, to hide her faintness and trembling—" have we given you cause?"

"I have given myself cause, Miss Letty; I have done wrong in ever leaving my humble home; and the sooner I now return to it, the better for myself—so, good-b'ye." He stepped

closer, took her proffered hand, and, while his
tears wetted it, added—" and believe me most
thankful—most grateful—most bound to pray
—and bless—" his voice failed him.

" Good-b'ye, sir; I am sorry—I wish you
very well;" and poor Letty wept outright, and
snatching her hand, covered with both hands
her agitated face, while, as she sank back in
her chair, her large shawl fell in folds around
her.

John mutely gazed on her in a wild state of
feeling. It was, first, despair, then joyous dis-
traction. Yet one who could have watched his
face, would not, perhaps, have fathomed his
heart. A faint and inane smile only played
around his mouth as he thought " she loves
me—that fairest creature, that most elevated,
gifted, and noble creature, loves me ; and those
tears, those agonies—" Letty's passion rose
higher; she sobbed aloud ; the calm purpose of
despair, held even while he spoke, gave way
at once; every danger was forgotten ; or, if remembered, braved ; he darted to a chair by her
side, again seized her hand, and, "Yes, yes !" he
cried, " good-b'ye! good-b'ye for ever ! I go
home indeed to-morrow morning, Letty, for both
our sakes : I go, because to stay were crime and

madness—ruin and death, here and hereafter; because I love, because I love!" pressing her to him; " and because you love me! Do not turn and deny it; do not make the sin of my confession useless as well as heinous; do not take away from me the only palliation that Heaven will remember when I cry out and groan and grovel for a pardon; leave me but the certainty I now feel, the certainty that before I grew mad, I was honoured, blessed, cursed! blessed and cursed together with your love; leave me but that! the consciousness that when I fell the brightest angel out of Heaven tempted me; let me have so much to plead, and I will not be without hope in my remorse and repentance. I will not be without the hope that God, when he permitted the glorious temptation, saw how impossible it was for me to escape it! Letty, Letty, speak! say the word! I will have it from your lips! my only excuse, my only plea, my only hope! the only hope of my soul, though the eternal despair of my heart!—you love me! you love me! confess."

" I love you," she answered, as her trembling frame sank in his arms, " with my heart's full and first love."

Muttering raptures and ecstasies, and now solely swayed by the tumultuous triumph of youthful affection, John fell on his knees, his arms still around her neck, her cheek resting on his; and while Letty alone wept happy tears, he kissed her lips, her forehead, her closed eyes, her crimsoned neck, which the fallen shawl left more than usually shown. At this moment both started, for both thought a stealthy step came to the door. Letty suddenly caught up her shawl, and wrapped it in successive folds around her shoulders and waist: John drew back his hands, and they dropped at his side; but he did not, or could not, rise from his knees: he listened; the noise was not repeated: he grew assured with respect to that circumstance; but his checked ecstasy did not return; arrested, frozen, it allowed the sudden re-action of thought; his flushed face grew pallid, as he still knelt. Letty saw his eyes distend and fix on the fire; saw him gape; saw cold moisture teem from his forehead; heard him breathe laboriously; heard him gasp: and at last, as he uttered a low groan, John slowly lifted up his arms, cast them forward, and fell prostrate with them; his head coming so violently in contact with the massive fender, that blood trickled on the carpet.

This was a trying situation for a young creature like Letty. Love urged her to cry out for help; fear of observation, on his account and her own, stifled her voice. Apprehension for his safety, for his life, flung her on her knees by his side; yet a consciousness, if not a recollection, of the scene that had just occurred—of the new, embarrassing, even doubtful relation, they began to hold towards each other, distracted her efforts to serve him, and confused her speech. And yet she raised his head from the hearth, rested it on her knee, and began to staunch the slight wound with her handkerchief, as she cried—"For God's sake, Mr. Nowlan! rise, Sir, and retire, if you can!—Speak, at least, and explain this sudden misery! John! dearest John Nowlan, speak—was it illness—was it faintness? —are you better?—Gracious God! he will not, or cannot answer!—what is to become of me! no help near that I dare call upon;—and yet I must call up the house, John Nowlan, if you do not speak: ah! now you revive, and will be better."

"What's this?" he whispered, starting to

his knees—" I remember,"—groaning as he met her glance—" good night, Letty—farewell, indeed, for ever !" He arose, staggering.

" Sir !—Mr. Nowlan !"—in angry surprise— " explain this—explain"—correcting herself— " explain the cause of your embarrassment, your accident, I mean ;—was it sudden illness ?— giddiness ?—what do you mean ?"

" My vow ! my eternal vow." He hid his face, and leaned against the wall.

" You are not a priest !" she screamed; " you have not vowed a vow that makes your declaration to me—your attentions—your manner—the confession you have just extorted— Oh !—I could not comprehend your dark meaning while you spoke ! I thought it doubt of me or of my sentiments; any thing but that ! But you have not vowed a vow that makes all *this* insult, presumption, outrage to me, as well as to——answer, Sir !—you are not a priest !"

He walked to the middle of the room, bowed his head, crossed his arms on his breast, and answered: " Curse me, as I deserve; I cannot stand more accursed than I am, to God, to you, to man, and to myself: the vow is vowed; and, as you say, I have as presumptuously, as bar-

barously insulted you, as—as I have sunk my
own soul!" and he left the apartment. Letty
stood a moment gazing on the door through
which he had passed, and then fell. The female attendant, entering some minutes after,
found her insensible.

John slowly ascended to his chamber, locked
himself in, and sank in a chair. The next action of which he was conscious was to start up,
extinguish the light, and resume his seat in
darkness. If time be truly defined as a succession of ideas, for him whose brain holds but one
abiding idea, there is no time. John Nowlan, at
least, was not mindful of the lapse of this night
into the morning. Objects began to be discern-
ible around, and through the window; sharp
breezes shook his window-frame, and little birds
twittered by, and the rooks cawed loudly in the
adjoining trees, ere he became aware of the long,
dull, sleepless, tearless trance in which he had
sat. Near the window was his toilet-glass; his
eye, glancing over its surface, caught the reflection of his own face, dimly seen in the grey twilight, pallid, rigid, and stained with the blood
from his forehead. He started, as if, in his
shivering lonesomeness, he had detected the

visage of some fearful stranger.   He cast himself
on his knees, and, with his knuckles clenched
at his forehead, began to pray.

In some time he arose and packed up, in his
little trunk, the few things of his which were
to be found in the room.   Next, he bathed his
face in a basin of water, and arranged his dress;
and in a few moments sat to a table, and wrote
two notes, one to Mr. Long, another to Letty:
the first, pleading an urgent case of necessity
for his sudden absence, and expressing anxious
hopes for the speedy re-establishment of Mr.
Long's health, ended with warm and sincere
thanks for all that gentleman's kindness; the
second must express itself in its own words :—

" All you accused me of is true.   My avowal was sacrilege to God; my extorted acknowledgment, sacrilege to you : all the feelings I
dared hold to you, wicked, insulting, blasphemous.   Humbled in the dust, kneeling on the
knees of my heart to my God and my benefac-
tress, praying pardon and oblivion, I have but
one word to offer—not a word of extenua-
tion—that I despise—for with ten times as
much to plead, I am immeasurably guilty.   Let
me say the word, however.   I never concealed,
intentionally, that my vow had been made.   I

thought you knew it perfectly. No more do I presume to say. I go to my father's house. Farewell. Be assured, the life I shall lead— the expiations I shall offer—the discipline my offended church must impose—the heart that from this day must wither—that I spurn—that I cast into the blight—all this will avenge you. Farewell. When I may dare to pray in the humblest hope of being heard, your name shall ever ascend from my lips. Blessings, as many as my curses, be with you for ever !"

Having written his notes, he remained gazing through the window, until some slight noises told him the servants began to stir in the house. Then he stepped cautiously down stairs, met a kitchen-wench, gave her the notes, left directions to have his trunk sent after him, half walked, half ran to his humble home, and entered under its roof with an unusual show of vivacity.

Immediately after breakfast he set out for the house of his old reverend friend, Mr. Kennedy, often mentioned before in this story. His brow fell when the people there informed him that the clergyman had accompanied his bishop to Dublin, on business of moment, and was not expected home for many weeks. This

disappointment John thought grievous; and he
was right in thinking it so; much of his fate
was involved in it. He looked round for some
other spiritual adviser; his recollections or
likings proposed none to whom he could will-
ingly unbosom himself; and he determined to
spend in solitary self-examination and discipline
the time that must elapse before the arrival of
his best friend.

He shut himself up in his little study, and
prepared to lay his breast bare to Heaven. But
it was a place of distracting recollections; and
pleading to Peggy and his mother a preference
for his father's room, a busy removal of books,
shelves, and other furniture, ensued, and his
wish was soon accomplished. He at last sat
down to his task, most tremblingly anxious to
speed it; but his powers of self-abstraction
were not equal to his will; it was too near his
time of passion; nature refused to be so sum-
marily trampled down; the very feverish impatience of his purpose unfitted him for success;
and his first day and night produced nothing
but sullen reveries, traitorous recurrences, ar-
dent aspirations, and bitter, bitter tears.

In the middle of the next day, he reflected
that he was bound to make enquiries after the

health of Mr. Long: circumstances, to which that gentleman was a stranger, could not warrant a neglect that must seem so strange and ungrateful. He therefore despatched one of his father's men to Long Hall, instructing him to add an enquiry concerning the health of *all* the family. The messenger staid away much longer than was needful; John grew impatient for his return; he could do nothing, in the mean time, but watch him out of the window that commanded his path: he expected, hoped, in fact, something more than an answer to the questions he had sent; yet he dared not tell himself he did.

Towards evening, the man at last appeared, and John's anticipations were not proved vain. Miss Letty sent assurances that her uncle was better; and with these assurances, a note to Peggy, accompanying and explaining various rare patterns of gowns, frills, and caps; and another to John, enclosed in it, that, the young lady informed her fair friend, would tell Mr. Nowlan how to sow and cultivate certain flower roots, and slips, for which he had seemed anxious, and which were forwarded by his messenger. Peggy ran to John with the note; he retired to his room, and read as follows : —

" Rev. Dear Mr. Nowlan,

" The man will convey to you the pleasing news that my dearest uncle is not seriously ill and you can imagine what joy this must be to one who loves him better than her own father and mother—than any second being on earth. Many thanks for your kind enquiries.

" I send the Dutch tulip roots I promised you ; also, some specimens of the yellow picoté which I can warrant ; and the rare geranium slips you seemed to admire.   As the two first will demand all your care, you must study, out of the book of the London florist that accompanies them, the best mode of culture recommended.   Pray, accept, at the same time, a little portfolio containing a few drawings you used to flatter me about, particularly a carefully finished drawing of the first sketch you saw me make on the morning of our walk from your house to Long Hall.   The music of the wild and beautiful ballad of " Lord Ronald," and of other songs, which I believed you half asked from me, are also in the portfolio.

" I got your note : but, indeed, I do not understand it.   Of what could I " accuse" you ? Nothing that my calm recollections suggest ; nothing that you ever deserved ; nothing that

it must not have been as cruel as it was indeli-
cate for me to glance at. I say from my heart,
Rev. dear Sir, I have not, I never had, the
slightest reason to reproach you. Let the evening before last be eternally forgotten. I know
not what happened; I do not wish to know.
But whatever I said or did, must have been
caused by the weak and wandering state of
heart and mind into which I was thrown by the
sudden illness of him who merits and possesses
my undivided affection. So, instead of your
asking pardon from me, I ask it of you. Indeed I do, Mr. Nowlan, most sincerely. For
the slightest undeserved word that could have
caused you pain, I am—believe me I am—sorry
and afflicted. Therefore, in the name of good
feeling, and good sense, abandon every thought
of visiting upon yourself, in any such shocking
way as you hint at, or as the severity of your
religion may (if you wrongfully accuse your
heart) enjoin,—an imaginary error. Promise me
this, or else a knowledge of your continued intention will make me, as I ought to be, the true
sufferer, and humble and degrade me beyond
expression.

" In fact, we should both forget that evening ;
I repeat it again. I have had an undisturbed

day and night to reflect—perhaps more than
reflect—thanks to your prudent generosity—
and such is my opinion. We have both been
led astray by erroneous impressions ; no farther
does our fault extend ; let us show that the moment we are set right, we can act as becomes us.
It was all exceeding folly : and any vehement
words or resolutions about it would only be a
greater absurdity. Let us meet again as if it
had never occurred. That is the better way. I
will never believe that, in your breast or mine,
prepossession is stronger than reason. Come to
enquire after my dear uncle's health, whenever
you will,—as soon as you will—and one of us, at
least, shall prove it is not.

" Adieu, dear Rev. Sir. I enjoin the utmost
care to be paid to my scarce and beautiful tu-
lips : and pray burn this note : that is my last
and strongest request.

> " I am, dear Rev. Sir,
>> " With respect and esteem,
>>> " Your faithful friend,
>>>> " L. A."

John knew nothing of women ; he had never
associated with them ; this note astonished him
to excess ; ay, more, it mortified him, and
put him in a passion. What ! after all that

had occurred,—after all his high opinions of her—(and of himself he ought to have added) —was she but a coquette—did she say words she had never felt ? " Undivided affection !" and " above any second being on earth !" of whom were those things so deliberately spoken ? Then the tone of utter contempt in which she alluded to the past—to him : and her challenges to meet him again with such indifference ! He would meet her half-way, at least. He would prove, as fully as she could, that in his breast " prepossession was not stronger than reason."

Only two phrases of her letter at first divided his sentiments. One was, " thanks to your prudent generosity ;" *prudent !* Did this mean more than met the eye ? Did it contain, or hide, a reproach for his silence of one day ? and was she piqued with him ? The next passage was—" a day and night to reflect—*perhaps* more *than reflect :*" what " more ?"—His conjectures subdued him ; he saw her, for a moment, weeping away the night, alone in her chamber, and his own tears started at the picture.

Then he read her letter again ; and all that portion of it which sought to save him from future suffering, took full hold of his heart.

An idea of her self-devotedness, self-sacrifice, surprized him into admiration, gratitude, and a return of the deepest, tenderest love; he flung himself on his bed; detected the treacherous wandering; started up, and again and again, the groans of his young heart went up for relief.

We shall pass a few days, and accompany John to pay a formal visit at Long Hall, not in anger, nor yet in guilty impulse, but from a sedate conviction of the propriety, in every way, of such a step.

He found Mr. Long in his library, looking pale and shaken; but after some conversation, he found Letty in the drawing-room, looking more pale and shaken. Prepared for his appearance, she received him with a calm smile; and though blushes and tremors came in spite of her, she was able to conceal them from him. Frank sat by, his arm not yet well. The interview aimed at quiet vivacity, but was dull and overstrained. Frank rose to leave the room; John started, like a culprit, at his motion, and withdrew before him.

Letty's appearance shocked him to the soul; and though not a word had been spoken about it, John thought of nothing else on his way

home. Conclusions that he shrunk from drawing, but that he could not resist, seized upon
his mind. She was, indeed, the sufferer more
than he. Gracious God ! her suppressed feelings—her choked passion—her despairing love
—her love of him ! it was striking at her life.
She was dying !

He might assist her to triumph over her
malady : and his presence, rather than his absence, would be the best assistance. Constant
interviews, that would end in nothing, yet that
would accustom both to regard each other as
simple friends ; cheering conversation on topics
she delighted in ; exercise, picturesque walks
that she was now giving up ;—all this might
effect a cure, and he determined to be the physician. The notion of her weakness made him
strong ; made him confident ; forgetful of his
own weakness ; presumptuous.

Though he would not dream of again taking
up his abode at Long Hall, they met, therefore,
very often, and read or sang in the drawing-
room, or lectured on flowers in the garden, or
walked out, accompanied by Mr. Long or his
nephew, to sketch ; and John's hopes seemed
crowned with success. Blushes and embarrassment when they met, or sighs or reveries

when they were together, or faltering adieus,
or pressures of the hand, when they parted, gave
him, indeed, some uneasiness on his own account, as well as Letty's ; but still he was braced
and bold in virtue, and his constant prayers
seemed ever to be answered with a promise.

They had strayed, one evening, into a fine
solitary scene, Mr. Long with them, and Letty
made some pleasing sketches. Her uncle suggested that she and John should turn aside,
over an embankment, to look about for a
changed grouping of objects, which he believed
might form a still better sketch. Both hesitated : it was the first time, since the scene in
the drawing-room, they expected to be alone ;
at last, Letty suddenly gave her arm, and in a
few seconds they lost sight of Mr. Long, and
sauntered by the edge of a mountain stream.
Letty set the example of talking fast and much,
he tried to follow her : but they soon grew mu-
tually silent. They stept over a very narrow
part of the stream, and continued their walk on
the other side, now doubling towards the point
from which they had started. The view did
not answer Mr. Long's promises, and Letty
urged a speedy return to her uncle. It was
again necessary to cross the stream ; but as, at

the place they now paused, it could not be stept over by Letty, John proposed to carry her over: she refused, with a consciousness of manner that communicated itself to him; but catching herself in error, at once assumed much indifference, withdrew her dissent, and was lifted up in his arms.

The rash boy trembled under his feathery weight. As mere matter of course, her arm twined round his neck; and, burning in blushes, that for a moment overmastered her paleness, he had never seen her look so enchanting. With tottering limbs he walked to the edge of the stream; she called out to him to let her down, observing that he was not able to bear her across; and as she spoke, her eyes met his.

" Ay," he answered, " able to bear you across an ocean of fire!—Letty, Letty, the heart, not the limbs are weak,"—and, as he stept into the water, murmuring these words, his arms, in irresistible impulse, pressed her to his heart.

" Set me down, Sir!" she exclaimed, " whatever may be the consequence, set me down!" —he staggered among the sharp stones and rocks—" No, no," in another tone, " take care, take care of yourself, for mercy's sake."

When they gained the opposite bank, her head rested on his shoulder; tears streamed from her eyes; she sobbed, and made no effort to leave his arms. Maddened, distracted, he embraced her again; she started up, and with a sudden effort, walked towards the place where her uncle was. At the thought of her returning, alone, and unassisted, he ran after her, and kept by her side till she had come up to Mr. Long. The now gathering twilight hid the agitation of both; and John, making a confused apology, hastened home.

The next morning Letty sent, in a book carefully sealed up, the following note:—

" We are unmasked to each other. All our false pretences are torn away: all our false philosophy shown to be imposition. Now there can be but one course. Let us never meet again. Let seas, countries, oceans, worlds divide us. I can die away from you, as well as at your feet—and at your feet I should die if——No, no! let us never meet in this world again. With our common sufferings, let us retain the virtue that will give us hopes of meeting in another. That is all we have to look to. I am dying, and (though I have never noticed to you) your brow and cheek tell me the state of your heart.

Farewell. I loved, and I love you above the earth's promise, without you; above myself; but also above the thought of sacrificing you to the terrible vengeance of the stern religion you proffer to me; pardon the word, that you conscientiously and honourably believe in. This you already know—fully know—and, therefore, I may say it.—Farewell. We must fly to the world's extremities asunder. I will prevail on my dear, injured uncle to go immediately to— no matter where; you need not know that.— Attempt not to see me—dare not.—Save us! it is in your power to do so. Farewell till eternity."

After a day's imaginary calmness, John answered thus.

" The resolution you have taken was mine also. We shall, indeed, part unto eternity. But stir not you. Stay by your uncle's side; he needs your care, and is not in a state for travelling. To fly, and fly far, is alone my duty. And already I have taken measures to leave Ireland for Spain. The clerical relative you have heard me speak of will readily assist me; and I have written to him on the subject. Indeed he spoke of it before. I return the first present you ever gave

me, the little ring I found in my room; also
your books and drawings. The flowers I had
planted I have torn up by the roots, as I tear
up your memory: and I would not have them
bloom behind me, in my native country, in my
father's little garden, while no flower can ever
more spring up in my heart.

"You say you are dying. I believe, indeed,
neither of us shall long outlive this struggle;
but that will not be a crime; and if God so
wills it, and since you love me as you say, I do
not regret the prospect. We shall brave death
in the performance of our duty; and while our
memories remain pure after us on earth, death,
and the hope beyond the grave, will be our
reward. No more can be expected from human
hearts.

"Love me to the last, when I am away: I
shall so love you. Surely this can be no sin;
for, in proportion as I love you, will the sacrifice
of my love to my duties be great and acceptable.

"Ay, let us part, indeed; but not, as you
urge it, without a parting. Do not start nor
tremble. I have long reflected on this point;
and a glorious opportunity of beginning the sacrifice, a holy one for practising, together, the
self-triumph we are called on to make, presents

itself. I shall go, this evening, in a post-chaise with my sister Peggy, to Nenagh, so far on our way to Dublin : it will await me on the road, at the middle stile, a little after six o'clock. All my preparations are made. Meet me, accompanied by your brother Frank, at the stile, and let us walk and converse one half-hour together, your brother, my sister, you and I ; and then let me take your unimpassioned hand for the last time. You shall see me worthy of this indulgence, and I shall see you worthy of granting it. Farewell till six."

Having despatched this letter, John proceeded, amid the tears of his family, to complete his very last arrangements for the road. Towards evening, he called Peggy into his room, and asked her if Mr. Frank had yet proposed for her to her father ; Peggy, in an affliction he could not explain, and which alarmed him, replied in the negative. He was about to proceed in the brotherly strain he felt as his duty—for John was now full of duties,—when he recollected that Mr. Frank's arm had been ill since the very night they spoke on the subject; and with but a few delicate cautions, which Peggy still took very strangely, he put an end to the subject.

The hour of separation from his father and

mother arrived; it will be imagined for us.
Two men preceded him with his luggage to the
road-side. Peggy took his arm as he walked
from the threshold of his home. About half
way to the stile, she professed, in a hesitating
manner, to have forgotten something; said she
would return for it; and he walked on alone.

Inside the stile, he met Letty and her brother. The young gentleman carried a fowling-
piece, to have a shot, as he expressed it, at
whatever might come in the way. He also took
from a side-pocket a pair of travelling pistols, of
which he begged John's acceptance. The young
priest refused them, with a smile at their use-
lessness to him; but his friend was politely
pressing, saying, as his journey was a long one,
he did not know when they might be useful,
and John accepted them; laying them on a
bank where all were now sitting, in expectation
of Peggy's arrival.

The lovers began their interview in the very
way, indeed, they had sternly promised to each
other's breasts; and neither trembled until the
post-chaise was heard arriving, on the road near
them. John then expressed his surprise at Peggy's delay; and Frank clambered up an eminence to look out for her. But " she did not yet

come in view," he said, "although the twilight might hide her figure." Then looking in another direction, he cried out—" A fox ! I must have a shot at him !"—and disappeared before John or Letty could urge him to remain.

Upon thus finding themselves alone, they shook like condemned criminals. They were silent. They arose, and stept apart, affecting to be engaged in looking out for Frank or Peggy. The sudden report of Frank's fowling-piece was heard. Letty bounded as if its contents had been levelled at her heart—then tottered, and was falling. John caught her in his arms. Absolutely overpowered, she clung to him. Again he returned her embrace !

In but a few moments more he was rushing, haggard and wild, out of the little retreat. He had started from his blaspheming knees, tearing his hair, foaming,—a maniac. The pistols given him by Frank lay in his way. He snatched them up, with a cry of mad joy, and ran forward, in the impulse of but removing himself from her sight, and then putting an end to his own life. A stifled laugh sounded close to his ear—he turned, expecting to see standing palpable before him, the triumphant enemy of man. Maggy Nowlan, now showing no symptom of laughter, confronted him at the turn from the dell.

" Stop, priest John !" she cried, " I was lookin' for you to tell you a secret ; last night, your sister Peggy lost herself to a friend of yours, and they are now hard by together, an' she on her knees, beggin' him to make her an honest woman."

His random suspicions of the day burst in his already raging breast.

" Bring me to them !" he gasped.

" This way, then ;" and Maggy walked on.

" *Salve et benedicite*, brother," interrupted the steady tones of Friar Shanaghan, stopping his " poor grey," at the road-side, in view of John. The madman uttered another shout, sprang back to the road, stuffing the pistols into his breast, clasped the astonished old man by the hand, then seized his arm, and cried out—" Down from your saddle, Sir !—down, quickly !"

" Why, and whither, man ?"

" To do a good deed ! to save souls !—Heaven sends you ! down, down !—life and death are in it ! down !"

He forced him down, and the old friar, thus exhorted, allowed himself to be hurried along.

Again John met Maggy; again called on her
to lead the way.

"Only on one promise do I lade either of
you," she answered; "promise—swear!—that
you will not tell him I warned you."

"We swear by ten thousand heavens and
hells—go on!"

"There they are, then," resumed Maggy,
pointing to a gap in a field, as she retreated far
from the coming scene.

John dragged in the friar, and saw, indeed,
Peggy kneeling to Mr. Frank, and with the
wildest energy, urging him to something, while
he stood over her in an impassioned but stern
attitude.

"Villain!" screamed John Nowlan, bursting
between them; "right her this moment! here
is your own gift to make you," presenting the
pistols; "and here is the priest God has sent
to help you."

Peggy started, screaming, from her knees,
calling on him to hold his hand and his purpose; Frank, shrinking back, utterly confounded, asked what he meant. The friar laid his
hand on his arm. John sprang aside: "Touch
me not, sir!" he roared; "let no man venture
that! but proceed, in your duty, to make this

guilty pair man and wife; or, by the Heaven
we have all outraged, you shall be my victim,
before I shoot him and her, and then destroy
myself! Take her hand, seducer, villain! she
already wears a ring—that will do! take her
hand I say, or—"

"John Nowlan! brother!" interrupted Peggy, again dropping on her knees to him; "why
do you ask this? what terrible madness has
come over you?"

"The madness that is necessary for this!
Up, woman, and stand by his side! one of our
father's children, at least, shall have a good
name after this night, a patched-up good name,
may be, but no matter; up! or as sure as the
same mother bore us, I will kill you at my
feet!" He held the pistol to her head; it pressed her forehead; she sprang up; still pointing
the pistols at her and Frank, he continued to
roar for the office of the friar.

"Let the madman have his way," said
Frank coolly, after a pause, and he took Peg-
gy's hand; she struggled, and "Hear me,
John!" she cried; "I wish not this, I—"

"Not another word!" he exclaimed. All
further opposition seemed not only useless, but
really dangerous, to a degree too horrible to

contemplate; in vain did the friar try to exert his voice; in vain did Peggy add—"Brother, brother, you are ruining me!" At the maniac's still increasing threats, the old ecclesiastic drew out his missal, and, in a few moments, Mr. Frank and Peggy Nowlan were married.

"That will do, I wish ye joy!" resumed John, when the sudden ceremony was over: " good-b'ye, sister; brother Frank, good-b'ye," shaking their hands; " and now for my own luck; you'll hear of me if ye do not hear from me: good night!"

He was rushing from them: "John! John!" cried Peggy, "throw down the pistols;" she ran after him, and a second time fell at his feet.

He stopped a moment. His glaring eyes darted into hers. He flung the pistols far over her head; kissed her cheek, and finally disappeared from his overwhelmed sister. A few bounds brought him back to the poor Letty. She reclined, senseless, on the earth. He caught her up in his arms, muttering—"And now no tie but that one which crime has tied, which hell binds close! No lot but your lot, my victim! Here lowly you shall not lie, to be spurned and scorned of all, and I the undoer!

Come, I can yet sacrifice myself with you! The father's and mother's curse, the curse of that church whose fallen minister I am, the shouts of the world, shall follow me ; still we shall be one ! Come, Letty !" he ran with her to the post-chaise, lifted her into the seat his sister Peggy was to have occupied ; was whirled off on his road to Dublin, and seven years elapsed before any positive tidings of John Nowlan reached his native place, with the exception of a circumstance known only to the old clergyman, Mr. Kennedy, which that gentleman never divulged.

CHAPTER II.

HAD we to rehearse a story woven out of our own brains, imagination, unable or unwilling to recognize any plausibility in the stern truths of real life, would, perhaps, have rejected the sudden catastrophe of the last chapter; and, even allowing John and Letty finally to commit crime, have invented some more gradual progress to it. The lovers of beautiful fiction may exclaim against their fall at the very moment when they had braced themselves in virtue, and only met to prove to each other how straight and how firmly they could walk their path. But human nature, such as it is known to those who study it, must be an appeal from possible censure in this instance. Temptations that have long borne hard, and often made a distinct, though unwelcomed impression, are not to be set at bay by any other means than total estrangement from the object or opportunity

that has set them on. In the presence of that
object or opportunity, WILL, however previously made up and determined, may, in one second,
be dethroned and trampled down. We prose,
or we sermonize ; but, in illustration of the oft-
repeated, though oft-forgotten theory, cannot the
sagest reader recollect any slight case in which he
has made the identical slip he had spent much
preparation to avoid ? Crime is not meant ; the
most trivial counteraction of " re-resolved" reason, by a momentary pressure of old temptation, will suffice—indeed, more than suffice ;—
for, as it is ordained that the greater the sin
the greater shall be the temptation to commit
it ; and, as in the instance recorded, the sin and
the passion accordingly balanced each other ;
so, if but an ordinary infatuation has over-
thrown the wisest plans of the wisest reader,
an extraordinary one must have had equal
power, more power, over the best resolves of
this poor boy and girl.

At the utmost speed the unhappy young pair
were whirled in the post-chaise to Nenagh. We
believe Letty was half sensible of being lifted
by John into the vehicle ; but she made no re-
sistance ; she even showed no consciousness.

He held her in his circling arms, as they now
sat together; still she remained passive and
motionless; her head hanging towards the corner of the chaise, or falling on his shoulder.
Night closed; he could not see her; and yet
she stirred not. It suddenly struck him that
she was dead; but he did not start at the
thought; nor call out to stop the chaise; nor
utter a cry; the wretched youth only smiled to
himself. His feeling could not be understood,
were it even well-defined; it is left then, in the
darkness and confusion that gave it birth.

Thus, without moving or speaking, they
gained Nenagh. The horn of a night coach
was heard coming to the inn-door. The driver
told him he could have two seats for Dublin,
and asked should he change his luggage from
the chaise. John calmly answered him. The
man re-appeared, saying the coach was about to
start, and offering his assistance to remove the
lady. John fiercely turned from him, caught
her up, suddenly and unassisted, and with some
difficulty, removed her himself.

" Is the lady very sick, Sir ?" enquired a
surly old gentleman, as, after much squeezing
among well-wrapt knees, broad shoulders,

elbows squared, and heads wearing white night-caps, John placed her in the corner of a " six-inside."

" Very, Sir ;" imagining he answered a com-miserating person.

" Then wouldn't it be more comfortable to you and her, Sir, to travel alone, than for us to travel with you ?" continued the man.

" Answer your question your own way, Sir," growled John Nowlan.

" Guard !" cried the knowing stage-coacher, thrusting his head out at the window. The moving woolsack appeared at the door.

" Do you mean that I am to travel in your coach to Dublin, with a sick and dying body cheek by jowl with me ?"

" Rascal !" exclaimed John, and was starting from his seat to seize the old barbarian, when, to his utter surprize—horror—Letty roused herself—caught his arm, and said, scarcely ar-ticulate—" I am not very ill, Sir ; I am only—only"—and burst into tears.

Even the crabbed selfishness of a cruel-heart-ed old man melted at her voice and her sorrow ; apologies were instantly made to John and her ; the pert voices of two younger passengers broke out in assurances of satisfaction and good wishes; the guard disappeared to his place, the horn sounded, the driver's whip cracked, and John proceeded on his journey, half-thinking, even amid the chaos within him—" So this is our first welcome among mankind."

After Letty had spoken, she sank back in the corner of the coach, covering her face, although it was pitch-dark, with some loose drapery; and did not utter another word during the remainder of the journey: nor did John once address her. He did not now even hold her in his arms: and she seemed to shrink from his touch.

The night, the dreary, horrible night wore on, unnoticed and uncared for. Without weariness, without a tear, without a thought, John sat by the side of his poor partner in guilt, in misery, and in despair. If, as his unwinking eyes strained through the blank at the window, perception brought, now and then, a notice of any thing to his mind, it was only to encourage the mood that was upon him. The howling of the midnight wind over the black bogs of Tipperary; the gusty beating of the rain against the glass; the feeble glimmering of lanterns at the doors of miserable inns or cabins, as the coach stopped to change horses, and the miserable, half-dressed, ghost-like, figures, roused out of their sleep, who vaguely appeared and disappeared in the dreary light and engulphing darkness; such circumstances or sights, if at all observed by John Nowlan, could only tend to answer, in an outward prospect, the inward horror of his soul.

When the first ray of grey dawn entered the coach windows, he found himself pulling his hat over his eyes; then glancing at Letty's face, which was still covered, and then fearfully around him, into the faces of the other passengers:—and thought of her, because for her, now at last began to break his trance, and, folding his arms hard, he fell back in his seat.

The two younger passengers awoke, yawning, shrugging, and pulling off, one a night-cap, the other a smart fur-cap; and turned to him and Letty, expressing hopes that they had found themselves comfortable during the night. John scarcely answered, Letty did not breathe. They spoke to each other of causes pending in Chancery and the Common-pleas and the King's-Bench; and of "latitats," writs, declarations, pleas, plaintiffs, and defendants; plainly indicating, to any one that would pay

attention, that they were two rising young
attornies from Limerick, going up to term :
but our poor friends were still abstracted, and
the surly old fellow was still asleep, or, the
better to avoid any talk of his former rudeness,
pretended to be so. They changed the topic,
and—in the acceptation of the term among
young Limerick attornies who knew town—
waxed witty: evidently exhibiting, with a
polite intent, to interest the lady whose face
they could not see. Practical joking, (now that
people began to pass along the road) which, to
any one that can enjoy it, is the life of an Irish
stage, went on among those of their friends
and acquaintances who, as they expressed
it, had " endorsed the coach," and they
contributed as much as they could : still no one
but themselves took the least notice of their
cleverness. John scarce heard or heeded any
thing ; or, if he did hear and heed, it was only
to loathe it. Even tranquil, rational happiness
he would have loathed ; and how must he have
felt affected by mere trifling? The chastest
wit would have played round him in vain ; how
must he have relished buffoonery ?

The coach entered Dublin. Streets and high
houses closed around him ; other night-coaches

passed him coming in from the country; or day-coaches whisked by starting from town. In the trading and manufacturing district of the metropolis by which he entered, that of James-street and Thomas-street, groups of " operatives" were already in motion towards the places of their daily occupation; the early cries were sung or screamed aloud; carts, drays, and such vehicles ground their way over the stones; from different public-houses, the voices of very late or very early tipplers now and then came in vehement accents; every thing gave him the novel sensation of a morning in a great city. To the young person who, for the first time, experiences such a sensation, it brings— no matter how calm may be his mind and breast, how certain and soothing his prospects —depression rather than excitement; a bleak strangeness seems around him: he doubts and shrinks more than he admires or wonders; he is in a solitude, unlike the remote solitudes he has quitted; in solitude with men, not nature; without the face of nature to cheer him. But, added to this common depression, John Nowlan felt remorse for the past, despair of the present, terror of the future. First—his distracted speculations only made on his own account,—he

saw himself sunk in crime, an outcast among
men, poor, hopeless, helpless;—his eye glanced
to Letty, and he started to find his thoughts
occupied without her; he shuddered to behold
her at his side; to behold her torn by him from
rank, name, and affluence, and dependent on
him, alone, for future protection, for mere existence; on him who was unable to protect himself; who had no earthly means of shielding
his own outcast head from poverty, shame,
ruin; and who dared not now even call on God
to interpose between him and his crime and
punishment.

The passengers left the coach, and the waiter
often invited him to descend before John heard
or understood the request. Still he was obliged
to take Letty in his arms into the hotel: she
appeared almost as helpless as ever. The
young attornies and the cross old gentleman
eyed him and her from top to toe, as he bore
her through the hall; and, had his observation
been acute, he might have seen many a leer
and grimace upon their features, as well as
those of the waiters, called up by his clerical
dress, primitive air, and questionable situation.
Again the waiters winked at each other as, in
a tone that showed little of the self-confidence

of an experienced traveller, he requested a bed-chamber for the lady. A female attendant appeared, however; Letty retired with her; and then John rapidly left the Royal Hibernian hotel, Dawson-street, in prosecution of some plans he had calmly, as he thought, within the last few hours, determined upon. Turning down Grafton-street into College Green, and thence over Carlisle Bridge into Sackville-street, he gazed from house to house, only anxious to find open shops of a particular kind, and uninterested by the fine city prospect about him, indeed unconscious of it. Few shops of any kind were, however, yet opened; and for nearly two hours he walked about the streets, awaiting the leisure of the Dublin shopmen and apprentices, who had no motive to leave their well-esteemed beds before the hour prescribed by their masters. At last they began to take down their window-shutters, and John entered a ready-made clothes shop; purchased a suit that did not show a bit of black; put it on in the back parlour, into which, at his request, the young man had ushered him, and walked out among the awaking crowds of Dublin, so far disguised from their most dreaded scrutiny.

Beautifully closing the perspective of Sackville-street, he saw the steeple of George's Church ; he knew it must belong to a Protestant place of worship ; and, in furtherance of his most important plan, John hastily walked towards it. Arriving before the church, (a little architectural gem,) he proceeded to make enquiries for the residence of the clergyman, which he supposed must be in the neighbourhood ; and, after much trouble, was at last directed to his house.

At his request for an interview upon particular business, an amiable old gentleman appeared. In a few words, which sounded with a startling abruptness and energy, he stated that between himself and a young lady, his companion in town, crime and misery had taken place : that they were obliged to fly from their friends in the country, had arrived in Dublin that morning, and now besought the clergyman to confer upon them the only consolation their sorrow and remorse could admit ; to marry them. After some questions that evinced a due sympathy in the case, the clergyman said he should but attend, with all despatch, to the necessary preliminaries, and at once meet his request. John's face showed the only gleam of relief that had lately visited it. He pressed the old gentleman to name an hour ; " Twelve o'clock," he was answered. " Could it not be sooner ?" Impossible. " Well, he was most thankful :" and he rose to take his leave, without naming a place of meeting. The clergyman now spoke of seeing him and his lady in the church. John clasped his hands, and begged him not to insist on that ; the poor young lady was too ill, she could not stir out. The clergyman paused ; but, with a benevolent smile, said he would, in that case, call at the hotel ; and his suitor, eloquent in thanks, left the house.

" It is the only step I can now take," thought John, as he walked rapidly through street after street, he did not know where,—" the only one : she is a Protestant, and this will help to bring her to some peace with herself ; it will give some little relief, no matter how little. According to her creed, my vows can form no bar ; and even the laws of the land make it a good marriage. As for myself, and my own creed and obligations, why, it is but heaping blasphemy upon blasphemy, sacrilege upon sacrilege. Well, no matter about me ; I have destroyed her, and the least satisfaction I can offer is my own destruction at her feet ; and I am bound to cheer her present despair, and to guard her future lot,

by any means, earth, heaven, or hell, can suggest. I have chosen my fate ; I have made it,
and it must be gone through ; it shall be gone
through : from this hour let me be as forgotten
by myself, as I am shaken off by the world ; let
me live and die only for her ; suffer and perish
here, and for ever, so I but help her to a consolation. Come, there are other things to do ;
come, come, no drooping, no tardiness, no neglect of a moment."

It was but nine o'clock : he had to wait
three hours ere he could meet Letty with the
clergyman, and without him he dared not meet
her ; to that resolution he had tied down his
soul. But she must not be left uninformed
about him, in the mean time. So he strove to
retrace his steps into the more bustling parts of
the town ; enquired his way to a tavern, called
for breakfast, of which he could not touch a
mouthful ; seized a sheet of paper, wrote her a
line, saying, that he was engaged on business
which concerned them both, and which would
not allow him to wait on her till noon ; sent it
by a messenger procured by the waiter ; paid
for the untouched breakfast, and once more sallied forth into the streets.

To a goldsmith's shop John next bent his

steps, and asked for a wedding-ring. The man enquired the size; John recollected the ring he had so long worn round his neck, and so lately returned, selected one that he believed was about its compass, purchased it, together with its guard, clasped both in his palm, and amid the titters of the shopman and his boys, hurried out.

More than two hours were yet to elapse, before he could face towards the hotel. Again he wandered, he did not know nor care whither. Passing through a private street, a person, he thought he should recognise, stopped at a hall-door opposite to him, and knocked. Another look convinced him; it was, indeed, his old reverend friend and relative, Mr. Kennedy. While he looked, and as the door opened, the clergyman started and glanced towards him. John felt as if cleft by a thunderbolt. His face turned down, he expected every instant the approach of his old guide and patron; but it seemed that Mr. Kennedy refused to believe the suggestion of John's identity, which his first glance and start intimated; the changed dress, the unlikely situation, must have baffled him, for the door sounded as if heavily shut to. John ventured to peep up; the clergyman had retired into the house. He turned, walked a few steps very slowly, gained the corner of a cross street, there began to run forward with all his speed, got into other streets, still more private and silent, without knowing it, upon the Circular Road, thence into the Phœnix Park, and under shelter of a clump of trees, there cast himself upon the grass.

It would be superfluous to display his feelings ; every reader will comprehend them. He was roused from his trance by a near clock striking eleven, and the chimes for a quarter. Starting up, and examining his watch, he saw, indeed, he had but three quarters of an hour to get to the hotel, and keep his most important appointment. He staggered to the gate of the Park, enquiring his way to Dawson-street. The people told him he was very far away from it. Again he ran along the Circular Road ; found himself in the town ; turned into street after street, without asking any proper direction, or without thinking of a hackney coach : as he rushed by a stand of them, however, a Dublin jarvey hailed him, and after some trouble made him understand the nature of the service offered. John gladly bounded into the crazy machine ; gained the steps of his hotel a few minutes

before twelve; looked up and down the street
for the clergyman; precisely at the appointed
moment saw him approach; accompanied him
into a waiting-room, and then, pausing to
compose himself, slowly ascended to Letty's
chamber.

He tapped at her door; no voice sounded in
answer: he tapped again, all was silent: seizing the handle in much alarm, he entered,
and, at the remote end of a large apartment,
saw her kneeling, her back turned, in earnest
prayer.   He started, and stood motionless.
Letty did not seem aware of his presence, but,
her hands clasped, and her head raised, continued to pray. Still John stood without moving;
without a loud breath; but he shook from top
to toe; and, his feelings at last exhausting him,
he staggered against the wall.   Then she looked
round, and, seeing him, buried her face in the
bed.   He manned himself, stept softly towards
her, gently took her hand, placed in it the wedding-ring, and in a solemn tone said, "The
Protestant clergyman is in waiting."

She looked at the ring, again hid her face,
groaned dolefully, but, in a few seconds, rose
up, snatched a white veil that lay near her,
threw it over her head and neck, and, without

venturing a glance at John, took his arm, and walked with him to the waiting-room.

The moment the door opened she curtsied, profoundly and lowlily, not raising her eyes from the ground, and advanced with John into the middle of the floor, both scarce able to move. The good clergyman, fully understanding the scene, spoke only few words, and those few of the gentlest accents, but at once opened his book, and performed the marriage service; his servant standing by as a witness. John and Letty did not know the ceremony was over, when, taking their hands, he caused them to confront each other, as he said, " Salute one another, my poor children; wife, behold your husband; husband, behold your wife."

Letty at last looked up, pale, shivering, and in blinding tears; she saw John stand with extended arms: shrieking, she cast herself upon his neck, and was clasped to his despairing heart, and their united sobs were soon echoed by the clergyman: until, as he tried to lead the sinking girl to a seat, she dropped, fainting, at her husband's feet.

When recalled to her senses, the former scene was renewed. The poor young pair again clung to each other, sobbing aloud, and

continuing to pour forth the first shower of
blessed tears that had come to melt the hardness
of their sorrow. Now and then Letty mur-
mured, "I knew it—I expected it.—I knew
you would immolate yourself, John, to your
wretched Letty.—I knew I was to be your
ruin !"—and he only replied—" My joy ! my
only joy and hope, you mean !—my only life—
my pride—my own Letty—my wife ! my wife,
dearly loved, and honoured for ever !"

The clergyman, again taking their hands,
withdrew. Hours lapsed while they still remained weeping in each other's arms. It was a
miserably happy nuptial day ; a day and evening of delightful anguish ; of terrible enjoy-
ment. She clung to him, now in a sense of virtue somewhat restored, as her sole earthly good ;
—all other good—every one and every thing
lost for him ; and a hope of the future, by his
side, springing up in her heart : he clung to
her with a conscience unrelieved, a remorse un-
soothed, a future uncalculated or dreaded, and
yet with a surpassing pity and love, an oblivion of self that humanized even the black visage
of despair, and made him determined, if not
content, to think this world and the next " well
lost" upon her bosom. He felt the joy of fren-

zy, the secret of despair, that sends the poor suicide to the bed destined to be drenched in his blood, smiling upon the hard-crammed pistol, which, at a certain hour, is to give him his supposed triumph over misery.

CHAPTER III.

THEY did not stir out for days, having no business, and totally uninterested about the attraction of their novel situation in a large city. John further felt unwilling to go out, lest he should meet Mr. Kennedy. From morning to night they sat, then, by each other's side; almost as silent, too, as they were inactive ; for not a word was spoken of the past or the future ; not a word about Letty's uncle, or about John's family, or the vows he had broken, or the common ruin of both. They even thought very little ; they were afraid to think. But, of the two, Letty thought most. As John had anticipated, she looked with no horror on his entering into the marriage state, in the face of obligations her conscience did not represent as binding; and Letty hoped her uncle might yet half forgive her elopement, and that John, aided by his friendship and in-

terest, might get on in the world. She took it
as granted, that, with his priest's vows, he had
changed his religion; the selecting a Protestant clergyman to marry them, confirmed her;
he had talents of, she believed, the first order;
some learning too; a manner and address calculated to fascinate; her uncle certainly liked
him; her brother Frank admired him; and, on
the whole, poor Letty's heart began to lighten
with hope; and, upon the first afternoon John
left her alone, she wrote two letters, one to Mr.
Long, another to Frank, confessing her marriage, praying pardon and mercy, and throwing
herself and her husband on their indulgence.

John went out in a different frame of mind.
For him there was no hope. He had not
given up his religious creed. He was still a
Roman Catholic: nay, according to the ordi-
nance of his church, and his own continued belief, still a Roman Catholic priest, living in a
monstrous state of sin, against all laws and
authority. Letty might suppose they were
married; he knew they were not married; he
knew they never could be: and though he
indulged her illusion, partly in furtherance of
his plan to sacrifice every thing to her happiness—his own thoughts, feelings, despair, the

truth, as well as himself—still he distinctly
felt, that while, in his own person, he stood a
renegade, a giver of dreadful scandal, a blasphemer, an outcast, and a marked sheep, she
led with him a life of partaken sin, and was,
in fact, no more than his mistress. Do what
he might, he could not prevent that. Immolate himself as he might, he believed he dared
never call her his wife; and his blood curdled at
the thought. It was the most horrible thought
of all, because it involved her; because, even
while he gave himself up to ruin for her sake,
she really derived no advantage from the sacrifice : he could not pray to God to bless her as
a married woman.

But, upon this day, he walked into the
streets with an additional cause of despair. A
voice had called him forth to think in solitude—
a voice he durst not resist—the awful one of
the future. It fell on John's heart like the
mutter of approaching desolation. He heard
it coming on, as the spell-bound in a hideous
dream await, wordless, and shivering, the progress of some chimera monster, whose grasp
is to crush and destroy. He knew not the
world, no more than the world knew him ;
and where to face, or how to turn himself

for the support—ay, the common support—of
the unconscious partner of his crime, John had
no more notion than a sprawling infant in the
streets might have how to escape the cart-wheel
that rolled on to grind over his little helpless
carcass. Yet there she was by his side; a
young, gentle, delicate creature, reared in luxury and elegance; unacquainted with even the
name of want: and as he turned, in miserable
smiles, to walk out and think of her and for
her this day, he found, after settling his hotel
bill, that of the unusually ample purse supplied
by his poor family for his voyage to Spain,
only a few pounds were left. Willing he was
to exert himself; but how? His nerves strained
to be set to work; but at what?

He wandered in the direction whither he had
been led upon the first morning of his arrival in
Dublin, and once more entered the Phenix Park.
Seeking one of its wild little solitudes, he sat
down, determined to think. Deep as was his despair, no extravagance was now in his mood or his
actions. He did not, as before, cast himself on
the ground, nor groan, nor shed a tear. The
wretch, when his death sentence is pronounced,
may shrink, or faint away; yet he can afterwards walk firmly to the gallows, and ascend it

without much visible emotion; and thus was John Nowlan at present sobered, by familiarity with the fate, which, at its first view, made him frantic.

Calmly, therefore, he sat down to reflect and plan. The impulse to throw himself upon his knees and pray, more than once occurred, but he checked it. From him, he believed, prayer would not only be blasphemous, but useless. Before he durst breathe one aspiration to heaven, his present connexion with Letty must be dissolved and that was impossible.

It also occurred to him to write home for assistance to his mother, or to his sister Peggy; but a second thought decided against this step too. He had separated himself from them as well as from God. He could no longer be any thing to them, nor they to him. He must struggle through his fate, without a friend on earth or in heaven. " Ay," he added, " I have made my bed, and must lie on it."

Centring his thoughts, then, on what he might possibly do by himself, he got before him, with more method than a few weeks previously he could have done, his present situation, his chance of future employment, and the best steps to be taken in setting himself to work. Pounds, shillings, and pence, were included in his calculations; he even took out a pencil and a piece of paper, emptied his purse into his hand, and summed up how long, according to a certain system of economy, he had a chance of not starving, before he should succeed in obtaining a situation.

After hours of patient and minute arrangement, he arose, determined on a little train of action. Alarmed by the extravagance of the hotel bill, he first resolved to seek some more humble place of residence. As he slowly walked homeward, through an outlet called Phibs-borough, notices of " Furnished Lodgings" caught his eye, posted on the windows of some small, but neat and cleanly-looking houses. He entered more than one; even here the terms seemed too high for his means. At last he inspected a single room, accommodated with a turn-up bed, which, in the day-time, was contrived to look like a sofa ; and though he disliked the persons who showed it, and the room itself, neat and tidy as it was, still the rent came within his views, and John engaged the lodgings, provided his lady should like them.

Proceeding still homeward, he debated how he should dispose of his watch, as he had de-

termined to add whatever it would produce **to**
his little stock-purse; indeed, it was already included in his calculations. Knowing little of
the trade of pawnbrokers, he thought his best
way would be to offer the article at a watch-
maker's, and he was looking out for a shop of
this description, when a placard of " Money
lent," attracted his notice. The announcement
puzzled him in the first instance; he was really
simple enough to debate the question of its
being a benevolent offer to assist the needy :
at all events he entered the house, handed his
watch at the counter, and received for it about
a third of what he had calculated. But then
he understood this was only a loan ; and trying
to feel contented, he hurried to Dawson-street,
most anxious about breaking to Letty, in the
best manner, his proposed change to Phibsborough ; uneasy, on her account, at his long absence, and, in the midst of all his blacker feelings, experiencing the tenderest yearning of the
heart, once more to see before him, and to clasp
in his arms, the poor devoted one who sat so
solitary in her chamber, dependent on him alone
for society and happiness.

Letty met him at the door of her apartment,
with outstretched arms, and a happier face and

freer manner than she had lately shown; her mind was lightened by writing her letters to her uncle and brother, and, as we have seen, hope fluttered in her heart. She had made her toilet, too, with more than usual care; John saw her dressed in one of the gowns *he* had purchased for her; altogether, while she looked perhaps more beautiful than ever, his feelings for her took a peculiar turn of fondness and devotion; and he folded her to his breast in murmurs of melancholy delight.

As evening approached, he studied to shape, in the most delicate way, the announcement of a change of abode; but the words stuck in his throat: he knew the lodgings he had selected were too humble for Letty's former rank, tastes, and comforts; and he durst not explain why she was not to be introduced to better lodgings; he durst not speak to her of pecuniary matters yet.

But Letty saved all his feelings on this subject. She had reflected as much as he during the day, and started her own plans, and taken her own resolutions.

" Dearest John," she said, as they sat side by side before dinner, " perfect confidence should exist between all married persons, and

especially between us, on account of our peculiar situation. You know I have no property
in my own right, or at my own immediate dis-
posal, and I know you are similarly circum-
stanced; and until our friends think of forgiving and assisting us, of which I do not despair,
whatever little funds we possess between us
should be known to both, and all placed in
your hands: so, dear John," as she hid her
face on his neck, " keep this little purse for
me; it is the amount of a half-year's pocket-
money allowed by my generous uncle, and I
brought it out upon that evening—the evening
we met—to apply it to some particular purposes;
—now we may surely use it ourselves."

He put up the purse without an observation·
—" And I have been thinking, too, how very
expensive this place is; you must, every way,
have already spent much money, dear John;
and the sooner we leave it for a humbler abode
—a very humble one—(you know, though lately
accustomed to luxury, my early life, at my father's, was thrifty and humble enough)—why,
John, the sooner that step is taken, the better.
We can await, anywhere, answers to my letters."

The same evening they occupied the single
apartment at Phibsborough.   When Letty first

entered it, John did not see her strange glance around; he only saw the smile she assumed as he turned to consult her features, and heard the cheering tone in which she compelled herself to admire the little thriftily-contrived room, and say it even went beyond her expectations, and was a state-room compared with that assigned to herself and three of her sisters at Mount Nelson.

But, notwithstanding Letty's manner and expressions, John continued to dislike, on her account, and indeed on his own, the room, and the house, and the people of the house, and every thing connected with it and them. His dislike of the very first day increased each day he remained; and yet he could not exactly tell why. It was not a very wretched house, and they were not ill-conducted or disreputable people; on the contrary, their abode and themselves bespoke independence, even comfort; and yet he had an indefinable notion that it was all mean, pinching economy, miserly comfort, unwarranted neatness and propriety; cold, heartless, worthless independence. It more overpowered him with ideas and apprehensions of poverty, than could a scene and group of squalid misery; and he feared the same impression would be made on Letty.

Although very small, containing, indeed, but four rooms altogether, every inch of this house had been made the most of; nay, over-occupied, over-attended to, over-done, in fact. From his window John looked into a little yard, around which were various wooden sheds, clumsily constructed in his evening leisure hours, by the old man of the establishment, assisted by as old a helper, a kind of jack-of-all-trades in the neighbourhood, and composed of all the scraps of boards and staves both could pick up, here and there, without paying for them. There was a little shed for coals, another for turf, another for ashes, another for odds and ends; another for "case of necessity;" and in the middle of the yard rose an impoverished grass plat, from which a sickly laburnum tree vainly strove to draw moisture for its scanty boughs and leaves. Below stairs, in the parlour, was the bed of the old couple; a daughter and a niece slept in the kitchen; and next to John's room, was another chamber "to be let." Each apartment was barely furnished, (and yet furnished) with articles selected, from time to time, wherever they could be found cheapest, of the old-

est known fashion, and all out of suit with one
another; yet all shining and polished from incessant care, into a presumptuous appearance
of respectability. An oil-cloth, composed of
three different scraps, of different patterns,
spread over the little hall, or passage, from the
street-door; a shame-faced attempt at a hall
lamp, suspended by the old man's peculiar
contrivance, dangled so low as to oblige one,
at the risk of one or two shillings for a new
green glass, to stoop under it, or walk round
it; and the little narrow stairs boasted a strip of
carpet, half as narrow as itself, patched up, like
the oil-cloth, darned over and over, like the
heels of all the old fellow's stockings, and yet
absolutely looking smart from endless brushing
and dusting every day, and shaking and beating once a week.

The carpet of John's own room was an extraordinary patch-work of diamond bits of cloth,
showing every colour in the rainbow, and each
no bigger than the corner of a card. His sofa-
bed was covered, during the day, with stamped
calico of a venerable pattern, half washed out;
his one window had a curtain of a different pattern, and his five chairs, covers still diversified.
His one table was of old mahogany, dark even

to blackness, and shining as a mirror; his chest of drawers was of oak, more ancient still, and also glittering so as to put him out of patience; his corner cupboard pretended to be Chinese; six high-coloured, miserable prints hung in black frames, and at the most regular distances round the room, of which three sides were papered, and one wainscot; but the old people had ventured on one modern article, in the shape of a long narrow chimney-glass, set in a frame of about an inch deep, and presenting to the eye about as faithful a reflection of the human face, as might a river or a lake with the wind blowing high upon it; nay, a row of flower-pots were placed inside the window, in a curious frame-work; as if to show a wanton exultation in the midst of this scene of beggarly contrivance, flowers had actually been prostituted in its service, and Nature's rarest perfumes deemed well employed in scenting its shreds and patches, and its crazy "fragments of an earlier world."

" Poor flowers!" sighed Letty, after she had given them one first and only look; " poor flowers! what brought ye here?"

The old man, who had some petty situation of thirty or forty pounds a year in some public

office, was upwards of seventy-five years, tall,
shrivelled, stooped in the neck, ill-set on his
limbs, and with a peculiar drag of one leg, which,
from certain reasons, and taken with other things,
rendered him very disagreeable to John. He
was obliged to be up every morning at seven, in
order to reach his office, or place of occupation,
by eight ; and he might be heard creeping about
the lower part of the house, making the parlour
and kitchen fires, to save his daughter and
niece so much trouble ; cooking his own solitary
breakfast, his fat wife lying in bed ; and then
cautiously shutting the hall-door after him, as,
rubbing his hands, he tried to bustle off in a
brisk, youthful pace, to his important day's
work. His voice could never be heard in the
house : if ever a man of a house lived under
petticoat law, it was he. The coarse, masculine,
guttural tones of his spouse often rose indeed to
some pitch ; but his, never. In other respects,
too, he showed utter pusillanimity of spirit. He
would never appear to John, in answer to a
summons for arranging any misunderstanding
(and several there soon arose) between him or
poor Letty, and the daughter or niece : his wife
always represented him ; and he would run to
hide behind a door, or into the yard, if he heard

John's foot on the stairs, during these domestic commotions; nay, even when all was at peace, his habitual poverty of nerve urged him to shun a single rencontre with his lodger; or, perhaps, he still dreaded to be called to account for any thing his wife or daughter had said; and whenever he was caught by John in the passage, or the yard, his fidgets, as he lisped and mumbled, and continually tapped his chest with one hand, ever complaining of his asthma, called up sentiments of irresistible disgust.

His sole attempts at manhood we have indicated, in describing the way he used to step out to his day's labour every morning. But rarer proofs of this still farcical and contemptible humour came under John's eye. As he and his ancient fellow-labourer before described (a contrast to him, by the way, being square-built, erect in his body, cross in his temper, and loud and independent in his tones,) used to fumble about in the yard of an evening, chopping or sawing sticks and rotten boards, and mending the little sheds with them, or for ever watering the roots of the sad laburnum tree, there was a would-be briskness in his every motion, (he knew his wife was always looking at him out of the parlour window,) an energy in the way he

grasped his saw, adze, or hammer, or his watering pot, and jerked them from hand to hand,
or upon a bench, when he had done with them ;
all of which plainly bespoke his ambition not to
pass for " so very old a man, neither ;" certainly
to give the idea that he was a miracle for his
age.

Every Sunday he appeared caparisoned for
church in a complete shining suit of black, taken
out of a press, and in a hat, also shining, ex-
tracted from one of his wife's early bandboxes;
the clothes and the hat some ten years in his,
or rather in her possession, and thus displayed
once a-week during that period, yet both look_
ing as if sent home the Saturday night before;
and, indeed, considering that they had encoun-
tered scarce three months of careful wear altogether, namely, the wear of about two hours
every seventh day for ten years, it was not after
all so surprising they should look so new. Sometimes his wife allowed him to invite to a Sunday
dinner five or six old men like himself, all clad
in shining black too; and when John saw them
come crawling towards the house, or, joined with
their host, crawling and stalking about the yard,
he felt an odd sensation of disgust, such as he
thought might be aroused by the sight of so

many old shining black-beetles; the insects that, of all that crept, were his antipathy and loathing.

His wife has been called fat; she was so, to excess; so much so, that she waddled under her own fardel—herself; but she was strong and sturdy too; and her waddle did not lessen the length and stamp of her stride, when, upon occasions that required a show of authority, she came out to scold, or, as her niece called it, to "ballyrag," in the kitchen, at her handmaidens, or in the hall, at her poor lodgers up stairs. Then the little house shook from top to bottom under her heavy and indignant step, as well as with the echoes of her coarse man's voice, half smothered amid the fat of her throat, and the sputterings of her great pursy lips. And poor Letty also shook, from top to toe, on these occasions, and flew for shelter to John's arms.

When not called upon thus to enforce law in any refractory branch of her garrison, Mrs. Grimes spent the day in a vast indolent armchair, reading pathetic novels of the last age, or casting up her accounts, to re-assure herself, over and over again, of the pounds, shillings, and pence, laid up during the last month or week, and how half a farthing might be split for six months to come. Every day, by twelve o'clock, she was dressed " like any lady," (still according to her niece,) to receive her cronies, or strike with importance the tax-collectors or landlord's agent, none of whom had ever to call a second time; and that was her constant boast ; but even there, shut up in her parlour, the old female despot was fully as much dreaded as if her voice and her stride sounded every moment through the house,—or as much as if she had lain there screwed down in her coffin, and that, at the least turn of a hand, herself or her ghost might come out to roar for a strict reckoning.

Her daughter and niece (the latter an orphan) supplied the place of a servant maid, in lieu of the eating, drinking, and sleeping, such as it was, that came to their lot. They were of a size, and that size very little; of an age, and that more than thirty; but from their stunted growth; hard, liny shape, and non-descript expression of features, might pass for ten years younger, or ten years older, as the spectator fancied. They gave no idea of flesh and blood. They never looked as if they were warm, or soft to the touch. One would as soon think of flirting with them, as with the old wooden effigies to be found in the niches of old cathedrals.

They imparted no notion, much less sensation of
sex. But they were as active as bees, and as
strong as little horses; and as despotic and cruel,
if they dared, and whenever they dared, as
the old tyrant herself. From the moment they
arose in the morning, thump, thump, thump,
went their little heels, through the passage, to the
kitchen, up stairs and down stairs, or into the parlour, to see after the fires the old man had lighted; to make up the beds; to prepare breakfast;
to put every thing to rights; to sweep, to brush,
to shake carpets, to clean shoes, knives, and
forks; to rub, scrub, polish, and beautify, for
ever and ever; the daughter always leading the
niece; and the whole of this gone through in a
sturdy, important, vain-glorious manner; accompanied by slapping of doors, every two
minutes, and (ever since Letty had refused to
go down to the parlour to join an evening party,) by loud, rude talking, and boisterous laugh-
ing, just to show that they did not care a farthing for the kind of conceited poor lodgers
they had got in the house.

The housekeeping of the establishment was
peculiarly loathsome to John. The baker had
never sent in a loaf, bunn, roll, biscuit, or muf-
fin, since the day, now some fifteen years ago,

when Mrs. Grimes came to reside in the neighbourhood: and even the home-made bread was
of the coarsest possible quality, and often used
a fortnight after it had been baked. Each day,
the dairy-man left one halfpenny worth of milk
at the door. They made their own precious
mould candles, or burnt such nefarious oil in
the kitchen lamp, or, upon a gala night, in the
passage, as poisoned and fumigated the whole
house. The morning tea leaves were preserved
and boiled for evening. No eggs, no fresh but-
ter ever appeared. The fires, after having been
once made up in the morning, were slaked with
a compost of coal-dust and yellow clay, which,
shaped into balls, also formed stuffing between
the bars. Upon a Saturday evening, the old
man sneaked out to drive hard bargains for
some of the odds and ends left in the butcher's
stall after the day's sale; and these, conveyed
home by stealth, furnished, by means of salting
and hanging up in a cool place, savoury dinners
for the week. Upon a washing-day, starch was
made out of potatoes, to save a farthing.

No charity was in the house, nor in a heart
in the house. In the faces of all professed beg-
gars the street door was slammed without a
word, but with a scowl calculated to wither up

the wretched suitor; and with respect to such as strove to hide the profession under barrel-organs, flutes, flageolets, hurdy-gurdies, or the big-drum and pandean pipes, their tune was, indeed, listened to, but never requited.

Yet the family was a pious family. Mr. and Mrs. Grimes sallied out to church every Sunday, and sat at the parlour window every Sunday evening, (while their daughter and niece went, in turn, to have a rest, as they said,) a huge old Bible open before them, and visible to all passers by, that the neighbours might remark— " There 's a fine old couple." John, however, thought it odd, that after all this, his cold mutton or his cold beef used to come up to him, out of the safe, (a pretty " safe," truly) rather di-minished since he had last the pleasure of seeing it ; and one Sunday evening, after listening for half an hour to the daughter's shrill voice, read-ing the Bible before supper, when, on particular business, he somewhat suddenly entered the parlour, he was still more surprized to find the good family seated round the ham, (a rare temp-tation, no doubt, in their system of housekeep-ing) which that day had formed part of his dinner.

But nothing irked him half so much as the

ostentatious triumph over starvation, the pro-
voking assumption of comfort, nay, elegance, as
it were, and the audacious independence which
resulted from the whole economy. He felt
it, as before hinted, to be the most irritating
specimen of poverty. Old Grimes's glossy Sunday coat, perpetually the same, was worse
than the clouted gaberdine of a roving beggar.
Every burnished thing around him seemed to
shine with a beggarly polish. The whole house
and its inhabitants had an air of looking better
than they really were, or ought to be; and the
meanness, the sturdiness, the avarice, the hard-
heartedness, that produced this polish and this
air, he considered as loathsome as the noise, the
thumping about, the loud talking, and the endless fagging of the two little skinny Helots
was brazen and vexatious.

We should not, indeed, have so long dwelt
on this domestic sketch, did we not wish to give
some clear idea of the causes, that, during many
weeks, while he and Letty awaited an answer
from the country, served to keep up, in John's
mind, a continued though petty ferment. And
still no answer came; and at last his poor
companion began to droop, and, like him, de-

spair: although she did not dream how long his feelings had anticipated her.

Almost their last pound had been changed, when a large and bulky letter was finally delivered by the postman, directed to John. He tore open the envelope, and found two notes for himself, and one for Letty. He waited to hear hers: it was from her brother, as follows:—

" MY DEAREST SISTER,

" I write in the greatest hurry, by stealth, and against the vehement commands of our dear uncle. He is indignant, and, I fear, not to be moved;—yet do not quite despair: whatever a brother can do, I will do. You know how close he holds me in money matters, and lately he has even tightened his hand, lest (as I suppose) I should bestow his allowances where he knows my heart inclines me: so that, dear Letty, I can only inclose a poor ten pounds, until better times, which I hope are not far off, though I fear they are. God bless you. Your immediate family are still more outrageous. Heaven melt and convert them all, prays your affectionate brother,

" F. A."

As Letty remained stupified over this note, John began to read his epistles aloud, in a deep, steady voice.

" DEAR, DEAR JOHN,

" What can I say? what comfort can I offer? Oh, nothing; none. Oh, did you see us, it would move your heart;—but that is moved, I am sure, by this time, at least; if, indeed, it was ever hard or wicked, which I, for one, will not believe. My husband—the husband *you* have given me, dear John, tells me where to address this; and you will find a line from another friend—or one that was a friend, your best friend—along with it. Oh, listen to him, John, dear brother, listen to him; listen to us all. Humiliation, time, penance, and a good life, may yet go near to make up for the past, if you would only turn your heart to think of it: but if you do not, oh see what is to happen! Read *his* letter, and see! God help you, John; and God help me, your loving sister, and the poor old couple, and their grey hairs. I don't know what to think! Oh God, pity, in particular, the poor young lady, who, whatever way you turn, must be the victim!

" John, Dearest John, I have thought of your situation in every view; and, with other things, remembered you would want what your poor Peggy has not to give, and strove to procure it elsewhere, from father and mother, and from another person, now nearer to me than either, but all in vain; And oh, dear, poor brother! what are you to do? or what am I to do, who cannot assist you? Once more, on my knees, I pray of a merciful Heaven to have mercy on you.

" Oh, John, I thought Frank, at least, could send you help, and I asked him again and again; but from what he says, I believe he has very little in his power, indeed. And I 'll say nothing, John, about the kind of husband he is to me; not a word: for not a word to give you fresh pain would I say for worlds. You had your own reasons for the part you took; and no matter now, until we meet again, and can speak of them. But John, John, will that meeting ever come? No one but yourself is able to answer. And again I cry out to you, in tears and misery, listen to us all, and, above all, to him who writes along with me. I have told you nothing of our father and

mother : I dare not tell you any thing ; but God
look down on them and you, is the prayer of
                Your miserable sister,
                        " PEGGY ADAMS."

Before he had read aloud a dozen lines of
this epistle, John saw he must not continue to
communicate its contents to Letty. Accordingly he told her, with a gloomy smile, it con-
tained nothing but silly lamentations from his
sister, which, while they were natural, would
only serve to give her unnecessary pain ; and
therefore he prayed Letty to excuse his silence.
Then he finished the reading, to himself, with
a brow of studied ease, a frozen eye, and a
nerve braced to desperate firmness ; and, without pausing, took up the accompanying letter,
to which Peggy had alluded, and which his
heart readily instructed him to anticipate. We
transcribe it also :

" Wretched man ! It was, then, you indeed,
whom I saw in Dublin; although I could no
more trust my eyes to the appearance you made,
than I could trust my ears to the monstrous
story of your scandal and sin, which awaited

my return to this place. It is said here, it is
believed here, that your fall was not from the
temptation of the moment, but rather the accomplishment of a plan, long studied, and, with
deep deceit, carried into effect at your leisure.
Even your bishop thinks this of you; but can
it be possible? was that letter you wrote me,
and was your story to your poor father and
mother, (God pity them!) about going to
Spain, all a deception? a contrivance to raise
means for your horrid purpose? John Nowlan, I strive to believe, to hope, it was not. I
pray morning and night, that you may not
ultimately prove such an unparalleled sinner:—
I recollect your youth, your character,—or
what, perhaps, in my blindness, I supposed to
be your character; I recollect our commun-
ings together; I recollect the laying bare your
heart to me in the confessional, and those recollections give me the hope.

"But, listen to me, John Nowlan. Only in
one way can you confirm my hope; only in one
way can you prevent certainty of the worst kind
against yourself; and oh, miserable young
man, only in one way can you ward off the
dreadful curse that is collecting to burst over

your head.—If you have fallen but through impulse, arise, and stand erect through reflection. Turn your back upon your sin, and your face to God and to your church—accuse yourself— humble yourself—repent—cry aloud for pardon and mercy, even after punishment—cry aloud for sackcloth upon your body, and ashes upon your head—ask to moisten the bitter bread of years to come, with your more bitter tears—and thus alone can you hinder even me from regarding you as a pre-determined sinner—thus alone can you hinder all Christian people from shuddering at your name—thus alone can you stay the final anathema of your insulted church and the eternal wrath of your insulted God.

"Already, of course, you are a suspended priest; and your bishop awaits but your answer to this letter, ere he commands me to pronounce your name as accursed among your own people, from the altar of your own chapel, and by the lips of your own priest and relation, and oldest friend. I say to you, John Nowlan, tremble! —But a few days stand between you and your earthly curse, and your long woe.

"MATTHEW KENNEDY."

This letter, too, John read to himself, without betraying to Letty's observation an iota of the confirmed despair which it fastened on his heart. He even smiled, again, as he put it up; and, turning to her, strove to talk cheeringly of the future. He could exert himself, and gain some little independence, he said, notwithstanding the anger of all their friends; or until they should grow more forgiving——until his own stifled and cramped heart should burst into shivers, he should have said, for that was what he felt.

He sat down by Letty's side, and seeing her still stupified, or else wrapped in reflection, continued to speak empty words of comfort. To-morrow, John said, he would go out, and think of looking after some reputable employment. He was a good classical scholar, and he had heard that in Dublin a handsome income was to be derived from but limited tuition. Letty suddenly started, looked full at him, again cast her eyes on the ground, and seemed really engaged with her reflections.

The day, the evening, the night, wore away, and he did not stir from her side. They prepared to retire to their humble bed, and Letty fell on her knees, and, with swimming eyes, asked him to join her in prayer. He laughed, slightly, and said he was so cold he would pray in bed. She continued long kneeling; then, still in unrestrained but silent tears, her head lay for hours on his breast, both awake, though neither spoke. At last John heard her breathe more quietly; after a further pause assured himself she was fast asleep; then he gently removed her head from his breast, wet with her poor tears; and then, and not till then, the passion—the loaded shell of passion—that had so long remained fuzing in his breast,—exploded in the silence of the night.

He sat up, flung aside the covering from his burning body, and, in an instinctive effort to hide his emotion from the unconscious creature at his side, desperately grasped the ticken in his spasmed hand.

"Ay," he thought, "let them do their worst! —let them brand me—curse me—outlaw me here, and bar the gate of mercy against me hereafter!—I am prepared for it—I expected it —body and soul were freely staked before they spoke—yet let them have a care!—Their vengeance upon me is nothing—shall be borne— but if, through ruin to me, ruin shall fall upon this sleeping innocence, now at my side—if, by

E 5

their curse and ban, my exertions in her behalf
shall be cramped, so as that she must be a common victim—by the Heaven that I have outraged, and that casts me off, they may rue it
sorely !"

Had John been called on to define the kind
of vengeance he threatened, he could have
given no answer; yet this burst of excitement
somewhat relieved him; it was a partial
escape of the pent-up volcano. No gentler
relief would, indeed, come. He reverted to
Peggy's letter, to its simple and touching tone,
to her deep affliction at home;—to the whole
picture of home, such as he had made it—yet
not a tear flowed. Her half allusion to " the
husband *he* had given her," and her mysterious
hints as to the life they led together, supplied
more matter to his boiling mood, than could her
sorrow and her sisterly affection. He flamed
impatiently at the thought of his having been
too precipitate in forcing Peggy to marry Mr.
Frank—in giving him a command and right
over her. His whole soul rose as he allowed
himself to doubt the truth of Maggy's information. And then the depth and ambiguity of
Frank's character began further to oppress and
irritate him ; he brought to mind how lamely

did Frank's letter of that day hold the promise of friendship given to him upon the accursed evening, when the young gentleman first turned his eyes to his present ruin; the letter did not, in fact, mention his name; and again, John, getting before him a supposed case, muttered to himself vague threats of revenge.

As the morning broke on his sleepless eye, his former mood of composed despair again closed round him; and again he was able, by an anomalous operation of mind that is one of the wonders of our nature, to form deliberate calculations for the coming day. When the hour for rising approached, he shut his eyes that Letty might think him asleep.

They breakfasted without speaking much to each other; and when John proposed to go out in search of an engagement, Letty quietly bade him farewell. He returned about four o'clock, and did not find her at home. He enquired when she had gone out, and the little kiln-dried niece sullenly answered, a few minutes after himself. Dreadful apprehensions crowded upon his mind; but in about an hour, a knock came to the door, and Letty, modestly dressed, pale, fatigued, and yet with a tearful smile, fell on his neck.

"Oh, love, love, have you succeeded?" she asked.

" Not yet, but I have hopes still, Letty. I called at every public academy I could enquire out; they were all supplied with efficient teachers: they told me, however, to advertise for private tuitions, and, no doubt, I should have employment. And now, Letty, where have *you* been? and why give me the shock of not finding you at home? Oh, it was dreadful."

" I did wrong there, indeed; I should have contrived to be home before you:—where have I been, you ask? Where, John, but trying, like you, to procure the means of honourable subsistence?—and, oh, dearest John! thank God, I return more successful!"

" How? where? what do you mean?"

" I 'll tell you all:—long ago, thinking of the worst, I purchased a few little materials unknown to you, and whenever you left me alone for an hour, sat down to make drawings, from recollection, of some of my former studies ; and —now hear me out—when you spoke of tuition yesterday, it occurred to me, for the first time, that I might teach drawing as well as sell my little works ; and so, John, when you went out, I hid my drawings under my shawl, and went out too ; and"—smiling—" while you were calling at the academies, I was calling at the boarding-schools; but they all refused me, intimating that an introduction would be necessary; and I was turning down the steps of the last, sad enough, when—when a good lady, who"—her voice broke—" who just then stepped out of her carriage at the next door, saw my tears, I believe, and stopped me, and addressed me very kindly and politely, and returned into the carriage with me, and was good enough to look at my poor drawings and praise them, and offer to —to purchase them"—Letty here blushed scarlet as she wept;—" and she did purchase them, John; and, besides, she has daughters, and I am to teach them! and this, dear love, was what kept me out so long." Again she fell on his neck.

" Did the lady ask any questions about your situation ?" enquired John.

" She did, and I freely answered—for I believe I was surprised into some energy; I answered, that I had made a marriage, which, on account of a difference of religion, displeased my husband's friends and mine."

" Did you say I was a priest, Letty?

" No, that was not necessary; particularly as you are not a priest now; I only mentioned, in answer to the lady's questions, that I was a

Protestant, and that you had been a Roman Catholic, and it seems our good patroness is a Roman Catholic too, and perhaps on that account
more disposed to assist me for your sake."

" 'Tis likely," observed John; " but thanks,
at all events, my own dear Letty, for this heroic
proof of your love; I need not say why I think
it heroic—I will only say I am grateful."

He pressed her, still in despairing tenderness,
to his heart, and endeavoured to show that he
shared with her a happy evening. Letty, romantic and enthusiastic as she was, felt proud of
herself; her sparkling eyes, brilliant smiles, and
cheering and playful conversation, told that she
triumphed in the idea of having made a successful sacrifice and effort for the chosen of her
heart; and the vivacity of youth lacquered the
future with delusive promise.

At first, indeed, all seemed promising. Letty
not only succeeded in pleasing her first pupils,
but, through them, got many others; and further, her friends interested themselves about
John, and procured him also private tuitions, of
which the produce, added to Letty's earnings,
enabled them to live above fear of want. This
turn of good fortune happened two months after
their arrival in Dublin, and continued four months

longer. Then, however, a change as terrible
as it was unaccountable occurred. One by one
their friends grew cold and distant; one by one
their pupils were withdrawn from them; until, at
last, while neither could guess a solution of the
mystery, that at once struck them with wonder
and consternation, Letty had not a tuition left,
and John had but one.

While they wondered, and drooped, and trembled, want closed round them more formidably
than ever. The receipts from one pupil did not
meet a third of even their humble daily expendi-
ture; and first, they were left without a pound;
and next—after both had repeatedly gone out,
each unknown to the other, to dispose of different
articles of dress—without any means of existence. Then it was, while weeks of lodging-
money became due, that they trembled at the
sound of their tyrant landlady's voice; then it
was, as their poor attire and sad brows bespoke,
too plainly, the state of their purse, that the rude
flaunts of the hard-grained little daughter and
niece sank into their souls; then it was that, by
tacit consent, they often went out at dinner-hour,
pleading an engagement to the sneering attendant, to wander by the lonesome banks of the
adjacent canals, Letty weeping away her heart,

and John stifling the despair of his, until he felt
as if it would shiver his breast in atoms ; then it
was that they feared to face home—alas, it was
not home !—to encounter the malignant consciousness of their poverty, that they thought they
could read in the eyes of the creature who should
open the door to their timid knock.   Then it was
that they felt the realities of the world, and, John
believed, the first pouring out of their curse.

To his single tuition they could only cling, in
dismal hopes of its producing others.   Meantime,
poor Letty, long ignorant of the first enfeebling
symptoms, that, to an older eye, would have proclaimed her situation, at last knew she was to be
a mother.   John suspected the fact—and only
suspected it—and in the silence of one dreary
and bitter night, asked her if it were so.—
"Your child stirs with life, under my bosom !"
she answered, in showering tears, and yet in a
tender embrace.

The event differently affected them.   Letty
trembled at the thought of not having a shilling to provide for her time of trial, or to purchase for her baby the commonest things necessary to shelter it from the winds of heaven.
It was now the beginning of a very cold April,
and she had not a warm shawl or cloak to shelter

herself. In fact,—miserable as *is* the fact—the only covering she had left was the old gown she wore every day. John heard, in fulness of horror that equalled only his despair, the announcement of his being about to be a father. That wretched infant, when born, would but prove the record of its father's guilt. Now, he could not even die and be forgotten; his child would live after him, and leave, perhaps, another child, and that another still, so that the memory of the blasphemer must be perpetuated, in his race, upon earth. His abject state of poverty, and the sufferings in store for Letty, gave him, indeed, dreadful anguish; but this, above all others, was the prepossession that brooded over his soul.

In the eighth month of Letty's pregnancy, instead of John's single tuition leading to others, he received a cold note from his young pupil's father, dispensing with his attendance even upon that one. He snatched up his hat, and ran to the gentleman's house, at last determined to demand a solving of this withering mystery. The person on whom he called was not at home, or was denied to him; but, as he turned away from the door, an individual came out, and an eye met his, that at once seemed to supply an explanation. It was an old class-fellow in the Bishop's school at Limerick, ordained long before him, and, as he now recollected, since officiating as a coadjutor in a Dublin parish. They exchanged one deep look; and the young priest turned away, while John rushed through the streets in an opposite direction.

Arrived at home, wild and breathless, he could no longer doubt the secret of his ruin. His and Letty's friends had all been Roman Catholics; the story of the runaway priest had reached Dublin; had become whispered about; this brother clergyman, his own early friend and neighbour, had doubtless recognized his name,—which John had never thought of disguising,—or perhaps seen his person; and the excommunicated and hardened sinner had consequently been shaken out of Christian society.

Trembling with mingled rage, despair, and terror, still he would ask an explanation; and he wrote and despatched to the gentleman he could not meet at home, a peremptory note, which was thus answered:—

" Mr. —— acquaints the *Rev.* John Nowlan, that he cannot, with satisfaction or propriety, entrust the education of his son to a Roman Catholic clergyman who keeps a mistress."

" Curses !" screamed John, starting up, after he had read this billet,—Letty, terribly alarmed, enquired what was the matter—" Ruin ! destruction !" he answered, stamping on the note ; " come ! we are hunted out of this—out of this city, as we shall be hunted through this world ! come !"

" Whither ?" she asked.

" Anywhere, Letty ! anywhere out of the streets of Dublin—I durst not again show myself in them ; the common rabble would shower curses on my head ! Come, get up, and dare not to pray !"

Mrs. Grimes's daughter here opened the door without ceremony, and to John's furious " What do you want ?" answered, that her mother would be much obliged, if, instead of stamping and roaring, to bring down the house, he would let her have her three weeks' lodging.

The note that had released him from his last tuition enclosed about the amount of the demand now made ; he flung it to the little creature, and shut the door in her face. After an instant's pause, he again rose up, and desiring Letty to meet him at a certain point on the Circular Road, left her to follow.

Hastily putting on her shabby little bonnet, and wrapping round her the relic of an old thin shawl, she soon obeyed him. He was not at the place appointed. She waited for him, shaking with horrid fears. At last he ran up to her, without a hat, and without the surtout that had served to cover the broken under-coat he lately wore beneath it.

"I have it!" he cried, as he held out his clasped hand, in which were the few shillings he had just obtained. "You shall see what it is, Letty; you shall not starve on the road from Dublin; but come now any road from Dublin! in any other distant place let us hide our heads; I can change my name, you know, and all will be well: come; when you grow tired I will carry you, awhile, in my arms."

CHAPTER IV.

Upon the evening of the second day after the scene described in the last chapter, in a town about twenty miles from Dublin, (out of particular motives of delicacy we do not give its name) a charitable club, composed of the respectable middle classes of the place, held its weekly sitting. Throughout many of the towns of Ireland there are several of such clubs, very numerous in their members, and very moderate in their annual subscriptions, and all having in view the relief of objects of different kinds.

The objects assisted by the club at present noticed, were poor way-farers, who, in passing through the town might stand in need of some little sum to gain them temporary food and lodging, and perhaps a help on their road. Its sittings, like those of all the others, commenced at seven or eight o'clock in the evening, when good folks might conveniently leave home, busi-

ness, and wife for a few hours, and, each sure of
meeting a neighbour's face in the club-room,
rationally combine together a little relaxation,
a little chat, a little charity, and a little whiskey
punch. Let us not be supposed to speak in the
slightest terms of satire of such excellent insti-
tutions. We have known many of them, humble as might be their pretensions, do a great
deal of good; while the antiquity of several of
them (we could name one which has endured
nearly a century) proves a persevering, an
abiding, and an inherited benevolence, that re-
flects much honour on their native towns and
cities.

The president of the night sat in his great
high-backed, quaintly carved, venerable oak
chair, worn into a polish all over from constant
use, and ornamented with a coronal wreath of
peace and charity, and faded gold letters, impressed on a blue garter, expressive of the name
and object of the club. The ancient secretary,
a superannuated pedagogue, whose father before
him had held the same office, put on his specta-
cles, mended his pen, opened his huge well-
thumbed book, called " order" in the name of
the chair, and business commenced, amid the
grave looks of the elder members, and the sly

winks and hems of some of the juniors, who saw no crime in dispensing charity with a light heart, and who were content to brave, now and then, the primitive fine of one halfpenny, for a jest upon the precision and peculiarities of " Mr. Sec."

Referring to his official copy of the last list of objects, with the several sums dealt out attached to each name, he noticed to the last week's president, (who had received it from him for service, and whose further duty it was afterwards to give in his report, in the club-room,) to go over it aloud, along with him. As he called the names, the ex-president communicated, in brief words, his observations upon the cases of each; for instance, when the secretary cried aloud, " Peter Dowling," or " Mark Cassidy," or " Mary Whelan," he answered in this sort—" Peter Dowling returns thanks, and walked for —— this morning ;" or " Mark Cassidy prays another week's money ;" or " strike off Mary Whelan; I saw her running out of Ronan's public-house, to jump into bed, and be sick, before I could pay her a visit to serve the allowance."

As the reading of the list continued, the name of Nancy Clancy occurred, and the last week's president prayed, in her name, a continuance of the charity.

" Stop," cried a young fellow, with a wink to his neighbours, " is that the pretty little strange girl that has a bed in the widow Laffin's cabin ?"   The ex-president answered it was: " then strike out Nancy Clancy, for I saw somebody—I won't tell who," again winking towards the grave ex-president, " comin' out from her, last night, afther nine o'clock ; no time for servin' the list, at any rate."

The village jest was taken, the club set up a roar, and the secretary rose to give notice of a fine, according to the rules, against " Masther Brenan," for a tendency to impurity in his speech ; the question to be debated after the more regular business had been disposed of.

" Here, Mr. Sec. to save you trouble," laughed the accused party, rolling up a halfpenny.

The reading of the list was over ; the secretary prepared his new one for the present week ; and while he was making it out, the acting president signified that this was the time for recommending new objects.   His predecessor rose, and gave in the name of George Spike, as

a fit object for the largest allowance the usage
of the club would afford.

" He is a stranger, of course, Mr. Fagan ?"
asked the president, addressing the speaker.

" He is, Sir; and, I believe, a gentleman in
distress," answered Mr. Fagan.

" And has a young wife, I'll engage, Mr.
president," remarked " Master Brenan."

" He has, Sir; a very young creature."

" I thought as much, Sir."

" Order, Master Brenan !" cried the secretary.

" Where did you visit him ?" continued the
president.

" I didn't visit him, at all," answered Mr.
Fagan; " but I'll tell the club how it was.
Some of the objects on my list lived more than
a mile outside the town, and as I had many
calls to make in the town itself, I left the
suburbs for the last, and wasn't able to get
through with the whole till late this evening,
just before I came to the room. Well: in
crossing over the Dublin road, to come on a
scattered row of cabins, where the road hasn't
a house at one side or other, I met this poor
fellow, standin' in the rain an' could, for it's a
rough April evenin', with his back against the

fence; and the crature of a wife in his arms,
sinking with fatague and hunger, I suppose, and
himself little betther off than she was.   There's
a lone, waste cabin, built in a lone field, off o'
the road, belongin' to a tenant of a friend o'
mine, that never was able to live in it for the
wet and damp, and afther a few words, I
helped him to lift her over the fence, and lay
her down in the cabin; and then I went for a
bundle o' sthraw, to put under her, and gave
him an advance of half-a-crown, and asked him,
was she well enough to be brought into the
sthreets o' the town, where we might get her
and him a dacent lodgin', and an apothecary,
if need was: but the poor man only shook his
head, and knelt down by her, and took her
hand, and said, 'twas betther not stir her yet;
but he would buy food and dhrink with the half-
crown, he said; and he thanked me much.   I
bid him look about a spark of fire, and a scrap
of candle; and he said he would do that too:
and then I left him, being in such a hurry to
the club, making him promise, that if she didn't
grow betther, he would come to my house, or
to this room, before bed-time."

This case silenced all present disposition to
merriment in the club, and the name of George

Spike was entered on the list for the next week, at the allowance of one crown, the highest the rules could warrant.

"What made you think he seemed like a gentleman in distress, Mr. Fagan?" asked Master Brenan, in a changed tone.

"Not his clothes, Will," answered Mr. Fagan; "for he has hardly a rag on his back, and never a shoe to his foot, nor a hat on his head; but his words, and the way he bore it all,—that was what made me think so."

"He ought to be visited arly to-morrow mornin', Sir; will you let me walk out with you, at six o'clock?"

Mr. Fagan assented. The club closed. The elder members retired, betimes, to their reputable beds; and though some of the juniors, and Will Brenan among the number, staid up tippling to rather a late hour, he was not much behind-hand in his appointment with Mr. Fagan, the next morning.

The elderly and the young man struck out of the clustering thatched suburb, upon the Dublin road, and about a quarter of an hour's walk brought them in view of the lonely cabin in the lonely field.

"And now for your poor gentleman, Misther Fagan," said the youngster, as he vaulted from the crisp, frosty road, into the whitened grass; "I 'm longin' to see how he is afther the night; but all is safe, I suppose, or he 'd send or come to you, as you bid him."

"I hope so," answered Mr. Fagan.

"Is the wife as purty as she 's young, Sir?" continued the lad, jeeringly.

"Nonsense, now, Will; it 's a shame, and nothin' else, to make light of a case of disthress, not to talk of my years:—but stop," as they approached very near to the cabin,—"where 's the dour of the house gone, I wondher?"

"Aha!" cried Will, "and your advance of the half-crown, Misther Fagan. I thought they 'd be no bhetter than they ought to be."

"Let us step in, any how." They crossed the threshold—but sprang back, with a common cry, the moment they had done so. The door of the cabin, which they had supposed to have been stolen, lay, supported by four large stones, on the wet floor; upon it lay the corpse of a beautiful young woman, of which the arms clasped a new-born babe, also dead, to the breast; a rushlight, stuck in a lump of yellow clay, flickered by their side; and at their feet, kneeling on one knee, while the raised knee propped his arm, and the arm his head, appeared a young man, his face as white as theirs, except where a black beard, long unshorn, covered it. The fingers of the hand that supported his head, grasped and ran twining through an abundance of dishevelled black hair. The other hand was thrust into his bosom. His unwinking, distended eyes were riveted on the lowly bier.

" The Lord save us!" whispered Mr. Fagan, outside the door; " many 's the poor wake I 've looked at in my time, but never the likes o' that."

" He 's mad," replied the youth, also in a whisper; " no one but a disthracted crature could think of doin' what he done, takin' the dour off o' the hinges, and gettin' the stones, and all: and may be he watched them, that way, the night long."

" God preserve us! may be so," resumed his companion, crossing himself; " and found the rushlight on the hob, I suppose, and went out to light it at a neighbour's cabin; and did you see his ould coat taken off, and thrown over the infant, all but the head?"

" What 's to be done?" asked Will Brenan, " he can't be left here: come in again, though I 'm a'most afraid, and let us spake to him."

" Come, then, in the name of God."

They stept lightly, once more, into the cabin. John Nowlan appeared precisely in the same position; but, as they again entered, he fixed on them one flaring look, and instantly re-assumed his set gaze on the bier. They spoke. He did not answer.

" It's as I tould you," resumed Will; "he 's mad, and neither hears us, nor heeds the sight before him."

" Do I not ?" cried John, springing up and darting to them, his right hand still plunged into his breast; " mad I may be—mad I am—but do I not heed nor feel ! Look at that !" He tore the hand from under his shirt, and with it a portion of the mangled muscle of his breast. " Look at that ! there's the way I was trying to keep it down."

They spoke to him all the comfort that, as perfect strangers, horrified by such a scene, they could naturally suggest. But he did not answer again. They left him to apply to ano-ther charitable club for a coffin. They return-ed with it, called upon the neighbours, and bu-ried for him, as the wandering poor are buried in Ireland, his supposed wife and child. He grew passive in their hands. He received the articles of dress he most needed, and a little sum of money, collected through the town. He walked after the coffin to the grave, and, when all was done, asked to be left alone. The sorrowing crowd withdrew, a few only remaining, out of sight, to watch,—for they feared what he might do. But when he thought himself quite alone, he only flung himself upon the fresh grave; and, after some time, started up, walked rapidly out of the town, and to this day remains unknown, by his real name, among its simple and charitable inhabitants.

But in some days after, his old friend, Mr. Kennedy, had a sight of him among his native hills.

The clergyman had been attending a sick call at some distance, and was riding slowly homeward, along a rough and narrow road. The moon shone high in the heavens. At an abrupt turn in the road, a man, haggard, wild, and greatly agitated, jumped from a bank, some paces before him, holding a blunderbuss upon his arm. At the same instant, Mr. Kennedy dismounted and faced him. " I am John Nowlan!" shrieked the wretch, " and you have

cursed me, and banned me, and ruined me
and her :—she is dead !" presenting the blunderbuss.

" I know you, John," replied the old priest,
erecting himself to his full height ; " and I
know, too, I have done my terrible duty by
you ; and now you are here to kill me for it—
that so you may add a priest's murder to a
priest's apostacy. Do, then ! fire on my grey
hairs, John Nowlan, and the sacrament lying
on my breast ! look here !" snatching out the
little case in which John knew the sacrament
was usually carried to the sick ; " and now,
pull your trigger, man !—fire !" extending his
arms:--then, as his tone rose into one of stern
and loud command, " Sinner ! down at my feet !
you dare not pull a trigger !"

The courageous old man augured aright.
John Nowlan cast the deadly weapon on the
ground, and flung himself after it : the frenzy
that urged him to the horrid attempt, having at
once quailed before the voice which his ear had,
from infancy, been accustomed to obey, and in
the presence of the sacrament which even madness durst not steep in blood. As for an instant
he lay upon the earth, the old clergyman prepared himself to address the poor outcast in another

tone ; but at the first sound of his words in kindness, John leapt up, and bounded, howling, from the road. Mr. Kennedy remounted his horse to pursue ; called up some peasants, who joined him ; and the search was continued until morning, but in vain. Upon the rugged banks of a mountain river, swollen with late rains, they found, indeed, a hat, and some letters directed to John Nowlan ; and at the discovery all crossed themselves, and stared aghast at one another ; and for many years it was believed among his native wilds, that John Nowlan had ended by suicide a life of crying sin. His own family, however, were not made acquainted with the report ; nor, as has before been mentioned, did Mr. Kennedy ever divulge the shocking rencontre which had that night taken place between him and his unfortunate relative.

CHAPTER V.

THE fortunes of Peggy Nowlan now demand
attention ; and the reader will be pleased to re-
cur to her at the moment, when, in consequence
of her brother's violence, she became the wife of
Mr. Frank, according to the canons of the Roman Catholic church, though not according to
the law of the land.

Confounded and silent, Peggy, Mr. Frank,
and old Friar Shanaghan, stood together in the
field, listening to John's retreating steps.   In a
few moments the post-chaise was heard to drive
furiously off.

" There he goes," said the friar, breaking the
confused silence—" and now, can any one tell
me the meaning of this ?"

" I cannot," answered Frank ; " except that
he is grown stark mad of a sudden."

" Nor I, Sir," added Peggy, " except on a
like thought."

" He seemed to speak of a necessity—a shameful necessity—for your immediate marriage, Peggy," continued Mr. Shanaghan.

" He spoke in great error then," answered Peggy, holding herself erect, and looking firmly from the eyes of one gentleman to the other.

" He did, Sir," echoed Frank; " in error that wronged us both : and his unaccountable precipitancy, although it confers upon me a happiness I long proposed to myself, under certain circumstances, and at a certain time, yet"—

" Has made you this young girl's husband against your will, on this particular evening," interrupted the friar.

" Not against my will, Sir; that is, not against my feelings for Miss Nowlan, but solely against present expediency. I had hopes that time would have enabled me to obtain the consent of my friends; to avow my marriage to them now would be ruinous."

" Then what do you propose to do, Sir?" demanded the old ecclesiastic.

" That is exactly the point necessary for us all to determine; for it concerns us all : our common safety is at stake."

" You include me, Sir ?"

" Yes, good Sir. You know my immediate

family are rather violent religionists; and should they at once become acquainted with your agency in this matter—that is, should they hear, while their feelings are warm, of your having solemnized an illegal marriage between a Protestant and a Roman Catholic—"

" They might prosecute me, under the Act of Parliament that makes my ministry penal ?"

" Exactly so, my good Sir."

" I thought so. But you 'll never mind that, if you please : leave me to take care of myself, and just consider the case without me."

" Well, then, Sir; if my uncle be at once informed of my marriage, I am convinced he would turn me off."

" That 's more important; and you therefore wish secrecy for the present ?"

" For Peggy's sake, as well as mine, Sir,—yes :—the most inviolable secrecy. I wish we should promise each other not to speak of the matter to another human being."

" Hum—let us see. Your wife's opinion will be useful here, Master Adams. Peggy, my child, what have you to say for yourself ?"

Peggy had, since her last observation, stood by her husband's side as he held her hand, her head drooped perhaps more in thought than in embarrassment; now she spoke firmly and distinctly, though her voice was low:—" Since, by my brother's doing, I am this gentleman's wife, Sir, it is my first duty to care for his interests; and, therefore, I at once engage to keep our marriage a secret from every one but my father and mother—and, when she comes home, my sister."

" But that may be the very way to publish it to the whole country, dear Peggy—let me entreat you to make no exceptions."

" I cannot think," she resumed quietly, " that my father, mother, or sister, would break a trust upon the keeping of which my happiness depends; and, as they could not get their right and their due, by being consulted on my sudden and strange marriage, the least respect we can now show them will be to tell them it has happened; nothing can alter my mind on that head—not even the commands of a husband."

" Well;" resumed Frank, after a reverie, during which the friar closely watched him— " I have your promise, Sir?"

" You have, Sir; and besides," with a sneer so slight and peculiar, that even Frank could not perceive it—" my dread of a prosecution will be your further security, you know."

" Then, dearest Peggy," continued Frank, in a manner seemingly changed into the sincerest vivacity—" ask this excellent old gentleman to see you home—communicate the event to your father and mother, just as you like, and expect me to join you at a little bridal supper, in less than an hour. Now I must look after Letty, who, since your brother's departure, waits me to squire her to Long Hall; after that necessary service I shall fly to your father's. Adieu, Peggy; you cannot refuse the bride's kiss at least," —saluting her—" And cheer up, my life; for sudden and extraordinary as this has been, you know it is but an anticipation of my wishes, and every thing may be for the best—Farewell !—Of course"—in a whisper—" we meet at your father's not to part again; that is, you cannot expect your husband to return home to-night."

Burning in blushes, that immediately changed to paleness and trembling, Peggy heard him in silence, and, taking the friar's arm, proceeded to her father's house.

" Ay," muttered Frank, as he turned from them to seek Letty—" let the madman have his way; he only gives me the triumph that nothing else could. She was not to be surprised—force would have been dangerous—but this mock

marriage compels her, according to her mum-
mery creed, to receive me in her arms ; and
thus his own very act, his own insolent violence,
gives me my satisfaction for his own accursed
blow, and for her share in it ; forgetting altogether the real liking towards the silly girl,
that not even my grudge can smother. But
how's this ?" as he entered the little retreat in
which he had left Letty : " My excellent sister
not here ? Ho ! Letty ! No one answers ; can
it be possible ? can such double happiness have
been in store for me ? No ; yonder she sits,
in tender sorrow at his loss."

The female figure he now more closely approached, proved, however, to be Maggy Nowlan. She rose to meet him.

" Ha ! Mag ! what brings you here after all
my commands ? You have frightened Miss Letty
away, I suppose."

" I didn't frighten her away ; an' yet she's
gone away, sure enough, Masther Frank."

" What do you mean ? gone home ? with a
servant, come to fetch her ?"

" Gone to Dublin, wid the priest," laughed
Maggy.

" How you sputter out your lies, old Mag !
It cannot be."

" I only saw him lifting her into the shay."

He stood overwhelmed with contending emotions. The accomplishment, even of his own plans and wishes, shook him to the soul; he had been taken off his guard; he could not have contemplated the event at this moment, although we have heard him speaking loosely about it; and the fate of a sister so suddenly determined, compelled a natural struggle even in the breast of such a brother as Mr. Frank, about whom, by the way, the reader has yet much to learn. After a silence of some minutes, he left the spot, saying, in a low voice, to Maggy—

" Now, you and your mother, and your brother Phil, are to get to Dublin as fast as you can, Mag; and as all has been settled, good night; I will see you here to-morrow evening; not a word in the mean time."

He separated from her without further adieu, and walked slowly to his uncle's. Mr. Long had retired to bed. He enquired for Miss Letty, telling the servants she had left him, an hour since, to return home. They had not seen her; he supposed she also was in her chamber; and asking a light, he said he would go and see. Ascending alone to Letty's apartment, he found

the door open, glanced round to ascertain if he
was unobserved, locked it gently, put the key in
his pocket, regained the drawing-room, informed Letty's attendant she must have retired early,
as her door was shut, and he could not get her
to answer, supposed she had entered the house
without their notice, and, finding herself fatigued, gone straight to repose: and dismissing
the girl, with an injunction not to disturb her
young mistress, Frank then laid his head on his
hand in a deep reverie.

" No use," he thought, " to agitate the
house and my uncle to-night; I can break the
news myself, in the morning; and pursuit will
then be less dangerous than it now might prove
to be. Maggy may be seen early, to serve as
my informant, and to bring a message. Besides, I must hide it as long as possible from
the Nowlans, too. Their blubbering about that
clown would sadly interrupt the joy of Peggy's
nuptials. Let me see. The priest will travel
with her all night, so that they will reach Dublin to-morrow morning. Ay; having once
taken the step, he is not likely to dally on the
road. Well; if I can now keep my uncle in
my hands, all goes fair for independence.
At his uncle's instance, Frank wrenched the

Meeting every cursed demand upon me, a good portion of the old acres will be left free; and I begin at last to breathe like a man."

As he moved suddenly in his chair, something fell off the table; he stooped and picked up one of Letty's portfolios; at a glance he flung it far from him, and continued in a new train of thought. " Poor little wretch! I pity her, while her ruin is my rise. I wish, after all, she could have been saved. But she could not when the question was between her partial suffering and my ruin, my utter ruin; loss of character, perhaps loss of life, exposure, at all events, detection,—blowing up. If possible, she shall not want money. I will try to take care of that:—that is, if I can. And, after all, what has happened to her? She has just run away with the idol of her heart, as the saying is, and nothing more: and why should he not be able to support her? Stuff. I 'm boring myself for no reason. The thing is to evade pursuit. Yes; I must see Mag, on my way home, in the morning. On my way home! Come; I was forgetting that this is my bridal night:—bridal fiddlestick! If that old curmudgeon is saucy, the magistrate shall get him pilloried, or whipt through Nenagh town, or trans-

ported to Van's Land, or hanged, or whatever
it is to be. Peggy, my love, I cruelly keep
you waiting. Powers of chance! to think of
this : on the very night, in the beginning of
which I had nearly run my neck in a noose, to
have my fancy and revenge another way !"

Muffling himself, he stole down stairs and out
of the house, a servant, so far in his confidence
as to wink at his occasional absence for a night,
opening the door to him. Walking rapidly, he
soon entered beneath the humble roof of the
Nowlans. The old couple received him in tears,
but they were tears of joy. Peggy and the
friar, omitting John's violent interference, had
made them assured that the important Mr.
Frank Adams was now the husband of their
eldest daughter ; and they readily consented to
be silent on a subject which so nearly concerned
them, and more than readily acceded to his own
arrangement, proposed to Peggy, for celebrating,
in a little family feast, the happy night. The
good dame herself led Peggy to her nuptial
chamber.

Early the next morning, he stealthily left the
house, and bent his steps towards the wretched cabin, in which lived Maggy Nowlan and
her mother. Half way, he stopped upon the

banks of a deep stream, looked round, assured himself he was alone, took out the key of Letty's sleeping apartment, hurled it into the turbid water, and then sprang onward; met Maggy, gave her certain instructions, and, desiring her to follow him close, turned to Long Hall.

The moment a servant appeared, he asked, in the greatest seeming agitation, for his uncle. Mr. Long was not yet up. He hurried to his room; tapped loudly; was desired to come in; and stood before the good gentleman's bed-side, well looking " the prologue to a swelling act."

It might be tiresome, as well as disgusting, to give a minute account of the way he communicated the elopement of his sister, which, he said, a strange woman, who had unfortunately witnessed it, just then imparted to him. The feelings of Mr. Long more forcibly interest us; and they were indeed poignant, even to despair. He would not believe the story—it was so very impossible; had Frank sent to her room? No—Frank had not thought of that; but they would repair to the door together. They did so; and of course found it locked. They called; and of course got no answer. At his uncle's instance, Frank wrenched the

lock open, and they entered the apartment ;—
alas—

> "———— It was lonely,
> As if the lov'd tenant were dead !''—

The delicately-framed invalid—the sensitive
and outraged uncle—swooned under this dreadful calamity, and was borne, insensible, to the
library, by Frank and the servants he had
summoned.

When restored, Frank was at his side, and
held his hand. Mr. Long fell weeping on his
neck, as he said—" Now, Frank, now, I have
only you in the wide world! do not deceive
me, too !"—

" Alas, Sir !" with a trembling voice, as he
pressed the trembling hand he held so close.

" But cannot the wretched creature be re-
claimed ?" continued Mr. Long, rousing himself—" can we not pursue, and bring her
back ?"

" Oh, Sir ! I have thought of that—it was
and is my only hope—"

" Where is this woman who saw them go ?—
A post-chaise, you say ? and she walked out to
meet him ? Heaven and earth !—it must have
been long planned !—the heartless, worthless

creature meditated it ! And that ungrateful dis-
sembler too ! that smooth villain !—oh, Frank,
I suspected this long ago, and told you I
did !"

"Yes, my dear uncle, yes !—and I shall
blame—hate myself eternally, for rejecting your
suspicions and counsel—indeed I shall—"

"But this woman—where is she ?—her information may give their route at least—"

Frank rang the bell; Maggy soon appeared,
and after describing, with needful additions, the
manner of the elopement, delivered to Mr.
Long the following false message from his
niece.

"Afther I spoke to her, Sir, an' bid her take
heed what she was doin', an' she scoulded me
for my pains, the young misthress tould me to
bring you these words, Sir—' Go to my uncle,
in the mornin', an', for your life, not afore the
mornin',' says she, ' an' advise him, from me, to
give himself no great throuble on my account,
for, the thing I 'm now doin' I long planned to
do; an' my coorse is my own free choice, an'
neither he nor any other can turn me from it ;
tell him I was tired of livin' the life I led, shut
up from the world in that big house, an' it 's
time for me to follow a likin' o' my oun ; as to

the fortin he promised me, he may give it or keep it ; I 'm not afeard of seeking my own.' "

On account of some vulgar embellishments added by Maggy herself to this preconcerted message, Frank thrilled with fear during its delivery, lest it should prove too strong, too strangely unnatural, for his uncle's ear ; but the good gentleman's feelings did not permit him to see nice distinctions ; perhaps, too, he allowed something for the messenger's character and probable exaggeration ; at all events, he did not suspect it to be a cheat; and it instantly caused him to alter his determination of pursuing his unhappy niece.

When Maggy withdrew, he remained a long time silent, resting his face on his hands.

" Human nature is the nature of a beast, Frank," he at last resumed ; " there is no generosity in it ; no heart or soul ; and, what is worse, not even the gratitude of beasts for love and caresses conferred. As to delicacy or taste, sensitiveness or dignity of character, pshaw !— that is a dream. Here was such a creature as we do not see every day, and yet she only proves the more finished deception. Good Heaven ! so young, too ! so seemingly pure, simple, and innocent ! and after all my cherish-

ing. Frank, Frank! I am abused as much as
I have been deceived."

His nephew, while Mr. Long once more hid
his face in his hands, spoke all the comfort
that love, duty, and sympathy, could naturally
be supposed to suggest. Mr. Long interrupted
him.

" I will deal very plainly with you, Frank.
I hope you may continue every way worthy of
my confidence and esteem; but, after this
chance, and in recollection of your earlier life,
I doubt, I fear, Frank—pray, let me speak on—
If Letty can, all of a sudden, deceive and outrage me, you, who have been in the habit of
deceit, may relapse at your leisure."

" My dearest uncle! rash, headlong, and
most guilty I have been, but pardon me if I
remind you, not so much through plan as
through impulse."

" I do not know, Frank. It was after I
received the first private notice of your cul-
pable proceedings at Oxford, and after you
promised me future amendment, that your
fleecing of that young nobleman came to my
ears, in a way too you could not have possibly suspected; upon the occurrence of that
shameful act, which, but for my unwearied ef-

forts, would have cost you expulsion ; you had been, young as you were, an experienced gambler for three or four years, and you know people said there *was* some plan in setting upon the thoughtless boy in the way you did. About the same time, too, you contrived to get yourself cut on the turf, while your suspected acquaintance with the domestic inmates of certain places in and near St. James's-street exposed your friends to dreadful doubts of what might be your more hidden courses. Excuse me, Frank, for this retrospect ; but the present event has startled me into candour ; I believe you will see it make me an altered man ; at all events, it pushes me upon a question : why have you lately showed no anxiety to resume your journey to Dublin, for the purpose of entering college ?"

" His arm had scarce been well," Frank said, " and he was just thinking to ask leave to run up—and, if his dear uncle pleased, he would start that very day."

" No, Frank ; there must now be an end of the scheme ; as I have said, you are the only friend left to me in the world, and that brings me back to my point. I hope your reformation is complete, Frank : I will believe it is, but mark me: while we live, here or elsewhere, on terms of perfect good-will and confidence, your actions and the character of your whole life must give me the best proof; I expect to see no mystery, nothing equivocal, nothing to start the shadow of a doubt; and I fairly warn you, Frank, that I shall be more watchful, and, if necessary, more decisive than ever. I tell you again, I am changed—this morning has changed me, but let us never allude to *her* again; leave me, I wish to be alone some time. Stay, Frank; when you go out to the drawing-room, remove any thing you may find there that—you know what I mean; farewell."

With a good affectation of repentant humility, Frank listened to his uncle, and now retired, bowing very lowly. When he had left his presence, " I am warned," he muttered, " and, being no fool, shall stand on my guard."

It is unnecessary now to say that the letter his poor sister had addressed to his uncle, never reached Mr. Long.

The news of John Nowlan's fall soon spread to his humble family. We shall not attempt to describe their agony. Peggy's letter to him

may have indicated it. The public denunci-
ation of the refractory sinner at the altar of his
own chapel, remained hidden from the two old
people: no one, not even the most babbling
and unfeeling neighbour, would tell them of
that. Peggy knew it, however, and it withered
up her heart. Along with, perhaps, more immediate causes for solitary drooping and fret-
ting, it made her life a waste and a burden.
After her beloved and lost brother refused to
answer her affectionate letter, and after his de-
nouncement, she never raised her head. Her
young and handsome features never wore a
smile.

Frank seemed to exert himself to the utmost
to soothe the first storm of anguish felt by her
and her father and mother : that was a passing
consolation. But, in about a month from their
marriage, he began to absent himself from the
house ; and his few meetings with Peggy showed neither the tender anxiety of a husband, nor
even the fervor of a lover. The old couple
noticed the change to her ; she made no reply,
and did not so much as weep in their presence.
Time wore on ; and Peggy presented to the
eyes of her watchful mother promises of a na-

tural event. Mrs. Nowlan, urged by the feelings of wounded pride and parental affection,
spoke warmly to Frank upon the necessity of
acknowledging his marriage. The young gentleman was very cool and deliberate, and requested, next day, a private interview with
Peggy. They met in a lonesome place.

" My dear Peggy," he began, " you do not
wish to ruin your husband, and the father of
your child."

" God knows," she said, " how my heart answers the question ;—I am careless, for my own
part, how soon or how late you own me as your
wife, Frank, if that is what you mean."

" But your mother, Peggy,—she is obstinate
and foolish ; and if my uncle hears of our marriage, I tell you, once again, I am a ruined
man. Will you go to Dublin, for a time, where
one of my friends is anxious to attend to you ?"

" No, Frank ; I cannot leave my mother's
side during this trial ; but I promise you to do
my best with my mother to make her hold her
peace ; and let the good neighbours say just
what they like of me ; let them say, that the
sister of the runaway priest—"

" Come, come, Peggy ; no whimpering ; that,
you know, is useless : and sit down here ; you

are weak ; and taste this—" producing a phial.
" As a husband, you know I must be alive to
your situation, and its necessary comforts ; so,
here is a little draught I have got from the best
physician in Limerick, to strengthen you, and
do you good—taste it, dear Peggy."

" What is it, Frank ?" she asked, taking the
bottle, and gravely looking on it.

" I have told you ; a nourishing draught for
persons in your state :—and 'tis not so disagreeable neither—just try it."

" My mother will know better than either of
us, Frank, and I will first show it to her."

" No, Peggy," snatching it, as she was about
to put it up, " if you so unceremoniously reject
my opinion, no other person shall decide betwixt
us ; and I must tell you, madam, this *is* more
unceremonious, more insolent than I reckoned
upon, from you to me." He rose up pale and
trembling, his handsome eyes flashing, for the
first time, fiercely and ominously on Peggy.

" What do you mean, Frank ? what have I
done ?" not able to rise with him.

" Since explanation is necessary, madam, I
shall tell you. You call me a husband ; you
profess to hold towards me the duty of a wife ;
I put it to your affection and obedience to oblige

and obey me in two distinct matters, and you refuse both; but by the light of Heaven!—by—"

He stamped, and was becoming outrageous,
when Peggy interrupted him,—"Give me the
draught, again, Sir! give it, dear Frank! I am
sorry for having vexed you—give it—I will
drink it, at once; there can surely be no harm
in so simple a matter." Wholly unsuspicious,
although she had been prudent, Peggy reached
out her hand. His eyes flashed with a different
passion as he gave the bottle, and said—"That's
my own good gentle Peggy, drink, and get
strength."

She raised the phial to her lips,—when, at a
hop, step, and jump, tumble over a bank came
Peery Conolly, and with one judicious tap of his
cudgel shivered it in pieces, as he cried out—
"The divil's-dam's cordial! not a taste of it do
we want! hould your hand, a-chorra! it's the
dance it 'ill gi' you! the dance, a-vourneen! the
dance that 'll never let you alone, night or day,
over-an-hether, in town or counthry!"—and continuing to speak after his deed was done, Peery
capered about, with might and main, as if to
hold up himself as an example of the visitation
he conditionally prophesied.

"Impudent rascal!" cried Frank, collaring him, "how durst you do that?"

"It's not that, but this, a-roon," answered Peery, as, with great skill, he tripped up his heels. Frank started to his feet in a moment, and, while Peggy screamed aloud, again approached him as he exclaimed "Scoundrel! you shall be duly punished for your insolence! what is your name? who or what are you? Villain! you shall shake for it!"

"My name it's Conolly the rake—"

And Peery got through his verse, still capering strangely, "an' that's my name, so it is; an' about the shakin', let us thry who's to shake first: whisper a bit—"

He darted suddenly to Frank's ear, gave one inaudible whisper, and the result showed that Frank, indeed, was the person doomed first to shake, and shake fearfully too. He started back as if he had been shot; and while he trembled from head to foot, gazed horribly on poor Peery. His eyes glazed and set, his lips parted widely, and moved as if in slight convulsions. Presently a sudden change came over his face, his brow knitted, his glance lightened, his teeth clenched, and he slowly moved his

arm to his breast, and thrust in his hand, as if
searching for something. Peggy leaped up,
frightened to death.

" Frank !" she cried, " rouse yourself, what
are you about to do ? what do you search for ?"

" Off, woman !" flinging her aside, so rudely
that she reeled and fell. " I search for that
which I ought to be accurst for not finding, for
that which, after his assault, would get me but
a lawful revenge, in self-defence ! Damnable
traitor !" he continued, addressing Peery,
" breathe that word again, and you are lost !
Even as it is, tremble ! you are an idiot, indeed, and none will believe you—but beware !
Come to me, and come soon ; fall upon your
knees at my feet, and promise and swear, and
humble yourself in the dust, or woe upon your
miserable head ! Beware ! I say."

He rushed out of sight, and Peery, remaining a moment ludicrously to mimic his frown
and gesticulation, gave two or three transcend-
ent capers, and with a " pilla-la-loo-oo-ah !"
danced off in another direction.

" The good God deliver me from that man !"
cried Peggy, now left alone, as she sat weeping on the ground ; " the good God that gave
me into his power, deliver me from his hands !

It was poison he wanted me to drink, I 'm sure of it now! Oh, brother! brother! where are you this day to relieve me in the suffering your own madness brought on me! Oh, I haven't a friend in the world to stand up for me! what am I to do? what am I to do?"

" You are to put your trust in the God you have invoked, ma-colleen, and you are to act a bold and an honest part," said the voice of Friar Shanaghan, close by her.

" Oh, Sir, Sir, pity and help me!" clinging to the old man's knees: " You do not know what has happened—what has just happened, in this very place, on this spot!"

" But I do though, my child, I heard all the bad man said to you; and my own hand should have dashed the phial from your lips, had not that poor silly creature been before me."

" He wanted to poison me and my child, Sir!" continued Peggy, sobbing wildly.

" No, Peggy, you wrong him a little there; he only wanted to wither up, before its time, the infant you are bringing him; nothing else could he have intended—simply because he dared not; but that he certainly thought to do."

" You tell me so, Sir?" she resumed, slowly

G 5

rising with the friar's help, and apparently more shocked at this certainty, than at her first suspicion ; " the inhuman man ! could he mean that ?"

" I have my own reasons for thinking—perhaps for knowing what I say, child. You have heard I am an inquisitive ould fellow, though I don't always seem so, and that I ask questions and get answers when nobody minds me ; and then you see I am mostly on the foot, here and there, or, to tell the blessed truth, it's the poor grey that's mostly on the foot, and I snug on her back ; so, to make a long story short, I believe I heard say where and how he got the little bottle yesterday evening, and for what he wanted it."

" Then, Sir," resumed Peggy, who had listened with profound attention, " my part is taken."

" And what part is that, a-vourneen ?"

" To save myself and my infant from this man, Sir."

" But how, child ? how ?"

" By never seeing his face again, Mr. Shanaghan."

" No," rejoined the old friar, frowning shrewdly, as he shook his head and looked

down ; " that won't do neither. Listen to me,
ma-colleen. There's a little bird that comes to
me with news, now and then, and is just after
telling me another thing : your husband wants
to say he's not your husband, and that your
child is not to be an honest child."

Peggy looked simple astonishment ; she knew
nothing of the statute book, and could not
comprehend the meaning or practicability of
this.

" And moreover, my pet, he has been putting questions, I hear, as to whether he can get
me sent to Botany Bay, or hanged, for marrying you and him."

She looked still more confounded. The
friar explained briefly and clearly. Peggy
was quick at apprehending, and she at once
understood the whole question.

" So that you see, Peggy my child, it isn't
by never seeing his face again, that you and
your little burden are to be saved from shame
and danger."

" No, Sir, it is not, I believe that, now ;
nor can you, either, Sir, be saved in this way."
Her agitation subsided, and she only looked
very thoughtful.

" Never mind me, Peggy ; and I tould him

just the same thing before; only look sharp on
your own account, and you can yet do yourself a service, may be. Have you a strong
heart, Peggy ? have you courage ?"

" I am not a coward in the right, Sir; and
I think God will give me great strength in this
business."

" Well; I don't fear you; and now wait
till I tell you what I think you ought to do.
You know, he depends entirely on his uncle.
You know, too, his uncle is as good a man, as *he*
is a bad one."

" I do, Sir; and I see the way you want to
point out; indeed, I was thinking of it."

" That 's my brave colleen; I expected no
less, and you 'll just put yourself at once under Mr. Long's protection, won't you ? Just
tell him the whole story, plump and straight,
in your own little way ?"

" I will tell him the whole truth, Sir, from
beginning to ending, if you stand by me."

" And may be I won't. Do you know what,
Peggy ? The poor grey is nibbling a bit, at
the end of the bosheen: bundle yourself up,
body and heart, together;—take my arm;
I 'll put you sitting on the crature's back, for
I know you can ride sideways in a man's sad-

dle: I saw you at it once, before you went to
the nunnery; and you needn't have the laste
fear. My poor grey is as asy as a sedan-chair;
but to make all sure, I 'll lade you by the
bridle, and in half an hour, or so, we'll be
walking up Long-Hall avenue: what do you
say? There's no time to be lost; a night
must not go over you for nothing, and the
dark is now coming on; so, here 's an ould man's
arm for you, if you can trust him."

" In my God, Sir, in you, and in the right,
I put my only trust," answered Peggy, as she
accepted the proffered arm.

CHAPTER VI.

AFTER leaving Peggy and Peery, Frank
Adams bent his steps to his uncle's, at first walking rapidly, and then slowly and thoughtfully,
when he began to grow ashamed of the vehe-
mence into which he had been betrayed. An
avoidance of the danger threatened in poor
Peery's whisper, became his chief subject of
meditation. Even Peggy Nowlan, and all connected with her, at present yielded to the su-
perior importance of this matter. Ere he had
gained a view of Long-Hall, Peery's destruction was not only resolved upon, but planned
without the seeming possibility of failure. All
the means were at hand. As if fortune studied
to favour him, a person, deemed by Frank to
be most useful, indeed, indispensable in the
project, met him outside the shrubbery, near
the house. He could not expect to see his
friend in that very place, although he knew he

was within call. They whispered together a few moments, but were obliged to separate very suddenly, as a slow step came down the shrubbery walk; and Frank, now alone, advanced to see his uncle.

After a salutation, " Who was that ?" asked Mr. Long.

" Where? when, my dear Sir ? whom do you mean ?"

" The person that turned from your side, at the far end of this path, as I came up."

" Dear uncle, I was quite alone ; no one turned from my side ; you must have seen my own shadow among the trees, faintly cast by the moon just beginning to shine,—and how beautifully she does shine !—or the shadow of one of the stems, Sir."

" Perhaps ; yet I am not quite certain, Frank."

" My dear uncle ! what can you mean ?"

" This, Frank,—you begin,—you have more than begun to break the compact last entered into between us—pray do not interrupt me. We were to have had no mystery, no doubtful, or secret goings on : but, Frank, all you do, all you say, all connected with you, is doubtful and secret. The very tones of your voice, the

very expression of your eyes, grow troublous—
fearful to me. I am here, a solitary, nervous
invalid, and you terrify me with mystery;
you begin to make me tremble. I will come
to particulars with you. I cannot bear this
existence. Strange people lurk about my
grounds : men, whose appearance and faces, as
I catch glimpses of them, are not like the pea-
santry of the country, and I fear, Frank, I fear
some of them lurk in my house ! Listen to me.
But last night, as I lay awake, I heard you,
notwithstanding all your precautions, arranging
to leave the house, (and *there* is another instance of your secret proceedings,) and much
interested, of course, I arose, dressed myself,
saw you issue towards the village disguised—
but that is not the point : having watched
you from the parlour windows, I was returning alone to my chamber, a lamp in my hand,
when a foot sounded stealthily in the stairs
above me ; and, looking up, I caught indistinctly the profile of a face I had before seen,
although I had no right to see it a second time,
in my own house, at the dead of the night.
Do not smile, Frank, do not attempt to tell me
I might have been mistaken ; that pale, calm,
marbly face, is never to be forgotten :—and it

was, Frank, the face of the Englishman, who deposed, along with you, to the robbery of the mail-coach—the face of Lawson."

"And, my dearest uncle," said Frank, continuing to smile, "I know it was: now, for common charity, Sir, hear me out, in turn. Some months ago, I got reason to believe that one of the fellows engaged in the outrage, to which you allude, lived in the neighbourhood, and, under cover of assumed insanity, thought to hide himself from notice. I contrived to see him, and became rather assured he was the very person who fired upon me, and wounded me in the arm. But, before I would take any decided steps, I wrote to Mr. Lawson."

"He could give you no assistance, Frank, in identifying the man : for Lawson's depositions, drawn up by himself, and which I still hold, assert his ignorance of the persons of any of the mail-coach robbers."

"And so they do, uncle ; and that was not my motive in writing, at all ; I only deemed that two respectable witnesses to the fact of the robbery would be better than one ; so, my dear Sir, after many delays, Mr. Lawson at last consented to come over to Ireland. Early in the evening of yesterday, he announced to me, by a private message, his arrival in the village; I sent him word to meet me as privately in the house, here, that we might go over the whole matter, alone; he came towards midnight: acting upon particular information, I repaired to the village, to obtain, in a public-house, a second closer observation of the robber; Mr. Lawson remained behind me, and you saw him: I returned perfectly convinced; indeed, more than ever so, of the identity of the fellow in question; and we but await the assistance of competent officers to lodge our joint informations, and secure his arrest. And now, my dearest uncle, you will ask, why conceal this from you? But need I answer? You were an invalid; your nerves shattered, indeed, from various irritations; and surely it was my duty, the common duty of grateful affection, to save you from any protracted annoyance on this head; to wait until the thing was done, and then at once inform you of it; not fret you about it, morning, noon, and night, during Mr. Lawson's long delay and indecision, which from the beginning I foresaw."

"Is the gentleman now in the house?" asked Mr. Long.

"No, Sir; he has walked down to the village; but, if you wish, you can see him to-night, or else—"

" Phru-u ! stop a bit, ma'am, if you please, here," interrupted the voice of Friar Shana-ghan, admonishing his " poor grey," as he led her up the avenue.

" Who are those persons ?" enquired Mr. Long.

" Heaven and earth !" Frank began, getting a view of the group : then checking himself— " Who can they be, indeed ?—oh, some wandering beggar with his wife, ass, and brats. Allow me, my dear uncle—these scenes are too strong for you ; I will soon relieve you from them. Pray turn towards the house, Sir ; the night-air does not serve you : thanks, dear uncle ; and now—"

" Do not dismiss the poor people roughly, Frank, whoever they may be ; give them a little assistance," interrupted Mr. Long, as he walked away.

" Fear nothing, Sir," answered Frank, as he bounded from the shrubbery across the lawn that separated him from the avenue.

" Welcome, Sir," began the Friar, while he came up ; " seeing you and your uncle together, we halted to speak a bit."

" My uncle will gladly see you in the house, good Sir, and has sent me to say as much to you and your companion—Ah ! Peggy, my life, what brings you out, so late ?"

" A little business, Sir ; a little business, that concerns you and her," answered Mr. Shanagan, as Peggy remained silent.

" What, Peggy !" advancing closely to her, and speaking ardently, though in a suppressed tone, " can this mean that you propose to address my uncle on the subject of the connexion between us ?"

" Yes, Sir ; on the subject of our marriage," answered Peggy, with emphasis.

" For God's sake ! for both our sakes ! But first grant me your private ear, only a moment —just allow me to lead the animal a step aside— just ask this good man to allow us one confidential word ; this cannot harm you, Peggy, and I entreat it !"

She requested the old ecclesiastic to take no notice of Frank and her, for an instant ; and Frank led her out of his sight and hearing, as the Friar muttered, " Ay ; let him palaver you again ; do ; I see the end of it."

" Now, Peggy," resumed Frank, when they

were quite alone, " I am your humble peti-
tioner ; I will kneel, if you ask it, only to beg
that, for this night at least, you do not expose
me to my uncle ! It would be my ruin ! he is in
some unaccountable ill-humour against me—
and if you ever loved me—and I believe you
did, and hope you do—if you love the child
you have not seen—"

" Mr. Frank," interrupted Peggy—" these
ifs come with little effect from you—from you,
who this day thought to make me show my
love for my unborn infant and for my God, in a
way that—"

" You mean that accurst draught—you suppose it was intended badly ; some fool and
meddler has told you so—but, dearest Peggy, you wrong me, sorely ! I offered it but
for your good—it could have produced no
other effect—let me be confounded for ever if
it could. The thought is horrible, Peggy !
horrible, of your husband—of the father of
your infant—throw it from your heart, and if
this be your only reason for coming to destroy
us both to-night, just turn home again, and
see what to-morrow will do ! On my knees, indeed," (he knelt) " I ask that."

" It is not my only reason, Frank: I fear
something even worse; I fear you want to say
we are not man and wife, that our child is to
be a base-born child, and that I—" she stopped.

" Madness, again, Peggy—worse than madness! I swear to you, on my soul, and my
soul's hope, you are shamefully wronged by
whoever has told you this. Listen to me.
Only return home, and give me a few hours'
preparation, and before the dawn of morning
I will prove this cannot have been my intention.
Let me have time to speak to a Protestant
clergyman—and, about midnight—say twelve
o'clock, exactly—let you steal out of your
father's house, and meet him and me at the
upper end of the Foil Dhuiv—'tis the nearest
point to his road—and there, the moon and
stars for our sole witnesses, except the all-seeing
eye above them, there, Peggy, shall you and
I be re-married, according to the rite of the
established church—will that satisfy you? will
that show how much I have been belied? will
that restore you to no confidence in the husband
of your heart?—and, after it, can you not
consent to await a proper time for my public-
ly taking you by the hand as my wife?"

" It would, indeed, satisfy me for the present, Frank; and, I hope, my father and mother too. What is the name of the clergyman you intend to bring with you? have I seen him?"

"You have, no doubt; young Mr. Sirr; an admirer of one of my sisters; he shall be the man: I am quite sure of his obliging me."

"Well, I'll meet you, Frank, at the upper end of the Foil Dhuiv, at twelve exactly; and no one but Mr. Shanaghan by my side."

"No one on earth, Peggy!—no human being by your side! Consent to this, or we are indeed undone: I fear the imprudent babbling of your friends, one and all—see how they have injured me in your own opinion already—it cannot be—I will brave my uncle at once, rather than that."

"But witnesses are always necessary," urged Peggy, coolly and watchfully.

"I know they are, where doubt exists; and, since you doubt me, Peggy, although I first thought to be quite alone, witnesses you shall have—of my choice, though—Do not dissent, but listen! one of my brothers and one of my sisters shall come with me, and be ready to take you by the hand—my eldest sister—Are you at ease, now?"

" You promise, this, Frank ?" looking seriously upon him.

" On my life, I do !—yet, if you will doubt
me still, what use of a promise or an oath ?
have you not your remedy in your own hands ?
If, when we all meet, you do not feel pleased
at the arrangements I shall have made, can you
not keep your cruel resolution until morning,
and accuse me to my uncle then, as well as
now ? Dearest and only-beloved Peggy, your
heart must be quite hardened against me and
my child, or you would not hesitate so long.
This is the very harshest treatment—I did not
merit it—God knows I did not."—She thought
he wept.

" Then I will fully depend on you, Frank—
No; I have no doubt ; I will have none; I
can have none; I will meet you and your
friends quite alone."

" Eternal thanks, my own dear Peggy ! But
now, I ask you in turn, is this a solemn promise ?"

" It is : a solemn promise, before God."

" No one shall even know you leave home ?—
Assure me of that too ; for their suspicions would
be as bad as any thing else : they would follow
you, dog us, and——you promise again ?"

" Yes; 'tis but part of my first promise ; I

could not leave home alone, unless I hid my departure from every one in the house."

" True, true; — and there is another little matter that, as you say, also forms part of your first solemn engagement. If no one is to know where you go, you can tell no one; neither father nor mother, nor yet this old priest—this good old gentleman—is it not so?"

" Certainly; I must be as silent as I am careful."

" And of course, again, when he asks you what we have been saying, you cannot answer him ?"

" Not a word."

" But what will you say ? You must invent something ;—let us see."

" No, Frank; we are not obliged to invent any thing. It is not necessary, even if it could be done ; even if I would do it. Should he ask me, I will just plainly tell him not to ask me again ; and surely he cannot be displeased at any confidence between man and wife."

" You are right, my good excellent girl ; you teach me what is right: in fact, then, he shall not know upon what account you alter the determination that has led you both here this evening—what you intend, one way or another. You will merely say you defer your purpose?"

" Nothing more."

" And as soon as twelve o'clock comes, you will meet me and my friends in the Black Glen?"

" I will ; but, Frank, I wish the hour was a little earlier, or the place another place. I am not very childish about these things ; but you know the Foil Dhuiv has a bad name, and is an ugly place at any rate."

" Pho, my dearest girl, I did not expect this from you ; nor do I, can I expect you will think of it a moment longer. All places are alike to those who fear no harm from having done bad, or from coming to do it ; and friends will be waiting for you, you know, and 'tisn't so far from your father's door ; scarce a mile ; and besides, as I said, Mr. Sirr can so easily turn to the spot—that is the great point."

" No matter then—I will be punctual."

" Blessings on you, for ever, Peggy !—and now, won't you give me a wife's farewell till midnight, after all ?—Ah, Peggy, what a soft and silky kiss !—none other in life is like it. Adieu, love, for a few hours ; and now let us return to Mr. Shanaghan."

In perfect silence, except that he met all stated with a " hum," or the end of a tune, the old friar received his charge, with her own request to be led home to her father's.

They proceeded down the avenue, and along a good stretch of the road, and still the dry old man remained without speaking a word as he led the " poor grey" by the bridle, over rut and puddle. His humming of bits of tunes grew, indeed, more surly; and sometimes he broke out into the opening of a Latin hymn, such as the " *Magnificat*" or the " *Confiteor tibi*," to which exercise of his voice for vespers he was, during his lonely *quests*, accustomed. At last, though still he did not speak, he began to interrupt himself with little bursts of splenetic laughter, and Peggy saw it was time for her to conciliate.

" You are angry with me, Sir," she said.

" Me angry !—for what, child ?—God settle your poor little head, I have something else to think of ; only, to tell the blessed and holy truth, I certainly was fancying, just then, what a respectable figure I cut, thrapsing about the country, myself and my grey, with a woman on our backs, at this time of our life, that knows just as much of her own mind, or her own good, as a blind cow does of a holiday."

" I could not help changing my mind, Sir ; indeed I could not ; charity and fair-dealing obliged me to change it ; and, Sir," anticipating what she knew she had to encounter—" if I was at liberty to tell you our conversation, you would yourself say the same thing."

" Oh, no doubt in the world of that, ma'am ; not the laste ; all quite right and as it should be, to be sure ; all settled to a hair, I know ; and all to be kept snug from the meddling ould friar that brought you the road ; sure I know, very well, thank God !—you're a rock of sense ; grey hairs on a priest's head, no more to you than a mill-sthrame to the Shannon : Ay, ay, and why not ; you understand him so well, and you're such a match for him, particularly at the tongue. Well, praise be to God, I say again, it's a dacent calling I 've turned myself into in the latter end o' my days ; the grey and I ; ay, yes, and good enough for us ; qups, Sheela, qups ; show your paces, miss, and mind your steps ; a wiser load you couldn't have on your back, supposing it the whole Council of Trent, and you an elephant big enough to carry them; and a betther trade your masther couldn't have than roaming about with you, from post to pillar, day and night, as a carter with his load, or a raree-show-man with his wonders of the world."

"Indeed, Sir, if you knew all, you would not be angry with me; and indeed, and in truth, I am very grateful for your kindness, and very sorry for your trouble; especially your walking so much, while I am on your horse; and if I was a year younger, Sir, you should be on Sheela's back, and I, as 'ud be my duty and pleasure, stepping along at your side; and, badly as you know I am able, I will even now tire you no longer, if you please; only just help me off, Sir, and,"—

"Bother, child," interrupted the friar; "bother says Brotherick, when he lost mass; stay where you are; I'm not so tired, either, ould as I am, and such a fool as I am, tho' it's kind of you (poor thing like you) to think of it. No ma'am, I didn't mean to quarrel with you; I like you too well, you baggage, for that; so, there now; and if you cry another tear, and if you don't give a good laugh at the ould friar, from the heart out, salvation to me,

but I'll kiss you and run away with you :—
what—eh ?—are we friends yet ?"

Peggy made a dutiful answer.

"Well : that's right ; and now, Peggy, my
child, we're in the bosheen, and I must lave you
to step home by yourself, for neighbour Shearman promised me a bed to-night ; and so God
bless you, Peggy ;—and only one word—Do not
depend on him, too far—do not depend on him
at all !—I know him, and you do not. Whatever he has said to you—whatever he has promised,—look close at it. If *you* have promised
any thing, think twice before you perform it.
I don't want your little secrets ; even if I did, I
see how it is ;—I might go without them ; no
matter for that ; but—since you can have no
other adviser, now advise with yourself ; ask
God to enlighten you. He is a bad man, I
tell you, Peggy ; and so good night." They
parted.

After Frank saw them turn upon the road
out of the avenue, he stood some time in deep
and breathless meditation. Then he returned
to the house, and sought his uncle. Mr. Long
again candidly brought forward in conversation the doubts of Frank he had before express-

ed; Frank combated them as adroitly as he could; the topic changed to Mr. Lawson, and the prosecution of the mail-coach robber. At last it grew late; Mr. Long rose to go to his chamber; Frank, accompanying him, bore a night-lamp into his own; shut his door, seemed to lock it; laid his lamp on a table; listened to his uncle's movements; heard a voice call to him out of an inside closet; started on tip-toe to the key-hole, and vehemently whispered through it —Have a care, and curse you !—not a move or a breath, yet !' "

For more than ten minutes he continued to bustle about his chamber; then became motionless, as if he had retired to bed; again whispered into the closet, " Open, but not a word !"—handed in the lamp to the person who there awaited him, stole to the outside door, gently opened it, listened for sounds in his uncle's room, and along the corridor, found all silent, and at last entered the closet.·

" You 've staid d—d long to-night," said the man he had secreted in it, and who sat at a small table, with a whiskey bottle, water and sugar, before him; " it has been hell-dark these three hours, except for the winking of the glim

in at this little high window, that reminds me
of a crib more than any thing I ever saw out
of one ; and confound my — eyes, if I can
stand all this much longer."

" I 'm quite sure, Ned, you can't stand it
this moment, if one may judge from the in-
crease of your complexion, your flash, and the
decrease of the black bottle ; but, hold your
tongue, you drunken goose, and speak lower,
while I tell you this,—we are on the brink of
ruin ; you, Studs, you have ruined us."

" As how, Master Frank ?"

" As how, you headstrong hound ? Last
night, after I stole out to pack off Mag, mother,
brother, and the whole kit, and left you here to
lock yourself in, and be d—d to you, with
your promise to stay quiet, and behave yourself, out you must creep, to take the air of
the house and the staircases, so that the old
chap, who was watching me (he 's getting 'cute,
Ned ; sharp 's the word) saw you on the land-
ing-place above him, as he returned to bed ;
saw you, and knew you, too."

" He lies, Master Adams ; by this bottle, I
never tramped an inch through his house last
night."

" *Thou* liest most ungratefully to say the

word, as it was by that very bottle thou wert then led to it, and art now perjured."

" Know me ? know Ned Studs ? well, that 's a good 'un."

"Not *as* Ned Studs, you stupid beast, but as Mr. Lawson, the English traveller."

" Oh ! all right ; and now, Mr. Lawson must be off, I take it ; and yet, that won't do neither."

" No, curse you ! Mr. Lawson must stay where he is, and appear as Mr. Lawson, and as sober as he can to the elder, to-morrow morning ; and I 'll tell you why. But first, Ned, how goes on the little firm over the water ? After you came last night, I was obliged to slip out before I could ask you all that ; this morning you were too drunkenly asleep ; and all day I have been panting to pop the question, and thought I could when we met this evening in the shrubbery—Had the swag much luck ?"

" A little, at first ; doubled or so ; and so kept on for a few months ; then--whew ! and off."

" D---d cross, that ; I believe you must play me loyal here, Ned ; for the final stake is too great to think you could nibble on what was to win it for us both."

" True blue, Master Adams; no fairer man; show it, by being here; for when one swag went, I and another tried for as good a one; got blown, talked about, looked after, and so, Ned Studs is a-drinking your Hirish stingo to-night, just for peace-sake, and a look up to Master Frank for a little help on the road, you know."

" And you shall have it, Ned, if we step high for it; but all the last year has been curst glum. I thought we could have coaxed off from the reversions half the rooks by this time; but on they stick; and then that running interest! I say, Studs, you were to have seen them for me; what do they say?"

" Nothingk; only this, that if you don't down the interest more regular, they 'll blab to old chap about that and other things."

" Hell's fire round them! He knows enough already, and thinks more, Ned; and harps away on old matters from morning to night. More than once, since the Irish swag here, he has hit me in the teeth about that plucking I gave the young Oxford Lord, and that unlucky affair at Newmarket, and our little firm in the West-end; and do you know, Studs, I begin to fear he has heard more than he ought concerning *all* the business of that firm. Could my real name have dropt?"

" Do you mean the Brumagem affair, in Lad Lane, or the heavy Ipswich swag, at Hankey's bundle ?"

"Why, Ned, you know I must mean both."

" Well, no fear of the last ; but while t'other lay in the ring, and the Bow-street barkers at it, with our broker, 'twas said your name *was* a little blown,—a little winded or so."

" The devil ! I always thought that ; and he—but no; could he really have caught a breath of it, I had not been here to-night. All must be safe, so far. Let us talk of business more at hand. You know, Ned, that upon the night of the swag, on this road, we expected a fellow to join us who did not come."

" Ay ; there was you in, with Mag. and Mother Carey ; I, out with young Carey ; and two country chaps of your choosing, were to join the two Dublin chaps, of my own choosing, and only one came to the scratch ; but 'twas all well as it happened ; three could give as good a blank volley as four, while young Phil and I did business with coachee and guard ;—never mind : remember it all ; snug, I say."

" But listen to me, you stupid blunderer.

This one fellow, who hung fire, was enlisted by
Mag, d——n her; I never saw him; she only
told me his name, Conolly; Conolly the rake, as
he calls himself, and a good alias I thought it
was.   Since then, he has never come in my sight
until this day; and, indeed, as I was so sure
my name was out of the thing, with all but you
and Mag, why I never much troubled myself
whether he might be alive or dead.   But this
day, I tell you, Studs, this very day, I met
the fellow without knowing him; and, before
we parted, after telling or singing me his name,
he put his lips to my ear and whispered, ' Who
robbed the mail coach, Master Frank?'   Studs,
I felt as if cold lead went through my brain!
as if————."

"As if Judge Best had asked you the question," interrupted Mr. Studs. "I think I know
what you 'd say; but, Master Adams, isn't
that 'ere chap the very one you told me was to
be put up for the self-same little swag you speak
of, when we met this evening in the shrubbery?"

"To be sure he is; have you done as I bid
you? have you kissed primer before the good
magistrate, my father?"

" John Lawson, of the county of Suffolk, in England, gent., came before me this day, and maketh oath, and saith———"

" Enough ; a point-blank deposition, I warrant ; and my excellent brother, the police chief, will not be long without finding Master Conolly ; and then, if the idiot hasn't peached beforehand with us, which all the devils forbid, how strange he will look to see us take the pretty tale out of his mouth, while not a breathing creature but will laugh out at his true story. Well, Lawson, we must, by some means, have another examination sworn."

" Against whom ? your own uncle, or your own mother, or who the devil ?"

" Only against an old popish friar, Studs, who has, in violation of the statute in that case made and provided, pretended to join in wedlock a certain young lady and your humble servant. I think I have the plan of the examination in my head ; but more about it, by and by ; only it must be done this very blessed night, and the priest put up by day-break. I hope they can't bail him ; do *you* know ? But why should I ask you about bailing any thing that isn't swindling, mail-coach swagging, hell-keeping, or, duly to honour the follies of your youth, pocket-touching, shop-lifting, and petty larceny, *ad libitum*."

" Speak no thieves' Latin to me, Master Frank, I 'm above it."

" Hold your hand, Ned; not another throw out of that black bottle:—lay it down, I say! and don't pretend to fly into a passion with me, just to put yourself off your guard, as it were, for a snatch at it. I know your tricks, Sir. Nor no grumbling, either, now, but sit still and hear, at last, what is worth hearing. I have told you, we were on the edge of ruin— that the drop was under our feet, and only the devil waiting to slip the bolt;—now learn really why and how. You have heard me speak of a wench, whom I had by humming her with the old priest's marriage; well, she 's up, of course, and getting, somehow, a wind of my true notions about her, here she comes to-night, to blow me to the old governor, and blab all how and about it. If she is once allowed to do that, my uncle, who thinks wenching as bad as man-killing, would first make me marry her in earnest; and then turn me off with the girl, upon a few thousands and a blessing: and so, if you can understand any thing, Ned

Studs, behold, in this prospect, the fine old acres wriggled fairly through our fingers: not even the half I was sure of when my pretty sister was here, left to clear the reversions I have (may I be well d——d for it some day !) suffered to get into the claws of the rooks."

" But who 's to allow the silly wench to come down with her gab? that 's all I ask, Master Frank. You sent her off this evening, I know ; can't you take care she don't call again ?"

" How do you mean, Ned Studs ?"

" Poh ! gammon, and so many hows in the case ; and you knowing them all so well."

" I 'm to meet her to-night, at twelve o'clock, in a very lonesome place, far out of sight and hearing of house or home, Ned."

" Are you ?"

" She thinks, to marry her legally."

" Ay, ay."

" Studs, in my case, seeing that every thing depends on mum—run to the saddle-skirts, as I am, what would you do? In what manner would you come to a settling with a foolish, ungrateful, unfeeling girl, if you met her alone, at the dead of the night, in such a place, where, if ever there was a spot to keep a secret— Hush !—who 's there ? douce the glim, Studs !"

In obedience to the latter words, given in a close, sharp whisper, his companion hastily extinguished the lamp.

They sat together in darkness, for many minutes, both silent, and suppressing their fluttered breath, as they strained their ears to catch a sound in the outside chamber. At last,

" Didn't you hear a step?" whispered Frank.

" Caunt say as a' did," answered Studs, " and I think you 've only frightened yourself a bit."

" Hush !—let 's listen again."

Once more they remained perfectly silent ; but, as not the slightest sound was heard, Studs's interpretation seemed plausible.

" Go on, Master Frank," he resumed, " not a mouse is stirring : why don't you go on ? I don't half like this sitting alone, in the deep dark ; I must either drink, or hear the sound of your voice."

" Then I must speak, indeed, Ned, for you have already guzzled enough for the work in hand. But can you guess what kept me silent a moment ?"

" Saying your prayers, Master Frank."

" No ; not so bad, neither : I was only thinking—it was a sudden and a strange thought—

that, if we had really heard a step, it could be no other than nuncle ; and if so, it struck me, Studs, to ask myself the question—should we, or should we not allow him to go back to his bed in full possession of all we don't want him to know : particularly as there has been some chaffer about it before,—and (what he *doesn't* know) as I could lay my hand, this moment, on the will he has last made, by which every acre of Long-Hall estate is legally bequeathed to a nephew of his ? That was just what passed through my head."

" It would be dangerous, here in his own house, Master Adams."

" Dangerous ! no more ! Curses on you for a gallows dog, wouldn't it be treacherous, bloody, diabolical ? I tell you but of a flitting thought that our master shot into my brain, and you, Studs, you imagine it rests with me, and argue only for convenience ! You are a worse villain than I took you for. Never dare to glance at it again. But, now about this poor foolish wench, Sir. I say we are to meet,—she and I, or any one that will stand in my place,—quite alone, exactly at midnight, in the most lonesome and wildest part among these black Tipperary hills. What am I to do with her? how satisfy her? how stop her from coming to accuse me before my uncle in the morning?"

" She thinks you meet her to marry her?"

" Ay, that's the understanding, as it were."

" Would the marriage make her mum?"

" Yes, I promise you; but am I a fool, Studs?"

" Sometimes ay, sometimes no. You don't want to marry her, then? it's all gammon, so far?"

" Confounded stuff and nonsense."

" Well, are you sure she will come quite alone?"

" Cock sure."

" But mustn't some one know where she comes to so late?—some of her friends?"

" Not a soul; her promise is given to that, too; and she'll keep it for her own sake."

" So then she might step into a pit, or a pool, or——But zounds, Master Frank, at which side of me are you?" suddenly lowering his voice.

" Here, at your right hand; why?"

" Then," cried Studs, springing up, " here's the devil at council with us in the dark,—some one else stands at my left, near the door!"

" Secure the door !" exclaimed Frank, " you are next to it ; curse you, fellow ! why will you not move ? I must scramble on myself ; there !" shutting and bolting the closet door, " if the devil *is* in company, we have dared him before, and shall not now fear him ; if any other hearer has intruded, let him tell his beads, and pay for his peeping ; he goes not hence alive. Keep you your back to the door, Ned, while I go round by the walls ; and no pulling of triggers, sirrah, no shots to alarm the house ; but just lend me your case with the spring-bayonets ; one of *them* never misses fire, and makes little noise ; so now stand quiet."

Carefully, although, despite the lightness and hardihood of his speech, his blood curdled and his hair bristled, carefully did Frank grope all round the closet, but no intruder was to be found ; again and again he searched, and was disappointed.

" You must have raved in your cups, Studs," he then said ; " here is no one but ourselves ; where did you see, or think you saw, the person ?"

" Where I said, at my left hand, his back against the wall ; but when I looked a second time, he was gone."

" Tush! you are a cowardly goose, and that's all. Let us leave this place, however; my time for meeting with the girl I spoke of is near at hand. Muffle yourself up as well as you can, and follow me out of the house by the private way. Stick close to my skirts, lest you stumble in the dark, and make some cursed noise. Stop, I too must put on a disguise, some coarse things that now and then serve me; we will talk over the whole business on our way; and whether or no you do any thing else for me, you know you have to call on the magistrate."

At about the time they secretly left Long-Hall, Peggy Nowlan also crept out of her father's house, to keep her appointment in the Foil Dhuiv.

Notwithstanding her solemn promise to Frank, she did not bring herself to take such a step without much inward struggling. The friar's cautions first alarmed her; in the alarm, all her own former ones sprang up; and while she sat alone in her little chamber, by the feeble flickering gleam of an economical rushlight, her father and mother and their servants hushed into sleep around her, and no sound heard outside the house but the hoot of the owl, and the hoarse murmurs of many streams, near and distant, poor Peggy's heart failed and revolted, she knew not why, at the thought of what she was about to do.

In vain did she assure herself that, against whatsoever the friar had intended to warn her, he could not have contemplated possible ill-treatment of her person at Frank's hands: he could not have meant that she was in any danger of bodily harm from him; and if not, what else did she fear? why else should she shrink from meeting him, even all alone, at any hour of the day or night? But he would not come alone—for, again, why should he have promised to marry her, according to the form of his religion, and in the presence of his brother and sister, if he intended to break his word? The disingenuousness could be of no eventual good to him, supposing him not sincere; then why practise it? In the absence of a doubt too horrible—too monstrous and unnatural, what could he mean but to keep his promise? The little phial, though —the scene that day, when they were alone before!—her veins ran cold—she would not go.— Yet, had he not most solemnly, by the most solemn oaths, disavowed the crime attributed by the friar? and might not the friar be mistaken? nay, he was mistaken—he must be—human nature never produced such a monster ; she would trample on the thought. And, again and again, the idea that Frank's offer was a providential chance to allow justice to be done to her unborn infant and herself, and that, if she now weakly rejected it, Heaven might, for her punishment, harden his heart against her in future,—these reveries at last determined Peggy ; and some time before she need have stirred, she was walking rapidly towards the place of rendezvous.

It was a fine night, starry and moonshiny ; and, until she turned into the first shadows of the Foil Dhuiv, Peggy held a brave heart. Then, however, the intense silence, blackness, and loneliness of the place, disagreeably affected her. She had never before been out, so late at night, amidst the desolate solitude of nature ; and,— from the change thrown over them by new effects of light and shade,—features of the rude scenery with which she thought herself familiar, seemed new and strange to her eye :—in one place, a hill looked nearer ; in another, a huge rock more distant ; while, generally speaking, real outline becoming lost, objects distinct in day-light, merged into one strange whole, or took peculiarities of shape that started hideous fancies to the baffled mind.

Step by step, the scene deepened. At last she gained the end of the valley farthest from her father's house, where, at either hand, and widely removed, two vast black hills swept up into the sky, each so toweringly, that the cheery moon, though more than half way in the heavens, was only able to glint, over the outer brow of one, a few rays upon the inner brow of the other. Thus, the whole deep glen remained in shade, except the very unnoticed summit of the mountainous side that, at Peggy's left hand, half formed it. Before her, another heath-clad black hill intercepted any distant view ; and, by the last abrupt turn of her little trembling feet, through the furze-choked and rain-sprinkled path, she was also shut out from a view of the long way she had come.

And here, shivering in the cold night blast, and starting at every sound, Peggy had to await the promised appearance of Frank and his friends. A long time she did wait, alone, and undisturbed, and she thought the hour of appointment must have elapsed, and that, whatever was the cause, he would not come at all. As she looked timidly up and down the shadowed solitude, many weakening fears again assailed her. The interview with Frank, when he frightened her to take the phial from her hand—his glaring eyes—his pale face—his changed character—more vividly than ever occurred ; and then the thought that he might so visit her, alone, in her present situation—she shrunk from that. Peggy remembered too, stories of the Foil Duiv, that used to shake her childhood, and collect terrible dreams for her childish pillow. About where she stood, a woman had once been cruelly murdered, and her bones were found whitening behind a rock, and the cries of her angry spirit often sounded through the glen. In spite of her, for Peggy was not weak-minded nor superstitious, such extraneous recollections added an ominous horror to her real fears ; and at last she was about to rush, screaming, along the path she had come, when the appearance of a single figure, on the side of the opposite and remote hill, rooted her feet to the spot; called back, with her observation, her presence of mind ; and suddenly calmed her into a watchfulness of her own safety.

A few seconds after her eye caught the object, she sank down, carefully and completely hiding herself amid a group of shivered rocks and stones, hedged round by furze-bushes and tall fern, but allowing her, through a little opening, to look out unseen.

The single figure came obliquely down the sweep of the hill, often pausing, as if it looked around, and to every quarter; but, amid the great shadow, and scarce relieved from the blacker back-ground of the hill-side, its motions, as well as itself, were yet very vague and indistinct. In some time it gained the bottom of the Foil Dhuiv; again stood still, and looked to the east, and to the west. Peggy could now assure herself it was a man; but of what quality, his non-descript dress did not allow her to decide. At a nearer approach, she saw he carried something on his right shoulder, and something else under his left arm. He continued his heavy strides towards where she lay; again paused, and again looked to the east and to the west; and now the former article seemed a spade; the latter, a sack, folded hard. He came still closer to her; at the distance of about forty yards stopped once more; renewed his keen scrutiny, at either hand; then threw down his sack, and, with his back turned to her, began rapidly to dig the loose, slaty earth with his spade.

Peggy was skilful enough in all agricultural

operations to perceive that the man worked clumsily, though vigorously, and in earnest haste, often interrupting himself still to look about him, far and near. By his stooping low, and his continuing to dig at one spot, she saw, too, that he was penetrating some depth into the ground. After a lengthened exertion, he ceased : his work seemed done. He cast down his spade upon his sack, folded his arms, crossed the valley to the far side, coming so near that she could have touched his legs, though still she did not see his face; and all the while looking out wistfully, and seeming to change his ground only to gain more commanding points of observation.

And thus he remained for more than an hour ; and thus, for more than an hour, though she could not then measure time, Peggy lay close and still, breathless and motionless, watching him. At length, as if overcome by impatience, he abruptly walked to the pit he had delved, gazed a moment into it, snatched his spade, hastily pitched in the piles of earth he had thrown up: when the hole was filled, stamped with his heels, evidently to harden the spot; smoothened over and all round it with his spade-handle ; took up his sack, and striding off in the direction whence he had appeared, slowly ascended the hill; crossed it obliquely, as he had descended it; disappeared, and Peggy was left alone.

Her feelings, during this scene, we have not attempted to describe; we shall not now attempt to do so. With the self-command, and the mental endurance for which women are, even above the stronger sex, sometimes eminently remarkable, she was able to look on, and give not the slightest indication of alarm. Though, before the coming of the man, imaginary terrors had almost made her shriek out, —yet, now a spectatress of real terrors, and with a consciousness and a misgiving, horrible beyond expression, she did not even breathe hard.

Nor, long after the disappearance of this person, did she stir. He might return; if once caught by his watchful eye, she could not, perhaps, though at a distance, escape him, and therefore she still lay motionless. For more than the time he had stayed, she lay so. But when once Peggy started up, she ran, burdened as she was, without looking to the right or to the left, through the whole length of the Foil Dhuiv; in unabated speed gained her father's house—her

own little chamber-window ;—opened it cautiously ; dragged herself into the room, fastened
her window ; and then, and not till then, did
poor Peggy's brain reel, and her eyes swim, as,
staggering round the earthen floor, she sank
swooning on her bed.

CHAPTER VII.

ABOUT the grey of the morning Peggy recovered to a confused sense of her situation; and
the first effort of her mind was to master her
terror, her agony, and all her feelings. She
became impressed with the conviction that such
was her duty; that she had a decided, courageous, yet temperate part to act; and that self-
possession was the first step in the discharge of
her responsibility. After sitting up, then, on
her bed, until she felt her strength in a degree restored, Peggy knelt down in prayer.
While thus engaged, some unusual stir arose
outside the house: she paid it no attention.
In a few moments, a light step stole to her
chamber-door, which was not fastened: she
turned, and her little sister, Anty, sprang to
her neck, and was clasped, in showers of tears,
to her sad yet comforted heart.

"I heard it all at last, Peggy," sobbed Anty,

" though it was so well and so cruelly hid from me—John's misfortune, and your unhappy marriage, and all; and, the moment I did hear it, came to be one among ye in your trials. Last night I slept at Nenagh. Oh! Peggy, it was very unkind to leave me so long ignorant."

" Anty, Anty," answered her sister, " we thought to keep our heart of one family safe from the curse that fell among us: and then, you were so young and so childish, we believed it would have been a pity to darken your days so soon—though, indeed, Anty, my dear, a few years' absence has made a great change in you,—in your appearance, your manner, and your mind, I 'm sure,—for you were always a sensible child, Anty."

" God grant, sister, I may have sense enough to be, now, to you the comfort you stand in need of. Are you glad to see me, and to speak to me ?"

" Since you *are* come, dear Anty, Heaven could not send a greater consolation. Oh ! you will be such a support to me in what I have to do ; and it will make me so firm to tell you all, and to get your advice ; for, till this moment, I had no one to advise with ; I was quite alone in my trials, Anty: the poor father's

heart is a'most broke, and he cannot talk to
me ; or when he does, 'tis more like a child's
folly than a man's sense : and the poor mother
is turned into gall with her sorrows; *her* speech
is only complaint and crossness; and she cries
so much, alone, that her old eyes are growing
blind with it."

There was a long silence, while the sisters
wept in each other's arms.   At last Anty whispered, " This used to be *his* room, Peggy ;"
and the remark was again followed up with
tears.   " Tell me, Peggy," she resumed, " was
the poor young lady such a temptation to him,
indeed ?"

" Oh, Anty, my eyes never lighted on a
creature like her : as good as she was comely ;
as bright in the mind, as, before *that* happened, I believe she was pure in the heart; and
the real gentlewoman, if ever one walked the
earth."

" And *he*, too, Peggy—when it happened, he
must have been all in her eyes, or in any woman's eyes, that she was in his ; though 'tis so
long since I saw him, I can only suppose so ;
nearly six years, I believe; for, just after I
went to the nunnery, now two years ago, he
was coming home from the bishop's school, with

the priesthood, but I didn't meet him then; and you know he had been at that time four years away from us all. But, was not our poor John a very handsome boy at three-and-twenty?"

Instead of answering, a low abhorring scream escaped Peggy, as she clung close to her almost childish sister; and Anty, following her eyes to the little window of the chamber, saw it darkened by the form of a man wrapped in a large cloak.

" I will not speak to him, Anty," whispered Peggy.

" Who is it?" enquired her companion.

" My ruin—my husband! he that says he is not my husband—he that——Oh! Anty, dear Anty!" as Frank tapped at the jessamine-shaded glass—" tell him I cannot—will not see him: get up and speak to him for me; tell him to meet me in his uncle's house in an hour —nothing more can now pass between us—go to him, for God's sake!—and stay—help me across the floor, out of his sight."

When Anty had attended to the latter part of the request, she advanced steadily to the window. Her glance curiously and earnestly sought to make out Frank's features; but the collar of the cloak, and the leaf of his rustic hat pulled down to his nose, baffled her attempt.

In a few words she gave, however, her sister's message, half opening the window for the purpose.

" I must see her this moment," replied Frank ; " who are you ? her sister ?"

" You cannot and shall not see my sister, Sir," insisted Anty ; answering both questions in a breath.

" Pho, child ; open the lattice, like a good, pretty girl, as you are ;" standing sideway to her, and with one hand spread over that part of his face which the cloak and hat had not quite hidden, he thrust the other hand through the half unclosed window, and, first catching Anty's arm, further attempted a slight liberty. The unsophisticated child instantly shut the window, secured it as well as she could, and rapidly disappeared to join her sister, out of view of Frank.

He continued to knock, unheeded. In some time, they heard him walk away.

" Now come with me, Anty," said Peggy, " that I may keep my promise with him, to meet him in his uncle's house ; but first let us seek an old friend, a few fields off."

" What has he done to you, Peggy ? it must
be something very bad when you will not speak
to him."

" Do not ask me all, now ; I will tell you
soon ; but now I fear the thinking of it would
deprive me of the little strength I have, and
which I want to keep.—Come, dear Anty ; let us
steal out without disturbing our father or mother."

" Yes ; but only one word : you said he
wanted to deny he was your husband ?"

" He does : he wishes to assert that we were
not properly married ; but he cannot prove that
in the sight of God, though he may in the sight
of men."

" What do you mean, Peggy ?" asked the
young sister, reddening and starting ; " what
do you mean by a marriage that will not hold
in the sight of man ? *Are* you his wife ?"

" We were married by the priest.

" Well ? and what then ? what can *he* mean,
then ? dear, dear Peggy, how you frightened
me ;" winding her arms around her sister.

Peggy explained the legal exception, as the
old friar had explained it to her. Anty looked
as confounded as Peggy had done when she
first heard it ; and scarcely had her sister added

that her only course could be to throw herself upon the justice and humanity of Mr. Long, ere they were both on the path diverging into the fields from the by-road before their father's door.

At a point where the path divided into tracks, one leading to Long Hall, the other to the house of a wealthy neighbouring farmer, whither Friar Shanaghan had gone to sleep the previous evening, Peggy signified her intention of first calling on the old ecclesiastic to give them his support and company up to Mr. Long's. " He was a courageous friend," she said ; " and, besides, would be a protector on the way, if any one they did not like to meet came across their path." Accordingly the sisters turned towards the rich farmer's.

In their progress they had to ascend an eminence, which gave a view to their right of the direct path to Long Hall, winding through several lonesome little dells and retreats ; and while they hurried along, Peggy, casting a watchful glance in this direction, started, pressed her sister's arm, and quickened her pace. Anty, standing a moment behind, also looked, and saw some hundred yards off, through a medium of bluish exhalation, the same person who

had knocked at the chamber window, and another man, mounted on a stout horse, which further bore an empty pillion. Both men were
motionless, and seemingly in earnest discourse.
While Anty yet gazed, her sister turned, as she
now called out to her, and beckoned anxious-
ly; and in wonder and alarm, she hastened to
join Peggy. But before she left her exposed
situation, she thought the figure in the cloak
turned and recognized her.

And she was right in her conjecture.

" There they go, by Heaven !" cried Frank ;
" avoiding the direct path, too: I told you so,
Studs ; she suspects every thing now: she *was*
in the Foil-dhuiv."

" Not last night then, Master Adams, take
my word for it. And what a fuss about the path
she happens to fancy this morning ; can't you
just wheedle her in here, you that can sing the
birds off the bushes, get her upon the pillion,
well strapped, and then order me wherever you
like, with your own lawful wife ?"

" That must be it, hollow ; so I take a
race round to meet her : but, Studs, are you
sure the old priest can't stir without coming
across the Pcelers ?"

" Didn't I station them myself ?"

" And this cursed Conolly : what *has* become of him ?"

" Run off in a funk, I say again."

" God or the devil make you a prophet ; for, if my fears be true—no matter—all that another time; now for this hoaxing wench ; don't budge an inch, Studs, till I come back."

In a few moments, Frank stood before the sisters with a " Good morrow, Peggy ;" one screamed, the other, encircling Peggy's waist, changed to the side whence he approached, not now daring or caring to look up into his face, which was still carefully muffled, as if to leave in future doubt of his identity, any chance spectator of his present actions.

" I knew, or at least was told by your servant, that you did not intend to keep your appointment last night," continued Frank, as the girls stood silent and motionless, " and so did not go out myself; but my friend Mr. Sirr, my sister, and one of my brothers, await you a little way off, to give you the satisfaction you required, early as it is." 'Twas yet scarce four o'clock.

Peggy continued perfectly silent.

" And so you will take my arm, and come with me."

He moved towards her disengaged side; Anty moved before him; he changed his place again; she again anticipated him.

" Tut, child," he resumed, "this is no time to play at bo-peep; tho' "—whispering her closely—" at any other time you will find me willing enough : for may I never die in sin, but, in a year or two, you will be worth two of Peggy—nay, this moment, you don't know how I like you ;" and taking Anty by surprise, he passed his arm round her waist, and ardently saluted her lips.

The young nunnery girl, gaining, from indignation, extraordinary strength, flung him aside, and, with some point-blank and rather forcible epithets, clung closer to her sister.

" After this, at least, let us go our road, Frank Adams," said Peggy.

" Why will you be obstinate, Peggy ? my friends all waiting, and you keeping them : from the last height you have passed you might have seen some of them—my sister rode behind Mr. Sirr, on a pillion. Come, come ; if you are wilful, and I will add, ungrateful, I cannot consent to be exposed to laughter; so, come along, Peggy."

He took her arm, and endeavoured to separate her from her sister's embrace. Both girls now screamed loud, and all struggled violently. They were answered by a " hilli-ho !" from the direction of the farmer's house whither they had been going; and presently appeared a very handsome young man, dressed in a rustic green sporting jacket, and bestriding as handsome a horse, which bore him rapidly towards the parties; while, at a good distance behind, Friar Shanaghan's poor grey, with her master on her back, did her best, at a very unusual stretch of muscle, to keep in the track of the leader.

" Stop, Sir, whoever you are, and whatever you intend !" said the young man, jumping from his saddle.

" And who dares bid me stop ?" retorted Frank ; " I am warranted in what I do; this female is my wife."

" Remember that, David," said the friar, now almost at the spot; " remember it well, David Shearman ; he calls Peggy Nowlan his wife."

All seemed much struck with these words : Frank looked irritated and perplexed ; and Peggy and David Shearman glanced in confusion at each other.

"I see you don't know her, man, though you ought; nor Peggy you, though she ought, too; but, Peggy, my woman, this is little Davy Shearman that used to be, though, now that he's come home from the priest's school in England, he's big Davy; and don't you remember long ago, when he and you, children as you were—but never mind; that's all past and gone; and now he's nothing to you but a neighbour, to do a neighbour's turn; and, to make a beginning, since he and I have come by chance to your side so arly this morning, why, we'll just stay at your side till we see you safe on the road you're for going; though he left his snug bed at such an hour to see me a bit on my own road, for ould-time's sake; eh, Peggy?" alighting slowly from his grey, "isn't that the way it'll be? and ar'nt you this moment going to take the course I bid you take yesterday?"

"I am, Sir; I was on my way to ask your company, and now I thank you and this gentleman."

"To be sure you were, to be sure you do; so come; stop, who's this? eh? Oh, I needn't ask another word; a Nowlan all over; there's

her mother's own nose and mouth, only the eyes
are blue like her poor ould father's; Anty, ma-
colleen, how are you? come here and tell me;
there, God bless you, my fine child;" kissing
her cheek; "how's the ould suparior? and all
the ould nuns? and all the purty novices?
and the boorders? Well, you'll tell me another
time; come now, I believe we're bound for
Long-Hall: does Mr. Frank accompany us?"

Frank, who, since the interruption, had stood
silent, his back turned, did not answer, but
stepped aside to allow free passage to three
Peelers, who, advancing in the way the friar
had come, soon gained his side, and as soon
pronounced him their prisoner, on authority of
a warrant granted by Magistrate Adams.

"Pullaloo and botheration entirely," cried
the old regular, as all other persons of the
group seemed, in different ways, much agitated
at this occurrence, "warrant away, arrest away,
hang away, my boys; I know all about that;
and I'll go with you as quiet as any lamb, if
you just take me, first and foremost, before
Mr. Long's face, where I have a word to say;
you'll oblige me so far, won't you?"

Having secretly consulted Mr. Frank's eye,
the leader of the Peelers said he could do no

such thing; Mr. Shanaghan must go before Magistrate Adams.

" Then, Peggy," resumed the friar, speaking earnestly, " go you your ways with your sister and Davy Shearman, straight to Mr. Long; tell your story, plain and square, before all; and never cry for me, a good girl; no fear o' the ould regular; many a cat and dog and better thing 'll die before me; shake hands, my child, and God speed you. David, don't leave her side; you know a little of the little rason why."

" Never fear me, Sir," answered David.

" One word with you, Peggy," whispered Frank, stepping to her. Anty clung closer than ever to her sister, and Peggy evidently showed a resolution not to turn off alone with him.

" Let pretty Anty come with you," he added; " what I have to say may as well be said in her hearing."

The sisters accordingly separated themselves a few paces from their friends.

" 'Tis but one question," resumed Frank, in a boding whisper; " why do you now so obstinately refuse the satisfaction you so earnestly demanded yesterday, Peggy?"

" I will answer your question, if you answer

one from me first," replied Peggy, measuring the distance between her and the friar and David Shearman: then glancing at Frank's hands, and pressing closer to little Anty.

" Let me hear it," he said ; his eyes falling.

" This is it, Frank," as her hoarse tones became almost inaudible; " who dug the hole in the Foil Dhuiv, after twelve o'clock, last night ?"

Without raising his eyes, he drew back, his shoulders slowly cringed up, and inclined to double forward, as if a creeping went through every fibre of his body ; and when at last his enlarged eyes as slowly rose and fell upon Peggy's, she shrieked aloud at their deadly, animal expression.

" What's the matter with you all there ?" enquired the friar; " and stop—what's the matter here at our backs too ? Salvation to my soul, but it's that crack-brained poor omadhaun, Peery Conolly, coming prancing on, like a year-ould coult, before my excellent friend Mr. Nevin, of Nenagh town, and *he* another magistrate, and with another handful of Peelers at his heels—Christ save us all ! it's a busy morning."

At the mention of Peery Conolly's name,

Frank quickly started from his baleful trance, and, casting but a look towards the approaching party, bounded away from our friends, before the new-comers could well have got him in view.

" Here we are ! here we are, like May-boys !" shouted Peery, dancing forward ; " come on, Peelers, my darlins! come on, Misther Nevin, a-chorna, an' glory to you! *fauch-a-vollaugh !** here we are !"

" Pray, gentlemen, has any one just parted from you ?" enquired Mr. Nevin.

" Mr. Frank Adams, this moment," answered the friar.

" That looks bad," rejoined Mr. Nevin ; " and now, Sir, I begin to believe your mad charges," to Peery.

" It looks good, your honour means," said that person ; " an' believe Peery or no, jist as your honour likes, he's to the fore, any how, to hould his own purty neck for a runnin' knot, if he can't fit it on another's."

" I will certainly take care of you, Sir, till the affair has ended.—Which way, Mr. Shanaghan, has Mr. Frank gone ?"

The friar officiously pointed it out : two of Mr. Nevin's attendants were despatched to ex-

* Clear the way.

plore it ; two more moved in an opposite direction.

"And now, whatever may be your business among us, Mr. Nevin, you'll do me a favour, I know," said the friar : and thereupon he explained his situation ; the attributed crime that had brought him into it ; and ended by requesting the interference of the Nenagh magistrate with his captors, to prevail on them for liberty to accompany his young friends towards Mr. Long's house. Mr. Nevin easily obtained the accommodation which the Peelers had before refused ; and adding, that he had just been at Long Hall, and was again called there by his present duty, the whole party moved for this important ground of explanation.

"Your honour wouldn't let me up to the Hall wid you afore," said Peery, "me nor the Peelin' boys ; an' may be all was dacent an' kind, for the sake o' the ould uncle, that was the best man in the counthry till his nephew came home ; bud now, if your honour plaises, we'll go in, at any rate ; an' you'll let the boys break open any dour or lock I rise up my little finger at."

Mr. Nevin assented. They soon gained the

house. Mr. Long received the magistrate, Peery, and our friends in his library, where they found him pale and trembling in an easy chair.

" Have you seen him, Sir?" asked the afflicted gentleman, as his brother-magistrate entered.

" No, Mr. Long; but he may have since returned to the house."

" Then, Sir, you can again search the house." The uncle more than suspected that Mr. Nevin was right in his conjecture; but, from the place towards which he believed Frank had retreated, he hoped all search might be turned. He was, however, left by Mr. Nevin and Peery to abide the issue of a closer scrutiny than had before occurred.

" And now, Miss Nowlan, your business with me," continued Mr. Long.

" Tell it all up, like an honest woman, Peggy," said Friar Shanaghan.

" My name is not Nowlan, now, sir," answered Peggy, " and for some time has not been."

" And I know that," rejoined the friar.

" And, since last night, I too know it," resumed Mr. Long; " the young woman has been married by you, Sir, to my wretched nephew, Frank Adams, according to the forms of your church."

" You have just said it, Sir," observed the friar, nodding : " may we ask how you found it out ?"

" By his own acknowledgment."

" Good God, Sir !" cried Peggy, " then we have all wronged him ; and I—I have injured him in coming before you this morning."

" Fear it not, my good young woman ; and do not think I heard his avowal with his own free will ; in fact, he knows not, even now, that I have his secret. So, go on. What request do you wish to make of me on the subject ?"

" He has lately disowned me as his wife, Sir."

" He has," echoed the friar.

" And that I know too," said Mr. Long. " Well ?"

" We know you, Sir, to have the kind heart and the straight mind ; and we hope you will just ask him not to deny it ; for we hear he can, if he likes, and with all the law on his side, Sir."

" I will ask him, my child, if, after the end-

ing of a matter that now nearly concerns him,
you still wish me to do so; and, perhaps, the
question will do him more honour than he me-.
rits. Do you love him?"

"It's not so much for myself, Sir, that I
want him to do me justice."

"For whom, then?"

"Oh, sir!"—and Peggy's firmness began to
fail. The horror of the last night was fully
recollected, in the thought of what a man she
was about to present her child to. She sickened; her head swam; she leaned on her little
sister, and whispered her; and in a few seconds,
Anty, transmitting her to the care of the friar,
advanced firmly, though she blushed scarlet,
and said in an even voice,

"My sister Peggy is more anxious for the
good name and happiness of her unborn child,
Sir, than for her own."

"Poor young thing," sighed Mr. Long;
gazing through moist eyes at his niece-in-law.

"And she hopes, Sir, that you will put it
out of the power of the father of her child to
call it a——"

The zealous advocate failed in her turn, and
could get no farther. The old friar supplied
the word.

"Answer me, Peggy," resumed Mr. Long, as she grew better; "I ask no idle questions; but a certain one I have before asked requires a candid answer:—Do you love my unhappy nephew?"

"No, Mr. Long!—oh! no, no, no!" replied Peggy, as she vehemently clasped her hands.

"You would not, then, be content to live with him (if, as I said before, he now escapes a difficulty)—in competence, though not in wealth, and, perhaps, in solitude?"

Peggy yielded a negative more earnest than her former one; the horror and revulsion of her soul, called up by the word "solitude" and all its associations, being quite evident to Mr. Long.

"How did this happen?—what cause has he given for this obstinate change of feeling? When did he forfeit your affections?"

"He never had them, Sir."

"Indeed! Why did you marry him, then?" demanded the catechist, now beginning to regard poor Peggy as a cold-hearted, designing young person—"his hopes of a good fortune were, perhaps, an inducement?"

"No, Mr. Long; I can spurn fortune, though I am only a farmer's daughter, if fortune does not bring peace and true heart's-love. 'Tis true I never, never loved Mr. Frank, and yet I became his wife. The first unlucky evening— unlucky in every thing but the saving you from danger—"

"I remember it," said Mr. Long, as Peggy paused.

"That very first evening, Sir, I'll not deny —for a young girl is sometimes foolish and thoughtless, Sir—that, for an hour or so, he might have pleased me by his flattery, and his fine words, and his elegant manners, that I never saw before; to say nothing of his being then, as well as now, the handsomest man that—God forgive me!—ever had within him so bad a heart;—but before he left my father's roof, my mind—the soul in my body—changed against him; and changed, first, from a little thing. I caught him, when he thought I wasn't minding him, sneering at my poor father and mother and my poor brother John, while they and I were doing the best to treat him kindly; and a'most in the same moment that he was praising them to my ear for all they said or did. He stayed that night; and I watched him closer, and liked him worse; and the next morning,

Sir, after you and Miss Letty came back, I saw his eye and his smile full of such contempt to my poor lost brother, while he pretended to be going under his very feet, that from that blessed hour my heart was shut for ever and ever against him."

"All this is still very singular to me," said Mr. Long, as Peggy stopped, from exhaustion.

"And to me, Sir," echoed David Shearman; who, in no common interest, watched Peggy while she spoke.

"Hould you your tongue, Davy, and let the poor child go on," observed the friar.

"I came, with him that's lost to us all, to stay a while in your house, Sir," resumed Peggy, "and though his attention to me grew more and more, my bias towards him grew less and less. I saw nothing in him or about him that wasn't suspicious; and, for a stronger reason, I was on my guard every time we met."

"May I ask that reason, Peggy?"

"I am bound to tell you, Sir, though it's a shame for any young woman to own it. This was it; while he talked of loving me better than the world, he never spoke, at first, (nor

'till I reminded him by saying he must ask me
of my father) of making me his wife: and
worse,—he would have been freer than he
ought if I had allowed him. It often rose in
my mind to tell my brother John all about it,
so that I might escape Mr. Frank's insults; but
I was afeard of John's passion, which was
always great when roused, and of a quarrel
between him and your nephew that wouldn't
become his calling."

"You say, Peggy, you referred him to your
father: it is not unlikely your father would
have assented; then you would have been
bound to marry him; and how do you reconcile
that to your rooted dislike?"

"I knew, Sir, he never intended to ask me
of my father; I knew he didn't love me for his
wife; I was quite sure: or, even supposing
he had come over the old man, I knew I
could get my father to give him the go-by at
last."

"But still, I cannot guess a reason for your
marrying him of your own free will, at last."

"It wasn't of my own free will, Sir; I'm
coming to that. After a night, when, by the
help of a poor boy I saw here just now, I bare-

ly escaped the worst at Mr. Frank's hands, we
didn't meet for a long while. He sent me letters and messages, through one body or another,
but I kept close by my father's hearth. At last
he thought of means to frighten me into seeing
him. He wrote me word that my unfortunate brother John was in his power; that with
one word to his bishop, he could ruin him for
ever; and he swore wicked oaths, that if I did
not come out in the evenings to speak to him,
he would say the word. So I was forced to
steal out from time to time, to try and soften his
heart towards my poor brother, God above, and
a good trust in God, my only safeguard. At
first, our meetings passed off with nothing but
Mr. Frank's promise not to destroy John Nowlan until I should see him again; but, by de-
grees, your bad nephew, Sir, made me understand that if I did not consent to sin, he would
take his long-threatened revenge. Nothing
else, he swore, could save us all. I broke away
from him again and again, only to run back to
him the next evening, and fall on my knees at
his feet for mercy. He was not to be moved.
And now comes the marriage. Upon the very
black evening that John Nowlan left his home,

and that I was to leave it, for a while, with
him, I promised Mr. Frank to give him a last
word near the stile on the Dublin road. It
was my plan to beg from him a few days grace,
until I should return, after leaving my brother
at Nenagh : and when, with his promise, John
and I were on the road, far away from the near
danger of a quarrel with your nephew, I
thought to tell him the whole story, and put
him on his guard against the charge that was
ready to fall on his head. Avoch, Sir, I knew
it was partly true ; but still I hoped he might
come to himself, repent, confess his crime to
his bishop beforehand with his enemy, and so
save himself and me, together.

"So, Sir, I met Mr. Frank in a lonesome
place, while John Nowlan and another were left
alone too. I begged my boon ; your nephew
would not hear of it. He swore more wickedly
than ever, that, if I left him that night as I
came, he would not sleep till he saw John's
bishop in Limerick town. I cried and wrung
my hands, and knelt to him over and over;
but I spoke to the heart of stone : he had no
pity for me. More, Sir ; he began to talk of
destroying me by force as well as terror; and I

was still at his feet, crying and beseeching, when my poor lost brother—oh, Mr. Long, Mr. Long!—I cannot go on, Sir; this good gentleman, Father Shanaghan, will finish it for me."

The friar readily took up the story, and detailed his strange meeting with John by the road-side; his progress with him to the lonesome field; their meeting with Maggy, whom the narrator knew; and finally, the frantic and terrible threat by which, against Peggy's inclination repeatedly expressed, he was compelled to celebrate the marriage.

" We all know," continued the old ecclesiastic, " the cause for the madness, that, happening just the moment before, made the poor boy ripe for any thing desperate and wild ; but, as I have since had reason to believe, his temper was turned into the channel for this extravagance by certain falsehoods told him by the wretched creature, Maggy Nowlan, who felt jealous of my child here, and, when Mr. Frank's earnestness went too far with Peggy, yielded to a sudden fit of wicked revenge in setting John upon them both. And now, Mr. Long, having told out our little story, we again

turn to you for all the justice,—and it's but little, too—you have it in your power to give us.
It is true, as my child Peggy says, that your
nephew wants to appeal to the convenient laws
of the country, to sanction his disavowal of his
marriage, and to give him security in his
crimes. As a proof of his intentions, you must
know that I am, this moment, a prisoner under
your roof, arrested on a warrant from his father, for having celebrated the marriage—"

" Good God, Mr. Shanaghan !" interrupted
the judge, becoming much agitated, while a
clamour through the house seemed additional-
ly to alarm him. He attempted to rise and
touch the bell-pull, but sank back in his chair
faint and trembling. David Shearman sprang
to it. A servant, looking frightened, appeared
at the door : Mr. Long asked a glass of water ;
tasted it, and resumed.

" Mr. Shanaghan, the justice you ask of me
you shall have, to the utmost of my ability to
confer it. First, be assured, I shall see you
freed from this odious arrest."

" Don't mind *me*, Sir," said the friar.

" Next ; if, by entreaty, threats, or promises,
I can prevail on my demoniacal nephew to re-

marry, according to the provisions of the law, this excellent young woman, whom I have more sorrow than shame in even now calling my niece, her child shall not come into the world legally branded : but, as I before said, this chiefly depends on Frank's escape from greater difficulties that threaten him close. Hear that ! the noise abroad, which now encreases, concerns the question, and, I fear, tells against us—against us all :—oh God !" as, amid loud talking, the parlour door flew open, " I fear I am to be the most disgraced sufferer, here."

As he spoke, Mr. Nevin, Peery Conolly, the servant before noticed as partly in Frank's confidence, and a group of Peelers, advanced into the room.

" Ax his honour's self, I say," cried Peery, now much altered from his usual buffoonery of manner--" My life is concarned in id, an' I must see myself rightified : if he gets time to make away wid the proofs in black an' white agin him, who 'll believe poor Conolly the Rake, on his own word, face to face wid one o' your gintlemin ? Misther Long,—your reverence,—Peery can't help it ; he held his pace a long while, an', only for two things, 'ud go to his grave, an' the dance

on him, widout a word; but when Masther
Frank wanted to wrong Peggy Nowlan, an' get
my own-self hanged, out-an-out, instead iv his
own self, why, plase your honour, the biggest
fool couldn't wait to let him."

"Pardon me my most disagreeable duty, Mr.
Long," said Mr. Nevin, "but the facts are
these—you know the capital offence with which
your nephew stands charged; we left you to
search the house, a second time, for him, or for
certain documents against him; neither have yet
been found:—but this young man insists that,
in a concealed and barricaded cellar, we shall
come at least on the documents: the door he
points out is trebly barred and locked; we suspect it to be fastened at the inside also; we
have demanded the keys from your servant, he
says they are lost; we believe he misinforms us;
but at all events, before we proceed to burst
open the door, at which some of my officers
remain stationed, we are anxious to consult your
wishes."

"Give up the keys, Sir," said Mr. Long to
the servant, after a very agonized pause.

The man insisted they were lost even before
he came to the house, and that the vault had
never since been opened or used.

"The papers are snug in id, for all that," insisted Peery Conolly; "I'm not likely to be wrong; one that helped to hide them there, and brought them at the dead o' night, from the middle o' the wood, where they were left, as soon as they were gutted,—that body, an' it's a woman, tould me so. Sure, from the first hour she spoke to me, an' thought to 'list me for the job, she an' me are as thick as two brothers; tho' I found manes to stay away that night, an' to throw dust in her eyes, to make her think me loyal to the cause, for all that. Yes, musha, what a fool I am; and there stands the colleen o' the world," pointing to Peggy, "for whose sake I pretended to listen to Maggy, and larn as much o' the matther as I could, becase I had a bit iv a rason o' my own for thinkin' that the man that wanted her to like him was at the bottom iv id all."

"I warn you," resumed Mr. Nevin to the servant, who still persisted, however, in his statement.

"Then you will excuse us, Mr. Long, our necessary duty: follow me, men;" and the magistrate, Peery, the Peelers, and the servant, again left the room.

In a few moments, heavy, battering sounds
were heard. The sisters, the friar, young David, and Mr. Long, listened some time in breathless silence.

" This is wrong," at last said Mr. Long; " I
should not sit here : I ought to see the result
with my own eyes : pray assist me, Sir ;" stretch-
ing out his arm to David Shearman.

The young man readily gave the help required, and both went out. The friar, with
Peggy and Anty clinging to him, soon followed.

All passed through the kitchen apartments
into a broad area, over which the hall-door
steps were supported by an arch. In the side-
wall of the area, detached from the house, and
under the steps, was a low door, fitting very
tight to its jambs, made of thick oak plank,
and secured as Mr. Nevin had described. It
obviously gave entrance to a vault, excavated
under a continuation of the steps that, tier after
tier, fell down into the lawn, some distance
from the house. Around it were grouped the
Peelers, headed by Mr. Nevin, and assisted by
Peery, still battering with a sledge, a large
stone, and the buts of three carbines, at the

tough oak, and, to this moment, with little success.

" Let us never mind the door itself, but try the sledge on this padlock, an' nothing else," said one of the Peelers. The hint seemed good. The strongest man stripped, and by a succession of crashing and well-aimed strokes, broke the padlock into pieces. Two iron bars, which it had kept fixed, were then easily taken away; still the door was fast, and now it was evident that it was indeed double-locked on the inside.

All looked at each other when this became certain ; and while Peery Conolly, after drawing his breath hard, remarked, " Christ save us ! the bouchal is within, his own-self," Mr. Long was seen to grow dreadfully agitated, and the sisters shrunk back as far as the area allowed them.

Again the sledge was applied to that part, at the side of the door, where the man supposed the lock to be. At every clash it gave, poor Peggy's heart shrunk, and her ears buzzed with the sound. Still she could not keep her eyes from the door, which, yielding to a tremendous stroke, and opening on its hinges into the vault, at last flew open, and, to the surprise if not terror of all, allowed vent to a gush of thick, suffocating smoke, that completely hid a view of the interior.

" Murther !" roared Peery ; " he's afther burnin' them—that's the smoke o' the blaze they made."

" In, men, in !" exclaimed Mr. Nevin to the Peelers, who, taken by surprise, stepped back as the unexpected volume of smoke rushed into their faces.

" Suppose we just guard the door well, your honour, till this cloud passes off, an' we can see what we're doin'?" answered the corporal.

Mr. Nevin assented. The men cocked their carbines and formed, at some distance, round the door. Our friends could see between them. In a very short time, the interior of the vault became so far cleared, that all were able to discern a dying flame at its remote end, and the figure of a man stooped over it. After another pause, the features of Frank became visible, haggard, and seemingly stupified. Kneeling on both knees, he held, as if unconsciously, a torn paper in one hand, and in the other a pistol, which more than once he pointed to his

head, but withdrew again, in want of nerve or
of self-possession. Mr. Long groaned aloud;
Peggy shrieked and swooned away; the old
friar crossed himself; the Peelers looked pe-
trified, and did not stir.

" Seize him, and save all the papers you
can," said Mr. Nevin; the first to awaken to
his duty. The men rushed in: Frank dis-
charged at random, and without effect, his pistol, and then passively submitted to his fate.
Mr. Nevin, assisted by others, stamped upon
the fire and extinguished it; collected fragments of paper that it had left unconsum-
ed, and others that lay nearly whole around
the vault, together with several leathern bags,
cut open; they were conveyed into the area,
and, after a moment's investigation, no doubt
remained that many of the letters and all the
mail-bags which, some time before, had been
robbed from the night-coach, now lay before
Mr. Nevin.

" This is dreadful, indeed," said that gentleman, passing to Mr. Long, taking his arm,
and walking him aside.

" Mr. Nevin," began the miserable uncle,
grasping the arm of his friend, but for a time

he could not go on.   At length he was able to
say—" Do you think, Sir, I deserve the appalling disgrace this must bring upon me?   Oh !
Mr. Nevin, do you not pity me ?"

" In my heart and soul I do, my excellent
friend."

" What, then ? am I to live to witness his
shameful end ?   If you pity me, indeed—"

" Hold, Mr. Long ; you and I cannot have a
word on that ; but it is natural you should
wish to see him alone, and you shall : men,
bring the prisoner up-stairs to Mr. Long's library, and while he and his uncle speak some
time together, guard the door carefully.   I
leave the house, Mr. Long."

Ordering Peggy and her sister to be kindly
looked   after by the housekeeper, Mr. Long
was able to muster sufficient nerve to gain
his library, followed by Frank, who entered
it unguarded after him.   The apartment had
a double door, both with locks.   The moment the uncle and nephew were alone, Frank
started from his lethargy ; his eye sparkled ;
he glanced around ; and, as Mr. Long sank into
a chair, he softly locked the inside door, and
put the key into his pocket.

" Now, uncle, you must aid me to escape,"
he said in a whisper, advancing.

" Miserable creature! it is for that we are
here."

" Quick then, uncle, quick," going to a
closet door; " your key, Sir: this little place
is fast, but I can drop from the window into
the garden; from it, escape into the village;
and if you stand to your promise, by staying
here for half an hour, there is a neck-chance
yet :—your key, Sir."

" On two conditions, I will, perhaps, consent to aid your escape from a felon's death."

" I fear I have no time to spare for conditions; but say them, uncle."

" First, you shall transport yourself to America."

" What to do there, Sir ?—Starve ?"

" I will supply you with a competence."

" What do you call a competence, uncle ?"

" Infamous, hard-hearted man! at such a
time as this can you stop to drive a bargain ?"

" Well, Sir, no matter ; your other condition."

" You shall, before you leave this house,
submit to be married by a Protestant clergyman to the woman you have already ruined."

" Hush, good uncle, don't speak so loud ; that 's all confounded nonsense ; it can't be done."

" Monster ! dare you deny me ?"

" Tut, Sir ; there 's no *dare* in the case ; I only say it is impossible."

" Then meet your fate."

" And that 's absurdity, too, uncle ;—stay where you are," pressing him back in his chair, as Mr. Long was about to move out of the room ; " sit quietly, Sir, and let me have your key."

" So, Frank ;—and if I refuse, you are ready, I suppose, to get it by some such means as occurred to you for getting rid of me, when you conjectured, and rightly conjectured, that I was in your closet, beside your counsellor, last night ?"

Frank started back, and glared on his uncle.

" You know the worst then : well, it will warn you to fear the worst :—your key, Sir, your key !"

As he spoke, in a hissing whisper, his hand grasped Mr. Long's throat. Horror, acting upon excessive nervousness, instantly deprived the feeble old gentleman of all sense. When

he recovered from his swoon, it was in consequence of the breaking open of his library door,
and the quick entry of the Peelers there stationed ; who, after a considerable lapse of time,
became impatient and suspicious, as they
knocked without getting any answer, and listened without hearing voices. They found Mr.
Long alone in the apartment, lying on the
floor, and his neck showing marks of some
violence. The closet-door was open ; so was the
window. Pursuit was raised after the fugitive,
which continued several days, but he was never
discovered or apprehended by them. Mr.
Nevin and Mr. Long stood clear of all suspicion of having aided his escape.

When Peggy Nowlan was conveyed, senseless, to her father's house, a premature labour
came on ; she gave birth to an infant which
died almost instantly, and, for many weeks, the
mother's life was despaired of.

CHAPTER VIII.

BUT sorrows wear down; and when they do, the persons they have most keenly afflicted engage, according to the law of their nature, in the usual duties of their situation. After some months, Anty Nowlan returned to her nunnery school, leaving Peggy quite re-established in health, and much cheered by the constant visits of the dry humorist, Friar Shanaghan, and of his young, handsome, and ingenuous friend, David Shearman. It was suspected indeed, that, half-recollecting the early childish intimacy to which we have heard the friar allude, and charmed with Peggy's sufferings, virtue, and (we must not forget) beauty too, David felt a peculiar attraction in his visits; while some went so far as to whisper, that if Peggy Nowlan thought herself disengaged from her solemn nuptial vows to a bad husband, she would experience little ill-humour at hearing him explain what that peculiar attraction meant. But, in her present situation, a widow indeed, yet a wife too, Peggy never gave the slightest proof of such a sentiment; and David was, on his part, correspondingly cautious and delicate.

About a year after Frank's flight, there appeared, however, good cause to leave her bosom free, if, indeed, Peggy had any hidden secret to intimate. Mr. Long, still and more than ever an invalid, often called to see her; and looking in, as usual, one evening, he asked, with much solemnity of manner, a private interview with Peggy. When they were alone, he took out a letter with a black seal, and, warning her to prepare for a shock, put it into her hands. She read the following :—

" To Charles Long, Esq.

" My race is ended, and I am at least bound to warn you that it is. An intimation of my being alive, and likely, in any situation, to continue to live, could not interest, and might disturb you; but the announcement of my coming death, invited by myself, will give you relief. My exit from this world will be disgraceful ; but the disgrace cannot extend be-

yond my own person; it will not reach even
my name, which, since I parted you, has
been carefully concealed. So, you have but
to keep your own secret, and no one will ever
reproach you on my account. Show this letter
to Peggy Nowlan, and, when she reads it, tell
her it is all that shall remain of

" Your accursed nephew,

" FRANK."

The letter was dated from London, but from
no particular place in London.

Peggy felt indeed shocked, but horror more
than grief overpowered her. She wept too;
but it was in sorrow for the dark death of a
bad man, who had injured her and lost his
own soul, rather than the tribute of affection to
a departed friend. Her solemn assertions, that
she had never loved the person whom extraordinary circumstances compelled her to accept
as a husband, have been recorded, and they
will be taken as the perfect truth, for indeed
they were so. Hence, she could experience
none of the violent grief that comes from our
first thought of being left desolate, irreparably
desolate, by the loss of a sharer of our heart.

Nor, after the momentary escape of the peculiar feelings attributed to her, did Peggy continue to weep, or remain insensible to the natural relief brought to her in the melancholy letter she had read. We wish her to appear above affectation of any kind; and it was impossible for her heart, yet young, and not wholly forsaken by some of the hopes of youth, to acknowledge as a cause of lengthened regret, the death of a man whose life was at once her shame and her bondage; and who, by a right, that he was not even generous enough to admit to her advantage, doomed her to all the miseries of a lonely and unenjoyed existence.

In a little time she was composed enough to hint to Mr. Long her anxiety for an explanation, according to his judgment, of the letter.

"What," she asked, "could be meant by ' a death invited by himself ?' " and her kind uncle-in-law, who, by the way, often requested her to address him as a relative, answered, that he was not quite certain on that afflicting point. The expression might allude to the wretched Frank's death by his own hand; (Peggy, who had not thought of this, shuddered) or to his death decreed by the laws of his country, and brought on by his own acts. Either was a horrible supposition, and both Mr. Long and Peggy showed, by their silence and their suppressed groans, that they felt it was. But Mr. Long at length added his presumption, that the second case supposed was the more likely ; and he produced to Peggy a London newspaper, containing reports of the trial and execution for forgery of a young man, who, on account of the coincidence of dates, and the minute description of his age, manner, and conjectured rank, the miserable uncle had little doubt would, notwithstanding a different name. turn out, upon enquiry, to be his nephew.

Mr. Long proposed to make enquiries, then ? Peggy again asked ; and he told her that, in a strictly private and cautious way, such was his intention. Indeed, a proof of the terrible event, apart from Frank's own assertions in the letter, became indispensable, in order to arrive at certainty ; and certainty it was his duty, for many reasons, to attain. For Peggy's own sake, he deemed himself bound to make a secret investigation ; and accordingly he would, that day, write to an old and esteemed friend in London, every way qualified to take his instructions, and attain his object.

He left the house, after cautioning her not yet to communicate the matter to her family; parting from Peggy with a kindness and respect that, since the discoveries and explanations at his house, had marked his manner towards her.

The increased seriousness which attended Peggy's silence before her friends, was seen by all; and her mother, friar Shanaghan, and David Shearman, questioned her about it, but got no answer, except that she could not yet inform them of the cause. Meantime, she awaited with natural anxiety the answer from Mr. Long's London friend; not that she had any of the slight doubts started by her amiable adviser; for, to Peggy's mind, the letter did not admit of a question, and was decisive on the main point; but, in very truth, she wished to watch the effect of the news on one certain person.

In about three weeks, Mr. Long submitted to her his friend's answer. It left no uncertainty on his mind. Although Frank's real

name, as his shocking letter premised, remained
hidden from every one in London, still the accounts supplied by the London officers of the
individual executed immediately after the date
of the letter, confirmed the presumptions of the
newspaper report, and seemed to propose down-
right certainty by adding, that this person was a
native of Ireland, educated in an English college,
and once heir to a considerable Irish property.
So Mr. Long now left Frank's letter in Peggy's hands, together with that of his correspon-
dent, and empowered her to break the news to
her family, agreeing with her, however, that,
outside her family, Frank's death should merely be stated as an authenticated fact ; the hideous manner of it entirely suppressed.

As she accompanied her good friend to the
door, another good friend entered, Friar Shanaghan. Peggy was glad to see him at this
juncture. In a few moments, with the old man
one of her council, she laid her documents before her father and mother. Little was said at
any side; but all seemed as much pleased as
shocked at the sudden announcement. Mrs.
Nowlan could not, indeed, repress some harsh
intimations of her thanks to Heaven for the

liberation of her child; old Daniel Nowlan wept, and took Peggy in his arms: the Friar, like Macpherson's ghost, "hummed a surly tune," that still told, however, to those who knew him, more content than dissatisfaction; and then, suddenly recollecting that he had to call at neighbour Shearman's that evening, he undid the grey's bridle from the hasp of the door, slowly deposited himself between his wallets on her back, and she, as slowly, wended with him out of sight. Peggy thought she could guess the Friar's business at neighbour Shearman's, and she held down her head to hide the alternate blushes and paleness that the guess, its associations, its doubts, hopes, and fears, sent from her heart to her cheeks.

"David will come to-morrow morning, if he comes at all," thought Peggy, as she laid her head on her pillow, a little disappointed that he had not come that evening. But David did not come the next morning; nor the next; nor the next: in fact, a week wore away without a visit from him. Peggy wept plentifully in her chamber, but also rallied her heart into spirit, and framed some high resolutions. " He is shy to ask the love of one like me, one that was

ruined and shamed by a lost creature," she
said ; and this first view it was that drowned her
in tears ;—" but let him ;" and the tears were
now hastily dried up : " if David Shearman
takes that part, Peggy Nowlan thinks him
more below her, than she is below him; my
misfortune is not my fault; and I was not bad
nor sinful, nor, with my free will, even that
poor sinner's lawful wife. God pities me, but
does not blame me ; and all good men the
same : my heart tells me that : so let him,
aroon ; he 'll never know I wanted other
thoughts from him at any rate."

It was early in the morning, after the lapse
of a week since David's last visit, that Peggy
held this little soliloquy in her chamber; and
she had scarce concluded, when David Shearman rode hastily into the yard, leaped from his
horse, and with a flushed cheek, and a brisk
step, entered the kitchen. She heard him from
her room bid the old people good-morrow ;
and then the voices of all sank into a low confidential tone, and so continued for some time.
Peggy's views of things began to change; and
when, with a good-humour that for years
had been a stranger to the old woman's face and

manner, her mother entered her chamber to say that Davy was outside, and was asking about her, after a week's absence from home on particular business, the indifferent way in which Peggy said she would be in the kitchen by and by, belied the fluttering of her bosom, and, we fear, did not ensure to Miss Nowlan the flawless sincerity we have just been over-zealous to invest her with.

When she slowly came into the kitchen, with her " shining morning face," (not unattended to, by the way, during the time she had kept David waiting,) and a bunch of flax in her hand, she found it occupied by David alone. This discomposed, a little, the studied serenity of her manner; but her greeting of him was still as quiet as it was mild ; and Peggy proceeded with much care and composure to attach the head of flax to her wheel, seat herself, pass the thread through the flyer, and, finally, begin to spin very hard.

David was not, by nature, a forward lad upon any occasion: upon the present one, he was shy and embarrassed. He asked her many questions about her occupation ; such as " did the thread often break ? wasn't it very hard to keep

it always of a thickness? and how in the world
did she manage to keep the wheel going round
without tiring her foot?" and to these curious
enquiries Peggy gave quiet, intelligible answers,
accompanied by quiet, peace-making, yet cautious smiles, until, at length, David abruptly
broke the real matter in hand.

" Father Shanaghan had been talking to him,
he said, last night, late, just after he came
home, and told him all about the two letters
Mr. Long received from London; (Peggy red-
dened and spun harder;) and she knew well,"
David continued, " how he felt on the subject.
To make a long story short, it left them both
free, and allowed him, without offence, to ask
her——"

David was interrupted by a phenomenon of
which he had just been conjecturing the probability, that is to say, the snapping of Peggy's
thread on the flyer; and (but we fear it is
rather an old phrase) the simultaneous snapping
of the thread of his argument was the inevita-
ble consequence. Both remained silent until
she had repaired the accident; and then Peggy
spun on both threads together.

" I'm no child to mistake what you mean,

David, and no flirt to pretend I do. But, for the present, we can say little more on the head of it. You make me happy, I won't deny; happier than I thought I ever could be." Tears ran down her cheeks as her head remained bent over her spinning. "Yet hear what I have to say: first and foremost, there's your father; he's richer than my father, and, we hear, higher in his notions too."

"Dear Peggy," interrupted David, "Mr. Shanaghan and I have already spoken to him; and the knowledge that Mr. Long intends to leave you a handsome fortune, Peggy, entirely reconciles my father to our coming together."

Peggy at last stopped her whirring wheel, and looking straight in David's face, asked, "Why, then, what's that you say, Davy Shearman?"

Her admirer explained that Friar Shanaghan, to whom Mr. Long had communicated his intention, was his authority for what he stated. Peggy, after listening attentively, burst out into hearty tears, only interrupted by grateful prayers for her benefactor.

"But, though that's a great blessing, David, particularly when we didn't expect it," she re-

sumed after a pause, "still I have something
to say. So, hear me out, without stopping me
again, I bid you. No matter what you, and
Mr. Long, and Father Shanaghan, and all
other good people think, there will be some of
the neighbours saying that my unfortunate
marriage with that poor man is a stain on me,
and must be a stain on you, David, and may
be on whoever is to come after us—let me go
on, I bid you again: and though you think
very differently now, you may——no, I will
not say you can ever entirely change your mind:
but some things that neither of us foresee may
help to bias it ; or your father, or some of your
family, may take second thoughts. Now, Davy,
I'll not run such a chance: no earthly creature
must have it to say that I took any one short ;
it is my duty to myself to leave no danger in
the way of being called a designer, or a shame
to the people I'm to go among, or beholding
to their pity, or their good-nature, or anything
else they may feel for me, at the present time,
for notice and love. It shall never be said that
Peggy Nowlan was under a favour for the
good will of her husband, or her husband's
family : and the long and the short is this,

Davy,—let us all take time to consider with ourselves ; and if your liking can keep as it is for two years——"

" Two years !" interrupted David ; and thereupon he proceeded to urge all the arguments and expostulations usual in such cases ; but Peggy remained firm.

" It is not a thought of the moment, Davy ; and you 'll find me fixed in it. Besides, no matter what kind of a man he was that 's now gone to his long account, he was my husband ; and though the world knows I never loved nor liked him, it 'ill be only decent and proper, and expected from me, not to make a new engagement for some time to come. And there's another reason ; and without offence, or a cold heart to you, the strongest, maybe ; at all events, God sees it ought to be the strongest. My poor brother John"—— Peggy melted again, and the rest of her speech went on in tears —" Tale or tidings we have never heard of him since the black day he left his lodgings in Dublin : thinking to get a letter from him, day after day, we made no enquiries since, or nothing like what we ought to make ; so that whether he 's in Ireland, or gone abroad, or on the earth, or could

L 5

under the earth, or stretched in the bottom o' the
sea, none of us can tell, nor any body for us. And
all this I have long been thinking about, for I
think a good deal, Davy. Before you spoke, it
was in my mind to ask a friend to go with me
to Dublin, and let us do our best in tracing
him out, or knowing his fate, and the fate of
the poor young lady that went along with him:
and now I tell you, plump and honestly, if
there was no other reason for you and me taking our time, I'll never hear of changing my
condition until the poor priest John is found
to be living or dead; or until two years, at the
least, are past and gone without tidings of him;
and more, Davy, I hope and expect, that whoever has my good opinion at heart will do their
endeavours to get us satisfaction in this matter,
if it is to be got, or leave no stone unturned to
get it, any how."

Again David pleaded eloquently, but in vain.
It will be perceived that Peggy kept rather a
high hand with him; and, indeed, no ladie-love
of one of the giant-fighters of old, ever insisted
on the probation and services of her ridiculous
knight with more sedate pertinacity than did
she on the terms now proposed to David Sheer-

man. Seeing her really in earnest, the young
man made a virtue of a necessity, and offered
himself, in her place, to accompany to Dublin
the friend to whom she had alluded. Mr. Kennedy, the clergyman, was the individual meant :
Peggy and he had before spoken together; and
so, after such signing and sealing of the compact,
so long under discussion, as generally ends simi-
lar compacts, David Shearman went off that
moment to seek Mr. Kennedy.

In a few weeks both set out for Dublin, and,
after a long stay, returned with but vague tidings. The result of all the enquiries they were
able with much planning and difficulty to make,
was, that in all probability, a John Nowlan,
whose name appeared entered as a passenger to
Newfoundland, about the time in question,
might prove to be their John Nowlan. Having
taken care to obtain the name of the ship in
which he sailed, together with the names of the
captain and owners, Mr. Kennedy proposed to
Peggy, on his coming home, to write, conjointly
with him, to the proper official persons in Newfoundland, enclosing letters for the exile, and
giving all the necessary details and references;
and accordingly despatches were forwarded, and

Peggy awaited, in patient anxiety, the expected
answers. None came to hand. Six months; a
year ; more than a year elapsed without a line,
a word to relieve her suspense; and the conclu-
sion of David's probation drew very near, when,
by other means, some news seemed to transpire
of the fate of her unfortunate brother.

Anty, her school accomplishments supposed
to be completed, came home at this period, now
grown, since last we saw her, into a pretty and
interesting girl of seventeen. Upon the evening of her arrival, both sisters walked out in
the by-road before their father's door, to give
and impart the minute and delightful confidence
that a separation of some years keeps in store for
a final meeting between friends. As they talked
over all their little secrets and feelings, Peggy's
engagements with David Shearman and their
brother's unknown fate forming the principal
theme, three or four weather-beaten men, dressed
in the rags of sailors' jackets and trowsers,
passed the stile on their way to a wretched village, and stopped and asked for charitable assistance. Their ship had been wrecked, they
said, during her voyage from Newfoundland to
Dublin, upon the northern coast of Kerry, and,

while some of their hands walked for other points of the kingdom, they were on their way to the metropolis, hoping to get a re-engagement. The two girls pressed each other's arms, which were closely interwoven, at the mention of Newfoundland, and, in much agitation and some fright, gave the poor men a little money, who immediately left the stile, and proceeded towards the group of dirty cabins called a village. Peggy had it on the tip of her tongue to ask a certain question, in reference to a certain name, but her heart failed her. She was taken by surprise in the first place, and then the men looked so strange and hard-featured, the night fell so fast, and her situation from the house, though at no great distance, was so lonely, that, particularly with her young sister to take care of, she could not bring herself to encourage their stay. She was therefore about to turn and walk home, when another ragged sailor, or else one of the former who had come back, limped wearily to the stile; and leaning his chin on his hands, and his elbows on it, gazed wistfully towards the house. Again the sisters pressed each other's hands, stepping farther from the stranger, but keeping their eyes on him. A long and deep sigh reached their ears; their hearts fluttered, and they looked more earnestly. But that worn and rigidly-marked face, shaded by long streaming hair, and but vaguely shown in the increasing twilight, gave no certainty, though it aroused wild and poignant anticipation. The sea-buffeted man once more sighed loudly, and began to move; and darting from their hitherto secret place of observation, they ran, with the panic of lonely women upon them, to the shelter of their father's roof. That night, lying down side by side in the same bed, they did not sleep; their conjectures and their hopes were too lively, or they blamed themselves for their sudden and unaccountable fright; or, in every flutter of the door to the light night-breeze, rose up on their elbows to listen for the timid knock of a fallen and repentant brother, craving, after years of exile, trial, and penance, merciful admittance into the paternal house. They were wholly disappointed, however, in all their little romantic expectations;—even the morning showed them no tired and sorrowful man, such as they had seen last night, walking up to the threshold; they went to the village and learned that the poor sailors had rested but a few hours, and then one and all pursued their weary way ; and whether their brother really appeared before them, or that some wave-tossed wretch, in his momentary transit by their peaceful-looking house, had

" Lean'd o'er its humble gate and thought the while,
Oh that for me some home like this would smile !"

Between these two cases the innocent girls remained in painful doubt, and spent many conjectures.

But another incident soon made them dwell most on their first supposition. Their uncle, Murrough Nowlan, had been to Dublin in the caravan, no one could tell why, not even himself; about a week after the little adventure noted, he returned, and stopped to sleep at his brother Daniel's; and at a late period of the night came out, from time to time, and between stated sups of his punch, with a strange story. As he was about to walk, he said, from the place he slept in Dublin, to the place where the caravan was to set out for the country, he wanted some one or other to carry a trunk for him, while he carried his valise himself. Looking about so early in the morning, he could see

no one at all likely to do the job, when a kind
of worn-down sailor passed him, and begged a
penny for God's sake. Murrough agreed to
give the alms for God's sake, provided the sup-
plicant could manage the trunk; and no sooner
said than done; they walked off to the caravan,
side by side, both laden; the luggage was
stowed; Murrough in the van, along with eleven fellow passengers; the penny was bestow-
ed on the temporary porter; and as the driver's
whip cracked, and just as the curious machine
began to lumber off—" The blessing o' poor
John Nowlan be with you!" said the mendicant
sailor.

Well? every body asked: Well, answered
Murrough, that was all he knew about it.—
What! did he not stop and get out, and speak
to his supposed nephew? Yes; he did ask the
driver to stop, and he wouldn't.—Then, in
truth, he did *not* get out? No; how could
he?—Was he even sure of the person who called himself John Nowlan? He must at once
have recollected his face? He never saw it;
he happened to be looking on the ground (no
great accident neither) when the poor fellow
stopped; while they made their bargain, there-

fore, he saw no more of him than the feet; while they walked to the caravan he never once thought of minding him; while he got in, his behind was turned to him; and when the words were spoken, he was hid from the speaker, who stood at the side of the vehicle.

No farther could Murrough go; but even upon this information Daniel Nowlan resolved to start for Dublin the next morning. Peggy pleaded hard to accompany her father, but he mildly refused her request, and her mother crossly lifted up her voice against it; and as David Shearman happened to be in another part of the kingdom, and was not expected home for some time, Peggy, with a sad and ominous heart, saw the old man set out alone on his long journey, in the middle of a hard winter.

In a week at least, Daniel Nowlan was to come home, or write home to his family; but the week passed and they had not seen nor heard from him; and while the anxiety of the two girls became excessive, their poor mother, long shaken with the sickness of the heart, and, as Peggy before intimated, half blind with incessant weeping, lay in her bed, a victim to peevishness, real distemper, and almost despair, at the new misery of the long and unexplained absence of her husband.   Another week wore away in terrible suspense, and the third was coming to a close, when David Shearman's father rode over to inform Peggy, that a slight acquaintance of his, who stopped a night at his house, on his way from the metropolis to a remote county, brought the sad intelligence of Daniel Nowlan having been left by him ill of typhus fever, a week ago, at the old Brazen Head Inn, in Dublin.   It was night when Peggy heard this; she did not take a moment to consider, but immediately proceeded, assisted by her weeping sister, to pack up a few things, and after twelve o'clock she bade that sister adieu, at the stile on the Dublin road before spoken of, where a night coach, for which they had some time been watching, stopped at their hail, and afforded Peggy a seat, but, owing to previous occupation, only an outside one.

But for the illness of their mother, Anty would not have been prevented from bearing her sister company on the first long and unprotected journey she had ever taken ; and it was with

anguish and impatience she now saw herself
compelled to remain almost alone in their
deserted house, attending the sick pillow of
one parent, while another was dying, perhaps
dead; and waiting, from day to day, the
arrival from Dublin of tidings that concerned
alike the fate of a brother, a father, and a
dearly-loved sister.

Her only companion was the household maid
of all-work, Cauth Flannigan; but from the
cast of this girl's mind, good-natured as she
might be, Anty could derive little relief; and,
in fact, the poor wench's best consolation was
her pitying and respectful silence, or her tears.
But Anty did not long experience the sameness
of grief she had anticipated; for, just as it
had set in, it became broken up into a startling
interest.

Upon the evening after Peggy's departure,
she walked out to see Cauth a little way on her
path to milk the cows: and when, with a slow
and heavy step, Anty re-crossed the threshold
into the kitchen, a tired soldier was sitting, in
the twilight, upon a low stool in the middle of
the floor.

A scream, half suppressed, only because she

had presence of mind to recollect her sick mother, escaped Anty, and she stepped back in much alarm.

"You do not know me, Anty," said the soldier, in a low and melancholy tone.

"I do not indeed, Sir," answered the timid girl.

"And yet," he resumed, "though I have not seen you these seven years, I know my second sister, Anty Nowlan."

Again she could scarce keep in a wild shriek.

"John!" after a moment's pause, stepping into the kitchen.

"Your unfortunate brother John, Anty;" he held out his arms, and she fell on his neck.

"I have been some time hiding in the neighbourhood," he continued, "but, day after day, could not take heart to face my father and my sister Peggy: at last, I even walked a good distance out of the neighbourhood, to get a friend to come here beforehand for me, until I heard they were both gone to Dublin, to look after me, I believe, and no one at home but you, Anty, and our poor mother, confined to her bed; then I thought I would try if your heart, Anty, the youngest and, as I always said, the tenderest of the family, would first open to give me a forgiveness, a crust, a cup of water, and a night's lodging.''

Tears started to his eyes during this address, and Anty also wept as she asked,

" John, John, could you doubt my heart, or one of our hearts ?—Oh, we prayed, morning, noon and night, to see you restored to us."

" Then you, at least, forgive me, Anty ?"

" Can you ask the question, John ? you have suffered as much as you have sinned—oh, how much suffered ! and your God forgives you, because you are punished and a penitent ; and why should not your sister ?"

" That's cold enough, Anty ; I ventured to hope that, without a clause of any kind, without catechising me at all, without stopping to ask whether or no I was sorry for the part I took, or thankful or no to those that drove me from home, friends, and country, for one youthful error—I hoped that without a word or thought of all this, my gentle sister Anty, at least, would give a sister's welcome to her unfortunate brother."

" And I do, dear John, I do—my heart's best welcome, for nothing but joy to see you :" she again threw her arms round his neck.

" Then, that 's like the gentle Anty I always believed you to be ; thanks, dear, dear sister !"

He returned her soft embrace, in a way that, to the sensitive convent girl, was, from a brother, strange. She felt some astonishment, disengaged herself from him, took a near seat and proceeded to remark :—

" You say you have been long in the neighbourhood, John ; did you come first in that dress ?"

" Yes ; in no other ; for no other have I : I am on furlough from my regiment, just returned to Ireland out of the Indies."

" You are a soldier, then, not a sailor ?"

" I have never been a sailor."

" Then how much we are all mistaken : word came to us, from more than one quarter, that you went, three years ago, as a sailor, to Newfoundland, and had lately come back to Dublin, after being wrecked on the coast : indeed, we half believed you had passed our door, some time ago, in a sailor's dress."

" I know all that, Anty, and I know that, in the notion of finding me as a wrecked sailor, in Dublin, my father left home near a fortnight ago."

" And if you knew it, John, why did you let the old man go on such a journey, for nothing ?"

" I did not know it till after he had gone, Anty."

" But, surely, you could then have set us right, and then we could have set him right, if you even sent us a message after he went ; and he would now be at home with us, and poor Peggy, too ; instead of his being sick of the fever in Dublin ?"

" I was as much afraid of letting Peggy know I was in the country, as of letting my father know ; indeed more ; for her notions of what 's good, and right, and all that, were so rigid, I feared she would never see my face ; but if my poor father is ill on my account, I 'm very sorry, Anty ; very sorry, indeed ; tho' I couldn't have intended it, you see."

Anty paused, a little dissatisfied, though she knew not why ; and, as if noticing this, he continued :

" But I see it 's the cold face is to be shown to me, after all you say, Anty."

" Did you go into the regiment in your own name ?" she asked, half expressing a sudden thought.

" Was I a fool, child, to do any such thing? When my name was blackened by the world, and by them that called themselves my friends first of all, do you think I had no reason or wish to hide it? What was left to me, but to hide it and my disgraced head in any far quarter of the globe that would open to me? and how could you think that the John Nowlan who gave his name, at full length, for Newfoundland, was the hunted wretch that only wanted to baffle his persecutors for ever? as if, indeed, there was only one John Nowlan in the world."

" What has become of the poor young lady, John?" enquired Anty, after another pause.

" Letty is dead."

" God rest her soul in peace!" ejaculated Anty, piously crossing herself, and looking up.

" She was a Protestant, you know, and you, a good Catholic, must not pray for her," he said, in a scoffing smile and accent; " only I like to see you do or say any thing, Anty, that makes you look so very handsome, child."

" Fie, fie, John," answered Anty, not noticing the hand he had stretched out to her; " to talk in such a light way *of* her, and *to* me, in the present circumstances, and after all that has happened."

" Ay, ay, rebuke and scold me, Anty, and make that the return you promised ; nothing shall ever make me think the less of you, or love you with less of the heart than I now do, and as I ever did; indeed, Anty, the thought of getting your forgiveness and love, supposing all the rest to cast me off, was the only thought that cheered my banishment and my despair. But hush! there's my poor mother's voice crying out for you from the lower room ;—and I see Cauth Flannigan, at a distance, coming home with the pail on her head. Dear Anty, for the present you must not tell I am in the house ; the sudden news might kill my poor mother ; and Cauth is a great *ballowr*, and would blab all about me before the proper time ; so, I'll just step into my old bed-room here, until you leave our mother for the night, and send Cauth to her loft; and then, Anty, I expect from your pretty hands a candle, and a little refreshment, of which I stand in need; and from your prettier lips, a little more conversation."

He arose, and with a jaded step passed into the little chamber often before alluded to, Anty assenting readily to the arrangement: and after he had gone in, she heard him lock the door, and take the key out of the lock.

She hurried to attend her mother, and, after receiving a peevish rebuke for her long absence, and administering some necessary services and comforts, came back to the kitchen, sat on the low stool, and closely communed with herself.

" The poor sinner has come at last; but, the good God save us! in what a mind and heart has he come!—There is no sorrow for his sin upon him; not a bit; he only seems hardened and careless, and enraged with those that did their duty by him, instead of kissing the rod of punishment. Oh! I wish, I wish he had tried his fate in any way but among the soldiers!— often have I heard how their company and example, and their wild bad ways, particularly in foreign parts, will corrupt the best, not to talk of a poor creature made to their hands, by his early troubles and passions, and ready for any mad course. They have quite case-hardened him, and quite changed him, every way. 'Tis seven years, to be sure, since I saw him before, and then I was a mere child, and he a young

boy, with blushes on his cheeks, and peace and
lightness in his heart, and it's hard to tell what
changes years, and the hardships of foreign
parts alone, may not bring on, without any
other cause;—yet, little as I recollect of what
he was before I went to the convent, I'm
sure he had not then such a bold manner, such
a careless air, and such a frightful way of speaking. Can I bring John Nowlan's face before
my mind at all, as it was at that time?—
No; I believe I cannot. Phelim's is quite plain
to my memory, because his early death fixed it
in one shape; but all I have heard of John—
his terrible actions, his wild passions, his long
sufferings,—all come between me and his young
features; every time I think of him in
such and such circumstances, his face appears
altered and strange; he is pale, or he frowns,
or he grinds his teeth; and there's not a trace
left of the boy-priest at nineteen, so mild, so
smiling, and so handsome. Even the sound of
his voice I forget, or else, as he spoke this evening, it is quite changed too——Blessed Heaven!" interrupting the train of her reverie, as a
doubt, before faintly felt, arose in her breast—
" what am I thinking of at all? who else can

it be? why should any one else come here and say he was John Nowlan? who else could know the house as he does, and all in it, and all about it? This is mere weakness of me, mere folly; I will forget it; and the voice he had just now, is not entirely strange to my ear, either; I *have* heard it before, though my bad memory says it was not from John Nowlan, at nineteen. 'Tis all great weakness. I must stir myself, and attend to the poor wanderer's comforts. My mother will not call for me again till towards the morning; and I will send Cauth to bed, and soon bring him a meal's meat, and something to drink."

Anty accordingly exerted herself; Cauth retired for the night; the refreshments were prepared by Anty, and with a timid knock she stood at the door of the little chamber.

" God bless you, my beautiful child!" he said, as he cautiously unlocked the door and let her in;—" God bless you for coming at last, to feed the hungry, and comfort the sorrowful."

With few words Anty laid down her light, her food, and her whisky, and sat to see him eat and drink. His soldier's cap was now taken off, and the candle, shining full upon his face and forehead, showed features still fine and commanding, though emaciated, and reduced to one pervading sallow hue.

You 're thinking how much I 'm altered, Anty," he resumed, as he partook of the food.

" I am, indeed, John. I 'm a'most thinking there 's not a trace of what I try to remember you were."

" Ah, dear Anty, the heart-break, and many years' toiling under a scorching sun, makes sad work of the boy, during his growth into the man."

"Your hair, itself, was once a different colour, I believe, John."

" That can be turned, too, Anty. I 've seen a young man's hair change, not merely from one shade to another, like mine, but into the locks of old age, in one night ; into a head of hair as grey as our poor father's, whom Heaven rise up in health and strength, I pray."

" Amen," said Anty : and, while both remained some short time silent, she had another reverie.

" Poor fellow, poor fellow ! poor priest John ! he has come home hungry to the father's house. And what it is to sit here and

look at the man he *has* come home, and to
think of all that brought him to appear so!
Poor outcast! his case has, indeed, been hard;
may be, too hard; and may be it's not much
wonder, after all, that he feels a little of
the sullenness he does feel. God will soften
his heart, and work a change in him; and our
kindness, too, with the help of God : and may
be the day's not far off when he can be brought
back to his old nature entirely, and a'most as
happy and as good in himself, and before the
world, as ever he was. He is our brother, at
any rate, and kindness and love are his due. I
love him in the heart, and pity and compassionate him more than when he was away:
though, from my cradle, we always loved one
another. Poor priest John!" and her eyes
swam in tears as she gazed on him.

" Come, dear Anty," he resumed, " drink a
glass to my welcome home."

" I seldom taste the liquor, dear John, but
my heart can't refuse you."

He filled her glass, and, with clasped hands,
they drank to each other.

" Ay," looking around him, " there are all
my old musty books, with their musty thrash

in 'em : and there hangs the old watch I left
behind me, in my hurry : now, however, it
comes back to its owner ;" and he stood up,
took down the watch, and put it into his fob.
Anty knew it was her father's watch, and had
never been John's. His last words, and this
action, startled her again. Shocked, and sitting silent, she found herself compelled to
admit to her own mind that her brother had
returned a profligate in more than one sense.
His speech was blasphemous ; his appropriat-
ing the watch, dishonest. As she sat, without a
word, her soul sickened towards him : and she
remained almost unconscious of his movements,
until, sitting close at her side, he passed an
arm round her neck, and called on her to drink
another bumper to their future love and happiness. Then she tried to draw back, as she
answered—

" No, John, I have taken too much already ;
and the heart can wish its wish without any
help of the kind : keep down your arm, John ;
it hurts my neck."

" Curse on it, then, for its rudeness to the
handsomest neck in the world : and, there, Anty,
it shall hurt you no longer, only don't *you* draw

away entirely. I thought you would drink the toast I offered : but no matter ; your heart, you say, goes with the words, and I believe you. Dear Anty, the more I look at you and listen to you,"—drinking rapidly—" the more I 'm inclined to ask your heart to join mine in another wish."

" What is it, John ?"

" I 'll tell you, my little beauty"—as with a kindled expression his eyes met hers—" a wish that, with your kind feelings towards me, you did not think of me as you do, in another way."

" Oh, if that 's all, God above knows how sincerely I—But stop, John, I say"—growing more alarmed at his glance—" stop, and recollect yourself, or I must leave you."

" Go away ? Nonsense. Stop *you*, Anty, and hear me out. You don't understand me. I meant that I had a wish you did not know me for your brother."

" And I had the same," she answered, in a low, solemn voice.

" Then, dearest girl," misconstruing the sense of her reply, you *could* feel kindly to me, for my own sake, even though I was not your brother John? Without that accidental tie, from what you have seen of me, you *could* love me, Anty, even if I was nothing to you? you own so much?"

He drew her closer to him. She started up: very opportunely for her purpose of escape, a loud scream sounded from her mother's chamber; and then another and another.

" Whisht, John! that 's our mother's voice; something has terrified her; or she is dying, may be! God forgive my neglect! let me go: I must run to her; good night."

" Surely, Anty," still holding her, as she struggled, " you will come to see me for one moment more, before we say Good night?— nay, you must promise——"

" Well, I do; but let me go now to my poor mother; she cries out louder and louder :— good-b'ye!"

He attempted to salute her, but she avoided him, and hurried off to her mother's chamber. The feeble old woman lay in a state of great alarm. Strange faces, she said, had darkened the window at the foot of her bed; she could but faintly distinguish them, but still she saw them in the lightsome winter-moon, as, more

than once, they came close to the glass, and
gazed in upon her. Anty, though her own
brain was half crazed with contending fears
and suspicions, tried to believe that her mother
had raved, and told her it was all a dream.
The peevish sufferer scolded her for saying so,
and commanded her to sit by her bed. Anty
did sit down, until the weak voice sank in exhaustion, which ended in sound sleep; and then
she began to tremble at her loneliness, and at
the whole scene from which she had just escaped. Remembering, though endeavouring to
doubt, her mother's story, she looked in terrified foreboding on the window; and, whether
it was imagination or reality, strange persons
seemed to steal by it. After this, she thought
she heard the noise of one going about the
house. Her heart beat high in alarm. She recollected there was no fastening to the door of
her mother's chamber, and she arose, half tottered to her own, locked herself in, and sat on
the side of her bed.

It is impossible to give a clear account of
Anty's thoughts in this situation. In fact,
though shaking with a fear of the character, actions, nay, identity of her guest, her thoughts

could not arrange themselves into order. A great horror of him fell upon her, no matter in what light he presented himself; and that was all she knew, or could pause to calculate. The sudden event was too much for her simplicity and childish inexperience.

She did not know how long she had thus sat alone in her chamber, shivering, and starting at every sound, when the noise of opening a window, in the direction of John's old room, riveted her attention. With a cautious step she gained her own window, and through a small hole in the muslin curtain peeped out. It was still bright moonshine: her position enabled her partially to command the point about which she was interested; and she saw, indeed, that the lattice was open, and three persons, one of them a woman, standing at it, evidently conversing with the guest inside. Redoubled terror seized Anty's heart; yet she continued to look until the people went away, doubling by the corner of the house, and so, rather suddenly, escaping her view.

She had scarce reseated herself on her bed, when she heard the well-known creak of John's door, and, afterwards, stealing footsteps coming from it. They seemed to pass into every room, staying some time in each; and Anty thought she caught the jingling of the little stock of plate, kept in a drawer in the kitchen, and then the opening and shutting of other drawers and cupboards. Presently, to add the utmost to her horror, the handle of her door was turned, but, after a few cautious efforts, left quiet, and the foot went into her mother's chamber; returned; again stole by her door, while a bunch of keys sounded in the passage; and Anty soon heard unlocked a little private desk in which she knew her father kept, now and then, considerable sums of money. After this, all became silent, for about an hour; but at the end of, perhaps, some such lapse of time, the step again approached her door, and stopped before it: the handle again turned, and a voice spoke in whispers through the key-hole:

" Anty, dear Anty !" She was silent, controlling even her breath.

There was a knock, and the voice continued:

" You are not asleep, Anty, I 'm sure of that; you cannot sleep so sound after my knock; open the door, and let me have a word with you."

She took heart to say, "Dear John, what is the matter?"

"I'm frightened to death in that old room of mine; it brings such thoughts and recollections, I cannot close an eye; let me in, for charity's sake, and I will just throw myself across the foot of your bed, and try for a little rest, which I want badly."

"You know I have lain down, John, and will not, surely, expect me to rise."

"I'll wait till you are ready to open the door, but you *must* open it, dear Anty."

"Well, I'll tell you, John; go back to your own room, and in a few moments you shall see me there, and we can sit up the night together, talking of old times."

"You promise this?"

"Depend on me."

He retired. She snatched a bonnet; gently undid her casement; issued out; avoiding the other window, gained a by-path leading towards David Shearman's father's, close by the Dublin road; and after a few cautious steps, ran forward in the impulse to call upon her good

neighbours for protection for herself and her
mother. She had made but little way, when a
soldier appeared closing her by another path
from her own house, and at the same moment
shots were fired further on, in the country
about Long-Hall. Utterly confounded, Anty
lost all recollection of a purpose, and only
raced more wildly towards the Dublin road,
not noticing that, at the report of the shots, her
pursuer suddenly slackened his pace. As she
gained the high fence that separated her from
the road, a strange man and two other soldiers,
all armed, started up before her; she shrieked aloud, almost wild with terror; the man
abruptly asked who had come to her father's
house that night ? She answered but with
another scream; he took her arm, and told her
that Long-Hall had been attacked by robbers,
and that he suspected one of them was then
skulking under Daniel Nowlan's roof; poor
Anty did not hear him; or, if so, could not
properly apprehend him; the quick succession
of so many startling incidents, the shots, the
soldiers, the loud talking, all bewildered her;
her catechist and his companions left her, as if
in impatience; she sank nearly senseless on the

road side; the horn of the usual night-coach
sounded; she sprang up, and only capable of
feeling that, as by such a conveyance Peggy
had gone to seek her father in Dublin, she
would now go seek protection from Peggy and
him, the terrified girl called out to the guard,
and in a few seconds, seated inside, was on her
way to the metropolis. Her poor mother's
helpless situation escaped her thoughts for the
moment, though when far upon the road, too
far to turn back, her heart sorely smote her,
during the remainder of the journey, at a recollection of the selfishness she could not have
controlled.

CHAPTER IX.

MEANTIME Peggy Nowlan had her own trials
and escapes on the road to Dublin.

Late in the second morning of her journey,
the coach upset within about a stage of the metropolis, and she was violently thrown off, and
deprived of sense by the shock.   When Peggy
recovered, she found herself in a smoky-looking
room, dimly lighted by a single dipped candle
of the smallest size.   The walls were partly
covered with decayed paper, that hung off,
here and there, in tatters.   There were a few
broken chairs standing in different places, and
in the middle of the apartment a table, that
had once been of decent mould, but that now
bore the appearance of long and hard service,
supporting on its drooping leaves a number of
drinking glasses, some broken and others cap-

sized, while their slops of liquor remained fresh around them.

Peggy was seated with her back to the wall; she felt her head supported by some one who occasionally bathed her temples with a liquid which, by the odour it sent forth, could be no other than whisky; and if she had been an amateur, Peggy might have recognised it as pottheen.

" My God, where am I ?" looking confusedly around, was her first exclamation.

" You 're in safe hands, Peggy Nowlan," she was answered in the tones of a woman's voice: " an' I 'm glad to hear you spake, at last."

Turning her head, she observed the person who had been attending her. The woman was tall and finely-featured, about fifty, and dressed pretty much in character with the room and its furniture; that is, having none of the homely attire of the country upon her, but wearing gay flaunting costume, or rather the remains of such; and there was about her air and manner a bold confidence, accompanied by an authoritative look from her large black eyes, that told a character in which the mild timidity of woman existed not. Yet she smiled on Peggy, and her smile was beautiful and fascinating.

" How do you know me, good woman ?" again questioned our heroine, for we believe she is such.

" Oh, jist by chance, afther a manner, miss; onct, when I went down to your counthry to see a gossip o' my own, the neighbours pointed you out to me as the comeliest colleen to be seen far an' wide; an' so, Miss Peggy, fear nothing;" for Peggy, as she looked about her, and at the woman, did show some terror : " an' I 'm glad in the heart to see any one from your part, where there 's some kind people, friends o' mine; an' for their sakes, an' the sake o' the ould black hills you cum from, show me the man that daares look crooked at you."

This speech was accompanied by such softness of manner, that Peggy's nervousness lessened. She gained confidence from the presence of one of her own sex looking so kindly on her, and, though years had been busy with her fine features, looking so handsome too. Her next question was, naturally, a request to be informed how she came into her present situation.

" You were brought here, jist to save your

life," answered the woman; "a son o' mine, coming along the road from Dublin, saw the coach tumble down; he waited to give it a helping hand up again; and when it druv away—"

"And has it gone off, and left me behind?" interrupted Peggy, in great distress.

"Of a thruth, ay has it, my dear."

"What, then, am I to do?—"

"Why, you must only stay where you are wid me, until the day; an' you're welcome to the cover o' th' ould roof, an' whatever comfort I can give you; an' when the day comes we'll look out for you, Miss Peggy, a-roon. But, as I was saying, when the coach dhrew off again, my son was for hurrying home, when he heard some one moaning inside o' the ditch; an' he went into the field, an' there was a man lying, jist coming to his senses, an' you near him, widout any sense at all; an' when the man got betther, my son knew him for an ould acquaintance; and then they minded you, and tuck you up between them; an' sure here you are to the fore."

"It is absolutely necessary I should continue my journey to-night," said Peggy.

"If you're for Dublin, child, you can hardly go; it's a thing a friend can't hear of."

Peggy reflected for a moment. Her usual caution now told her, what her first suspicions had suggested, that, in some way or other, the house was an improper one, and, perhaps, that good-nature had not been the only motive in conveying her to it. The woman's last words seemed to show a particular determination that she should remain. It would be imprudent, then, to express a design to go away; she might be detained by force. Nor would she suffer herself to become affected by her fears, lest she might incapacitate herself for escaping by stealth. Prompted by growing suspicion, she stole her hand to her bosom to search for her purse; it was gone: and Peggy became confirmed in her calculations, though not more apparently shaken by her fears.

"I had a small hand-basket," she said, "containing a few little articles, and my money for the road; it's lost, of course, and I am left pennyless; if I go to the spot where the coach fell, maybe I could find it."

"We can go together," said the woman, "if you are able to walk so far."

Peggy had made the proposal, not in hopes

of recovering any thing, but that she might be
afforded a chance of walking away; if, indeed,
the story of the coach having driven on proved
to be true. Now, however, she was, in consist-
ency, obliged to accept the attention of her
officious protector; and the woman and she
walked to the road along a narrow, wild lane,
at each side of which a few old decayed trees
and bushes shook their leafless branches in
the wintry wind, while the footing was broken
and miry, and overgrown by weeds and long
grass. It seemed to have been a winding avenue
to the house she had left, once planted with
rows of trees, when the mansion was better
tenanted and in better repair, but which had
disappeared, from time to time, beneath the
axe or the saw of the marauder.

Arrived at the spot required, she commenced a seemingly careful search; but, finding nothing, returned at the continued urgency
of the woman, who linked her closely, to
the house they had quitted. Ere Peggy re-
entered, she took a survey of the fabric: it
was, like every thing around it and within it,
a ruin. She could see that it had been a good
slated house, two stories high, but that in different places the slates were now wanting; in-

deed she trod, near the threshold, upon their
fragments, mixed with other rubbish. Some
of the windows were bricked up, some stuffed
through their shattered panes with wisps of
straw and old rags; and of the lower ones, the
shutters, which were, however, attached to the
wall, outside strong iron bars, hung off their
hinges, and flapped in the blast.

Again entering the room in which she had
first found herself, two men appeared seated.
Peggy, in something like the recurrence of a
bad dream, thought she recognized in one of
them the air and figure of the person who,
on a late and fearful occasion, had stood
so near to her in the Foil Dhuiv. But as
she did not feel herself entitled to draw any
certain deductions from feature, complexion, or
even dress, Peggy, after a moment's faltering
pause, struggled to assure herself that this misgiving was but a weakness of her agitated mind,
and firmly advanced to the chair she had before
occupied.

The second man was very young, his person
slight, and twisted into a peculiar bend and
crouch as he sat; his face pale and sharp, re-
sembling that of the woman who called herself

his mother; and in the side-long glance of his cold jetty eye there lurked a stealth, an enquiry, and a self-possession, as, in reply to Peggy's curtsey and her look of observance, he, in turn, observed her, and gave, slowly and measuredly, his "Sarvent, miss."

He and his companion sat close to the drooping table. Two of the glasses that had been capsized now stood upright, and were frequently filled from a bottle of whisky, of— as one might augur by the smell—home manufacture. The person whose first view had startled Peggy, made more free with the beverage than the other; the pale young man visibly avoiding the liquor; but often filling for his friend, and urging him to drink bumpers.

" Well, Phil, my boy," said the woman, addressing the pale lad, as she entered after Peggy, " did Ned tell you the raison yet, why he was on the top o' the coach to-night, instead of being far off on other business ?"

" Oh yes," answered Phil, in a dry, careless tone, " he tould me all how an' about it ;" and a wink, that, from its freedom from humour, was disagreeable, did not escape Peggy.

" I call that toss we got together a d—d

hearty 'un——my eyes, miss," said the other man, addressing Peggy, and offering her some liquor.

" Were you the person who lay so near me ?" refusing his politeness.

" Ay, that I was, to my cost; and though no great harm might come o' lying so near you, little 'un, at another time, I 'd rather not have such a throw for it, however."

She shrunk while he spoke, and while his eye of gloomy, stupid excitement, dwelt upon her; but did not omit an answer.

" Then I have to thank you, and, I suppose, this other gentleman, for my safety."

" Oh, that 's all gammon : easy to clear the odds with such a pretty 'un, you know."

Phil made no observation; but his glance went from the speaker to Peggy, and then to his mother, with a slow, remarkful, and cheerless expression; and again Peggy saw interchanged, between him and the woman, a wink, followed by a dead glare.

" Go, Phil, my boy," resumed the old woman, " take Ned and yourself up stairs; an' the bottle wid you; you must have the hot wather, when it 's ready, and the sugar along wid it : this young woman and myself 'll stay together."

Phil arose, taking the bottle and glasses: he was sidling out of the room before his companion, when, at a renewed signal from the woman, he hung back, allowed the other to stagger out first, and then he and she paused together, beyond the threshold of the room, in the passage, where Peggy could hear them exchange a few earnest, though cautious whispers.

" An' now, Peggy Nowlan," resumed the woman, coming back and reseating herself, " as you don't seem to like the whisky, you must have whatever the house can give you."

" I would like some tey, ma'am."

" Then, sure enough, you 'll get it ; we won't be long lighting the fire, an' biling the wather, an' we 'll take our tey together."

There were some embers dimly gleaming in the blackened fire-place, to which the woman added wood and chips, that, by blowing with her mouth as she knelt, soon blazed; and, according to her promise, a dish of tea, not badly flavoured, was manufactured, of which, with much seeming hospitality and kindness, the hostess pressed her young guest to

partake. Peggy felt thankful, and strove to
compel herself to feel at ease also: but, amid
the smiles and blandness of her entertainer,
there were moments when her thin and blood-
less, though handsome lips compressed themselves to a line so hard and heartless,—moments when a deep shade of abstraction passed
over her brow, and when her eyes dulled and
shrunk into an expression so disagreeable, that
the destitute girl internally shivered to glance
upon her.   These momentary changes did not,
however, seem to concern her. She argued,
that they rather intimated an involuntary turn
of thought to some other person or subject.
The woman never looked on her without a
complacent smile; and it was after her getting
up occasionally, and going to the door of the
room, as if to catch the sound of voices from
above, that her countenance wore any bad character.   But, whatever might have been passing in her mind, Peggy prudently resolved not
to allow her hostess to perceive that she observed these indications of it. Her glances were,
therefore, so well-timed, and so quick, that they
could not be noticed; and her features so well
mastered, as always to reflect the easy smile of

her companion. Her manners, too, she divested
of every trait of alarm or doubt; and even the
tones of her voice were tutored by Peggy into
an even, pleased cadence; and the questions
she asked, and the topics she started, calculated
to lull all suspicion.

As part of her plan, she would show no uneasiness to retire; and it was not until the woman herself offered to attend her to bed, that
Peggy rose from her chair. She was conducted
out of the little, half-ruined parlour or kitchen,
a few paces along the passage, and then a few
steps up a rent and shaking staircase, into a
mean sleeping-chamber, of which the door
faced the passage : the stairs continuing to wind
to the right, to the upper rooms of the house.
As they passed into the chamber, it was with
difficulty Peggy prevented herself from drawing back, when she perceived that the patched
door had bolts and a padlock on the outside,
but no fastening within. Still, however, she
controlled her nerves, and displayed to her attendant no symptom of the apprehension that
filled her bosom.

" I 'm sorry the poor house doesn't afford a
betther an' a handsomer lodgin' for you, Miss

Peggy," said the woman, as both stumbled about the half-boarded floor of the room : " but you 'll jest take the will for the deed ; an' so, good-b'ye, an' a pleasant night's sleep to you."

" Can't you oblige me with the candle ?" asked Peggy, as her hostess was about to take it away.

" I would, with a heart an' a half, if it was to spare ; but I 'll have nothing else to light me to bed, an' help me to set things to rights for the morning ; for the matther o' that, the good moon shines so bravely through the window, and I believe through another little place in the loft here, that you 'll be well able to say your prayers an' go to bed by it, Miss Peggy ; so, *bannochth-lath* :" and she finally took the candle away, securing the door on the outside, and leaving Peggy standing in the middle of the filthy chamber.

The moon did, indeed, stream in upon the floor as well through the shattered window as, first, through a breach in the slates of the house-roof, and then down the broken boards of the room over head. Peggy looked round for her bed, and saw, in a corner, a miserable substitute for one, composed of straw laid on the floor, and covered with two blankets. There was no chair or table, and feeling herself weak, she cautiously picked her steps to the corner, and sat down on this cheerless couch.

The motive of her conduct hitherto had been to hide her feelings, so as to throw the people of the house off their guard, and eventually create for herself an opportunity to escape to the main road, and thence to the next cabin at hand. In furtherance of her project, she now begged of God to strengthen her heart, and keep her in a steady mind; and, after her zealous aspiration, Peggy continued to think of the best part to act. At once she resolved not to stir in her chamber, until the woman and the two men should seem to have retired to sleep—if, indeed, it was doomed that they were to do so without disturbing her. In case of a noise at her door, she determined to force her way through the crazy window, and, trusting herself to God, jump from it to the ground, which, she argued, could not be many feet under her, as Peggy had not forgotten to count the steps while she ascended from the earthen passage to her present situation. If, after long watching, she could feel pretty sure that no evil was intended to her during the night, still she planned to steal to the window, open it with as little noise as possible, drop from it and try to escape.

More than an hour might have passed, when she heard a noise, as if of two persons stumbling through the house; it came nearer, and two men, treading heavily and unevenly, entered a room next to hers, and only divided from her by a wooden partition, which here and there admitted the gleams of a light they bore. Without any rustling, Peggy applied her eye to one of the chinks, and gained a full view of the scene within. She saw the person she so much dreaded, led by the pale young man towards such a bed as she occupied; the one overcome by intoxication; the other cool, collected, and observant. With much grumbling, and many half-growled oaths, the drunken fellow seemed to insist on doing something that the lad would not permit, and at length Peggy heard an allusion to herself.

" Go to sleep, Ned; you 're fit for nothing else to-night; there 's your bed, I tell you," said the young man, forcing him to it.

" I say, Master Phil, stoopid, I 'll have one

word with that wench before I close a winker,"
replied Ned; "that wench, I say—hic!—what
I picked up on the road; and why the devil
should I bring her here but to chat a bit with
her? Your house isn't fit for much better, you
know, Master Phil; and, —— my eyes but—"

"Lie down, you foolish baste," interrupted
his companion, pushing him down on the straw.

"I 'll stand none of that nonsense, neither,"
continued the ruffian, scrambling about; "and
it 's no use talking; I 'll see her by ——; I 'll
see the wench, as I brought to this ——
house: and don't you go to tell me, now, as
how it 's all a hum, and that I brought no such
body into it; I 'm not so cut but I remember
it : so fair-play, Master Phil; she must be ac-
counted for: none of your old mother's tricks
will do, now. I am not to be done, by ——;
the wench shan't be served out in that way,
however; and I 'll see her, by ——; first and
last, that 's my word: hic!—I 'll—hic!" and he
lay senseless.

The pale young man watched him like a
lynx, until, after some moments, his growling
changed into a loud snore, and there was no
doubt but he slept soundly. Then he stepped

softly to him, knelt on one knee, took out of
his breast a large pistol, thrust it under his own
arm, and finally emptied his pockets of a purse
and some crumpled papers. Arising, with continued caution, he glanced over the latter close
by the candle, and Peggy saw his features
agitated.   The next moment he stole out of
the room, barred the door outside, and she
heard his stealthy step, betrayed by the creaking boards, about to pass her chamber.

At this moment, however, another step,—
Peggy supposed that of the woman,—met his
from the lower part of the house, and both
stopped just at her frail, though well-secured
door.

" Well ?" questioned the woman, in a sharp
whisper ; " you pumped him ? and soaked
him ? and touched the lining of his pockets ?
Did we guess right ?"

" We did, by —— " answered the young
man ; " the —— rascal has peached, by the
—— ; his very shuffling with me showed it
at once ; but here 's the proof : here 's an
answer from Mr. Long to his offer to put him
on his guard against the swag at Long Hall,
this blessed night : and here 's another letter,

from Lonnon, closing with another offer of his
to set the poor private for the Bow-street bull-
dogs."

They had, during these words, been, perhaps, speaking to each other at some little distance ; for their whispers, now that Peggy supposed them to have come close together, were
lost on her aching ear, though she still heard
the hissing sounds in which the conversation
was carried on. A considerable time lapsed
while they thus stood motionless outside her
door : at length they moved ; seemed about to
part ; and, at parting, a few more sentences became audible.

" Go, then," said the woman, " an' let us
lose no time : nothing else can be done ; poor
Maggy is to be saved from the treachery of the
Lonnon sneak, if there was no one else concarned in the case ; speed, Phil ; make sure o'
the horn-hafted Lamprey that you 'll find on
the dresser : I 'll meet you at his dour with a
light and a vessel. Are you sure he sleeps sound
enough ?"

" There is only the one sleep more that can
be sounder," replied Phil ; and Peggy heard
them going off.

In panting terror she listened for their steps again passing her door : nor had she to listen long. Slowly and stealthily, and with heavy breathings, or a suppressed curse at the creaking boards, they separately came by. In a moment after, she heard them undo the fastenings of the inside room, and, fascinated to the coming horror, as the bird is to the reptile's glance, her eye was fixed to a chink, ere the light they carried afforded her a renewed view of the victim's chamber.

The woman first entered, bearing the candle in one hand, and in the other a basin which held a cloth. Her face was now set in the depth of the bad expression Peggy had seen it momentarily wear below stairs; and she was paler than usual, though not shaking or trembling. The lad followed, taking long and silent strides across the floor, while his knife gleamed in his hand, and his look was ghastly. They made signs to each other. The woman laid down the candle and the basin, and tucked up the sleeves of her gown beyond her elbows. She again took up her basin, laid the cloth on the floor, stole close to the straw couch, knelt by it, and held the vessel near the wretch's head. Her companion followed her, and knelt also. He unknotted and took off, with his left hand, the man's neckcloth. As it was finally snatched rather briskly away, the wearer growled and moved. He never uttered a sound more.

Peggy kept her eye to the chink during the whole of this scene. She could not withdraw it. She was spell-bound; and, perhaps, an instinctive notion that if she made the slightest change in her first position, so as to cause the slightest rustle, her own life must be instantly sacrificed—perhaps this tended to hold her perfectly still. She witnessed, therefore, not only the details given, but the concluding details which cannot be given. Even when the murder was done, she durst not remove her eye until the woman and lad had left the chamber; so that she was compelled to observe the revolting circumstance of washing the blankets and the floor, and other things which again must not be noticed. It is certain that moral courage and presence of mind never won a greater victory over the impulses of nature, than was shown in this true situation, by this lonely and simple girl. Often, indeed, there arose in her bosom an almost irresistible incli-

nation to cry out—at the moment the neckcloth
was removed, when the sleeping man muttered
and turned, she was scarcely able to keep in her
breath; yet she *did* remain silent. Not even
a loud breathing escaped her. All was over,
and she a spectatress of all, and still she
mastered herself; and although, so far as regarded her, the most home cause for agitation
finally occurred as the murderers were about
to withdraw, Peggy was a heroine to the
last.

" He 'll touch no blood-money now," whispered the woman; " an' we may go to our beds,
Phil, for the work is done well; so, come away
—but stop; high-hanging to me, if I ever
thought of that young —— in the next room:
an', for any thing we know, she may be watching us all this time."

" If you think so, mother, there's but one
help for it," observed the lad.

" A body could peep through the chinks
well enough," resumed the female monster ;—
" but, on a second thought, Phil, d'you think
it 's in the nature of a simple young counthry
girl like her to look at what was done, without
givin' warning ?"

" May be not; come, try if she's asleep any how; she can't bam us there, mother."

" Come."—and they left the chamber.

The moment they withdrew, Peggy stretched herself on her couch, threw a blanket over her person, closed her eyes, and breathed as if fast asleep. Yet it was with many doubts of her own ability to go successfully through this test, that she listened for the noise of unbarring her door. The creeping steps approached, and her heart nearly failed her. A bolt was shot, and her brain swam.

But again the assassins seemed to hesitate, and again she heard their whispers.

" Stop," said the lad, " she must be sound asleep, as you say; it's not to be thought she could look on and stand it."

" That's my own notion," replied the woman.

" Then if we rouse her, at this time o' night, wid those marks about us," meaning the marks on their hands and clothes, " why, it 'll be tell-in' our own sacret, when we might hould our tongue."

" Yes; an' only makin' more o' the same work for ourselves, when we have done enough of it."

" Besides ; she 'll be to the fore in the mornin', and then we can cross-hackle her on
the head of it ; an', if she shows any signs of
knowin' more than we want her to know,—why,
it can be a good job still."

" You spake rason ; an', sure enough, she 'll
be to the fore ; because I have a notion o' my
own, that we ought to keep her fast till the
poor private an' Maggy sees her ; they 'll want
to have a word wid her, may be: so, by hook
or crook, she 's to pass another day and night
in the house."

" Let us go sleep, then, mother ; an' you must
get me a little wather."

" Yes, a-vich ; but I don't think myself
wants much o' the sleep for this night, any
how."

They left Peggy's door, and she was thus
saved the test her soul shrank from. In
some time after their steps became silent, she
lay on her straw, with clasped hands and eyes
turned to Heaven, offering the most fervent
thanks for her preservation. The winter morning broke ; all seemed quiet in the house ; and
she ventured to sit up and think again. Her
neighbourhood to the mangled body occurred

to her, and delirium began to arise. She had
recourse to her prayers for help and strength,
and they did not fail her. Hour after hour
passed away, still she kept herself employed,
either by communions with her God, or by
laying out her mind to meet the trials she had
yet to encounter.

They would watch her, they had said, in the
morning; she was able to will and determine
that the investigation would be vain: Peggy
felt that she could defeat them. They intended
to induce or force her to spend the day and
night where she was; against this plan she also
attempted to lay a counter-plot.

It might be nine o'clock when she heard them
stirring about. But, at the first sound, she lay
stretched on her bed; and this proved a good
precaution. One of them walked softly up the
stairs; then into the next room; and afterwards,
close to the partition, by her couch; and, as
Peggy judged by the hard breathing through
the chinks, seemed to watch if she slept. She
was now able to give every appearance of sleep
to the eye of the observer. After a few moments, they were together in the room, and she

heard their whispers, and then the noise of trailing out the body.

For about another hour, they left her undisturbed. At length the door was opened, and the woman entered her chamber. Peggy still pretended to sleep, showing, however, some signs of the restlessness that attends our being disturbed from sleep without our being fully aroused. The hideous visitor stooped down and stirred her. Peggy bore the touch of that hand on her shoulder, without wincing in any way. The woman stirred her again, and she seemed gradually and naturally to become awakened.

" Musha, it 's the good sleep that 's on you, a colleen," said the woman, as she sat up.

" Yes, indeed; I 'm not used to be without the sleep so long, and I had none before this since I left the mountains," answered Peggy. " Is it very late? but I don't care much about that, as there 's no use in my starting from you till the coach comes again to-night, and gives me a seat for Dublin."

" We 'll tell you all about that by and by : get up now, my woman, an' break your fast; you ought to be hungry."

" And I am very hungry, and able to help myself out of any thing you lay before me."

The woman led her down stairs. A good breakfast was prepared. Peggy seemed to eat with a keen appetite; but she continued to slip the bread she had cut into her large country pockets. The young man entered: she bade him a smiling good-morrow. He hoped she had passed a good night: she answered promptly and easily.

" It's an odd question I'm for axin'," he continued, "but I thought I heard strange noises in a room next to yours last night—did *you* ?"

With the consciousness that the eyes of both were watching her face for a change of expression, Peggy baffled the enquiry.

" It's said this ould house is haunted," rejoined the woman, " an' that's the ghost's room."

" My faith isn't strong in ghosts," said Peggy, smiling; " but I'm glad you did not tell of it before I went to bed, or I might be kept waking."

A pause ensued, during which she knew that

her catechists were consulting each other by looks and nods.

"Why don't you ax afther your friend, that helped to bring you to us last night?" pursued the lad.

"I was thinking of him, but said to myself he was in his bed, maybe; and as he's no kith or kin o' mine, only a stranger met on the road, I didn't believe it would be right for a young, lone woman like me to be asking so closely after him."

"He's not in his bed," said the lad, fixing his eye. She stood his glance.

"No," resumed the woman; "but gone the road at the first light this mornin'."

"Why then I'm sorry for his going."

"How's that?" asked the lad.

"Because I'm left without a farthing in the world, and I thought that, as he looked to be a dacent man, maybe he'd lend me a few shillings to take me on to Dublin; and now I don't know what to do under Heaven."

"Never make yourself uneasy about that," remarked the hostess: "for if you thought he looked so like a dacent body, he thought you looked like a hansome colleen, as you are; an'

for a token, hearin' o' your loss by the coach,
he left us the very thing you're talking about,
to give you when you'd get up."

"Yes, he left this wid me for you," pursued
the other, handing some silver, "and just his
word to take care an' have as much ready to
pay him in the next place he an' you are to see
ach other."

As he gave the money, and spoke these words
very significantly, he again fixed her eye ; but
Peggy allowed him no advantage. With many
professions of thanks to her chance benefactor,
she quietly put up the supposed gift. Perhaps they became fully assured that they had
nothing to fear, for they soon stopped ques-
tioning her.

"I'll pay him, with hearty thanks, sure
enough," she continued, recurring to the topic,
"and sooner than he thinks, maybe. I have only
to get to Dublin, to the Brazen-Head, where
my father stops, when I'll have money enough ;
and, after a word there, I'm to pass your
dour, to-morrow, about the night-fall, when I'll
be axin' a night's lodgin' from you again ; and I
can jest lave the honest man's shillings in your
hands, and you'll give 'em to him, the next

time he calls, in Peggy Nowlan's name, and her best wishes along with 'em."

The day wore away in common topics, and she showed no anxiety to depart. She said she grew hungry for her dinner; and, when it came before her, still seemed to make a hearty meal. No living creature came to the house during the day; but she could understand that the person called Maggy, and who she concluded was her wretched cousin, Maggy Nowlan, and the other person, called " the private," were expected during the night; as also a number of " the customers," from Dublin.

Nothing had yet been said to deter her from proceeding to town in the night-coach, which, as usual, was to pass at about three o'clock in the morning. She often alluded to its hour of passing by, and they did not make an observation. This gave her courage; and, after the night fell—for Peggy, still to avoid a shadow of suspicion, would not motion to stir in the day-light—she said, inadvertently, and yet with some natural show of anxiety to proceed in her interrupted journey;—

" Maybe I couldn't get a seat in it, an' what should I do, then?—But maybe I ought to take the road some time afore ye expect it to come up, so that, when it overtakes me, if I get the place, well and good; and if I don't, why I could be so far on my way, and sure of walking the six or seven miles more, to Dublin, by the morning, any how; for I must be there in the morning: what brings me up is to get a good lot of money from my father, that 'll be wanted at home the day after to-morrow, or the next day, at farthest; and so, ye see, honest people, I 'm beholding to be soon back and forward, and, as I said, sleeping in your house, on my way to the country, by to-morrow night, any how."

They said little in reply to this; but Peggy believed they again exchanged some glances and signs, while her head was purposely held down; and then they retired to whisper at the outward door. Fervently did she pray, although the prayer involved an uncharitable contradiction, that, influenced by the hope of plunder she had held out, their resolves not to let her depart for the night might be changed. And perhaps her plan took effect.

In a short time they rejoined her; and after a few ordinary remarks, said, by the way,

that she might do well to "take a start o'
the road, afore the coach, just as she was a
saying of it; and they wished her safe to Dublin, any how; and they hoped she would keep
her promise, and come see them on her way
home again."

Without discovering any extraordinary joy
at this concession, Peggy bid them a steady
and cordial good-b'ye; engaged her bed for the
next night; and it was not till the very moment
she was crossing the murderous threshold that
she feared her face, accent and fluttered step
might have given intimation of the smothered
emotions that battled in her heart.

But, again befriended by her extraordinary
presence of mind, she checked her rising ecstasy,
and trod with a sober and way-faring step
down the dark, tangled, and miry lane. When
fairly launched on the broad road, her breast
experienced great relief; yet still she kept her
demure pace, neither faltering, nor looking back
nor about her, nor yet sure of the policy of
rushing into the first cabin she might meet.
Her heart whispered that the people of the
abominable house might have noticed her parting struggle, and, after a little reflection, would

perhaps follow her, and put her to another trial.

To her left, as she walked along, was some rather high ground, falling down to the road, little cultivated, and crowded with furze and briars. A straggling path ran through it, parallel to the road, but at some distance, and, she believed, led to the lone house in the " *bosheen.*" Her eye kept watching this path, every step she took. The moon shone full upon it, so as to enable her to discern any near object. Peggy, her head down, and her regards not visibly occupied, soon caught a figure rapidly striding along the path, through the clumps of furze and briars. As it abruptly turned towards a gap in the road-fence, some yards before her, she could ascertain that this individual was closely muffled in the common female Irish mantle, holding, as Irishwomen often do, the ample hood gathered round the face.

" That 's not a woman's step," thought Peggy; as the figure issued through the gap: —" and now, this will be the sorest trial of all."

And, with her suspicions, well might she say so. The gigantic resolution of her heart, so long kept up, had just begun to yield to an admitted sense of relief: she had just permitted her mind to turn and sicken on the contemplation of the horrors she had witnessed and escaped; an opportunity at last seemed created for an indulgence of the revulsion and weakness of her woman's nature;—and now again to call back her unexcelled philosophy; again to rally herself; again to arrest and fix the melting resolution; to steady the pulse-throb, tutor the very breath, prepare the very tones of her voice; this, indeed, was her sorest trial. But it was her greatest too; for Peggy, assisted a little by the shadows of night, came out of it still triumphant.

" God save you!" began the person in the cloak, in a female voice. Peggy gave the usual response with a calm tone.

" Are you for thravellin' far, a-roon?" continued the new-comer. She said she was going to Dublin.

" I 'm goin' there myself, an' we may 's well be on the road together."

" With all my heart, then," answered Peggy, and they walked on side by side.

" You 're not of these parts, ma-colleen, by your tongue," resumed her companion. Peggy assented.

" An' how far did you walk to-day, a-chorra?"

" Not far; not a step to-day; only from a house in a bosheen behind us, a few minutes ago."

" What house, a good girl? do you mane the ould slate-house that stands all alone, in the middle o' the lane?" Peggy believed that was the very one.

" Lord save us! what bad loock sent you there?"

" None, that I know of; why?"

" It has a bad name, as I hear among the neighbours, and 'ud be the last place myself 'ud face to, for the night's rest."

" Well, aroon; it 's only a Christian turn to spake of people as we find 'em; I have nothing at all to say against the house; an' may be it won't be long till I see it again."

" That 's bould as well as hearty of a young girl like you. Did you come across the woman o' the house?"

" Yes; and met good treatment from her; the good tey; the good dinner; every thing of the best."

" But what kind of a bed did you get from her, a-hager?" continued the catechist, speaking very low, sidling to Peggy, and grasping her arm. This threw her off her guard. She shrieked, and broke from her companion, who, as she ran, fast pursued her; and the person's real voice at last sounded in her ear.

" Stop, Peggy Nowlan, or rue it ! I know what you think of the bed you got now !"

The road suddenly turned in an angle; Peggy shot round the turn: as her pursuer gained on her, she heard the noise of feet approaching in a quick tramp, and a guard of armed soldiers, headed by two men in civil dress, and followed by a post-chaise, met her eyes at a short distance; she cried out again, and darted among the soldiers; one of them caught and held her from falling, and she had only time to say—" Lay hands on the murderer !" when nature at last failed, and Peggy's senses left her.

CHAPTER X.

SHE recovered to a sense of rapid motion, and found herself in a post-chaise sitting beside a soldier, whose features, in the yet unbroken darkness of the winter's morning, were hidden from her. To her incoherent and timid questions her new companion spoke mildly, and in a voice that was very pleasing to her ear. She had nothing to apprehend, he said. A gentleman who followed the military party in the post-chaise, recognised her after she had swooned away ; and as soon as the man, disguised in female attire, to whom she directed their notice, had been secured, he prevailed on the serjeant of the little detachment to allow her an escort to Dublin, and get her forwarded to a hotel in Sackville-street, where he would soon join her.

Peggy was as much astonished as pleased

at this information. Who could her self-elected guardian be? What right had he, whoever he was, to give orders about her? and ought she to submit to those orders? would it seem proper for a young woman like her to go passively to the hotel of a gentleman of whom she knew nothing, and there await his return?

She asked the civil soldier to tell her the name of this person. The man had never heard it. All he knew of him was that he had called at Richmond Barracks, which place lay on her present way to Dublin, very early that morning, accompanied by a police-officer and a country-looking man, for the purpose of summoning a serjeant's guard, to aid him in the apprehension of certain people who lived a little way on from the spot where they had found Peggy.

" That's the ould house in the bosheen," she thought, " and nothing else it is."

" But what like gentleman was it that came in the post-chaise?"

The soldier could not even on this point give her any information. The serjeant only, of all the party, had spoken with the gentleman, and had an opportunity of closely observing him. For his own part, he did not know

any thing about him. He would not venture
to describe even his height or age.

Still Peggy wondered, and, amid all her troubles and exhaustion, taxed herself to think.
In a few moments she resolved, if possible, not
to go to the hotel whither the gentleman had
requested her to be conveyed, and, encouraged
by the very soothing manner of her companion,
said she had the most pressing business at
another inn, the Old Brazen Head, and would
thank him to bring her there. The soldier
replied that he was not at liberty to conduct
her, himself, to one place or the other; he
could not see her even quite into town; in
fact, his orders were to drop her at Richmond
Barracks, and there engage some other person to
walk forward with her, while he immediately
returned in the post-chaise to the spot on which
his services might be required. But he engaged to enforce on the person that might take
her on into town, the necessity of attending to
all her wishes.

With this promise, they arrived before the
entrance gate of Richmond Barracks. The
attentive soldier got out; and " Here, sentinel,"
he said, addressing the man on guard, as he

helped Peggy down, " Sergeant Goodge sends orders that you give this young woman in charge to the first man at hand; she is much terrified, a stranger in town, and quite alone; let her have a safe guide wherever it is her pleasure to go; to the Brazen Head, she says: and harkye," in a low tone, " she 's a respectable person, and must be treated as such."

" The orders shall be cared for," said the sentinel, a staid man of middle age, who seemed to regard the thing only as a part of his military duty.

" Then, good-b'ye, young woman," continued her conductor : " I must be back again in the chaise as fast as the wheels can turn; and I say, my dear," in a mild, earnest tone, " if your face is pretty, as I suppose it is, just keep it as well hidden, until you get to your quarters, from every other person you may meet, as you have from me; good-b'ye."

As he was about to re-enter the chaise, a country-dressed man got down from the driver's seat : and the soldier asked, " Hallo, who are you ?"

" A boy from the bogs," he was answered, in a voice of mixed shrewdness and carelessness;

" a boy from the bogs, just come on the masther's business to town; sure you seen me maybe wid him, on the road, when the colleen stopt us, Sir."

" Oh, I half remember you; do you stay behind, now ?"

" If it's the same to you, I'd rather o' the two."

" I have no concern in the matter; on, driver, as quick as you can :" and the chaise whirled off at a rapid rate, in the direction it had come.

" What curosity ye all have in ye," muttered " the boy from the bogs," as it whisked away.

" Ah, Tims," said the sentinel, addressing a man in a soldier's watch-coat, who that moment came, with a quick step, up to the gate—" is that you, lad ? returned from furlough so soon ?"

" Yes; returned this moment."

" As you go in, tell Corporal White that here's a young woman to go under escort to the Brazen Head Inn, by order of Sergeant Goodge."

" As I shan't be wanted in Barracks till parade hour, why I'll take her in charge myself."

" Well, do so; and be careful of her; none of your old tricks, mind; the orders are that she is a respectable young woman, d'ye hear and to be treated accordingly :—this good fellow

will see you to your quarters, young woman,"
he added, addressing Peggy, who had held back
during the arrangement, carefully covering her
head with a large shawl, to avoid the chill blast,
as well as to escape observation; for we cannot
say but that the hypothesis upon which her first
conductor had given his parting advice might be
partially admitted by Peggy, prim and humble
as she was.

"To the Brazen Head, my girl?" asked her
new guide, offering his arm.

"Yes, sir," she answered, timidly, and, at
his request, still more timidly giving her arm:
they moved on together.

"It's a thing I often hard," soliloquized " the
boy from the bogs," as he walked in their train,
but sufficiently distant to be unseen in the darkness, which, notwithstanding that it fast approached to six o'clock, still fully prevailed—
"It's a thing I often hard said, that them sodgers is all born divils; an' when there's purty
cratures in the way, no such thing as puttin'
thrust in 'em; so, we'll keep lookin' on, by the
way we didn't see, though our eyes won't be
shet abit."

Unwillingly, yet cautious of showing distrust,

Peggy, without once lifting up her face, had taken her companion's arm. Although feeling a repugnance to so close an intimacy with a strange soldier, her conduct on this occasion was measured, too, by her country standard of behaviour, according to which she might innocently give her arm, at a late hour, on a lonesome road, to one of her father's workmen; no consciousness existing, on either side, of any thing beyond the real service required and afforded. She further judged, with her usual prudence, that the man was accountable for her safe conduct; for she had heard delivered the orders respecting her; and she knew enough of a soldier's duty to conclude that they must be strictly observed.

But they had proceeded only a short distance on their way, when, in passing by a brilliant lamp, that shone vividly upon them, the soldier stopped short, and in a jocular tone said— "Let's see your face, my woman." At the same time he touched the shawl that Peggy kept folded over her little bonnet, close down to her chin; and she, not speaking a word, still held it tight, bent her head, and tried to avoid his scrutiny.

" God save ye kindly," said their hitherto
unseen observer, coming indistinctly into view,
while he changed his voice, with much skill,
and put on a foolish look.

" Eh! what does he say?" asked the soldier.

" Nothin' of any harm; only God save ye."

" Well, and what do you want, Master Pat?"

" Jack, i' you plase; Jack Lanigan, Sir, is
the name o' me."

" But have you any business with us?"

" It isn't a grate dale, Sir," dropping his jaw
much lower, as with (to use his own word) " a
*moryah** humility" he took the front part of the
leaf of his hat between his finger and thumb, in
manner of salute, and so held it while he spoke;
" maybe, fur a good-will you 'd have towards
me, you 'd tell us where one Molly Houlihan
stops; she 's wid a misthress Taffy; a snug woman I hear; an' Molly is all-in-all 'wid her."

There really was such a woman as Molly
Houlihan, a " gossip" to the speaker; but he
chose to bring in her name here, only, in a certain strain, to support a character. Molly had
once been his neighbour, the wife of a small

* Pretended humility.

farmer; his god-mother, too; had become "broke, horse an' foot,"—literally understood to mean "ruined, in every shape and way;" had gone to England with her son, to reap and bind; on their return, when the son got married, had settled in Dublin, and was now "a basket," a basket-woman, or a porter to a respectable stall-vender of fish, in Pill-lane, the Dublin Billingsgate.

The soldier laughed at the man's request.

"Avoch, you're welcome to your laugh; only if you war could an' hungry, an' a poor sthray man, goin' the road among the hills this mornin', an' axin me, Jack Lanigan, where's the place my gossip lives, Jack Lanigan 'ud make you laugh, to rise your heart, sooner nor put the laugh on you, any how."

"As you seem to say you're hungry, there's a trifle for you;" throwing a penny in the direction where, without being more than half visible, his new acquaintance stood: "further, I do not well understand you."

He went to pick up the largess, and the soldier again addressed Peggy, pleading to see her face. While searching about, the man continued to keep his eye upon them. Peggy

still resisted her guide's importunity; the con-
test arose to something like a struggle; and her
shawl and bonnet at last fell off, leaving her
features fully exposed in the light of the
lamp. Peggy could now only cast down her
eyes; the soldier peered close; but, instead of
seeming pleased with the view of the very
comely face thus presented, he started back, as
if he had seen a spectre.

The countryman had picked up the shawl
and bonnet; and now, as the soldier stept back,
he stept closer with them to Peggy: affecting,
all the while, with his head bent, and his hat
pulled over his eyes, to rub the dirt from them.
We may, without any breach of the confidence
existing between this person and ourselves, tell
the reader that all his manœuvring of a closer
advance, and a little delay, arose from a wish
to look into the soldier's face without showing
his own; and this curiosity again arose out of a
suspicion, just come into his mind, that, notwithstanding the disguise of the high standing
collar of his watch-coat, the individual might be
a certain person with whom he was formerly
acquainted. Acting in furtherance of his view,
he accordingly kept rubbing and blowing at the

shawl and bonnet, as Peggy stood uncovered,
and stretched out her hand for them ; and
glancing stealthily, now and then, towards her
guide as he said—" Have a little patience,
a-lanna : " I 'll put the worth iv his penny upon
them, in a cleanin' ; we war never a boy, though
we cum from the bogs themselves, that 'ud beg
or take a thing widout givin' something for
it ;" and, as the soldier still drew back into
the shade of the wall, he moved sideways
after him.

It was in consequence of this wilful delay, that
Peggy yet stood uncovered and undisguised,
under the strong glare of the lamp, as a night-
coach rattled up, from the country, on its way
to the post-office. A young woman was leaning
from the window, either in vague hopes of
recognising some friend at every moment, or
impelled by curiosity to observe as much of the
metropolis as could be seen by lamp-light. She
screamed to the coachman to stop ; and while
the soldier, attracted by her scream, started at
her appearance, in another moment Anty
Nowlan was in her sister's arms.

" Is our eye-sighth good ?" queried " the boy
from the bogs ;" " wait—it 's the other, sure

enough. What the duoul—God forgive me!
—brings 'em both here? For the matther
o' that, what 's the raison the one or the
t'other 'ud be runnin' from their quiet home,
where there 's pace an' plenty of all sorts?
Well, I 'll have a purty job on my hands;
lookin' afther one wasn't enough, but there
must be a couple to keep out o' harm's way."

They were yet clinging to each other when
the guard cried out that the time was passing,
and he must start. They did not hear him;
he sounded his despotic horn. Anty, shaken
by her journey, and now by her emotion, became ill. He questioned Peggy as to her sister's
ability to get in: Peggy did not know what to
do or say; but even if Anty was lifted into the
coach, it struck her as a better resource than
remaining under the protection of the soldier:
she had, however, to put on her own bonnet and
shawl, which her unknown squire yet held;
and as, in her confusion and distress, she did
not reply to the guard's last question, the
door was clapped to; the man of capes and
handkerchiefs began to climb up to his seat:
she heard him cry " All right;" the impetu-
ous vehicle rattled away; she screamed after

it ; was not heard or heeded; and she and
her young sister were left together, in the dark
winter's morning, upon the immediate thorough-
fare into a great city, not knowing where to
turn, but luckily ignorant, at the same time, of
the full extent of the danger and impropriety of
such a situation. And could she have witnessed
the conversation that immediately ensued in the
coach, Peggy would not have been cheered by
hearing a good lady tell a fellow-traveller that,
" all along, she had no good opinion of the
young jade that just left them ; that it was a
mighty umproper sort of thing to take up such
runners-by-night, when a dacent person couldn't
guess who was coming : and *you* see, honey,"
she added, in a tone of great good-nature and
compassion, " the sort she must be of, when
she darts out, in the dark, to make hail-fellow-
well-met with a common sthreet-walker, fornent Richmond Barracks"—all the while that,
as she spoke, the young lady to whom she addressed herself might, if it was lightsome enough,
have discerned the arm of this charitable person closely circumscribing the waist of her next
neighbour, a burly and gallant country mer-
chant, going up to purchase goods.

" Excuse my awkwardness, young woman," resumed the soldier, after the coach had driven off, advancing from the shade, more closely muffled than before, while Peggy drew back from him in resentment and apprehension : " excuse my awkwardness; it was a soldier's little freedom, nothing more. I 'm sorry for it, now; and promise, on the word of a soldier, I 'll not repeat it, but conduct you and your sister to the place you seek, and which I know very well."

" Thank you, Sir; but we 'll try to find it without assistance : come, Anty," taking her hand.

" You 'll never be able to get on; be sure of that; and, at such an hour, the streets are particularly dangerous, and full of bad people."

" Indeed, and I fear so," hesitated Peggy.

" Besides, young woman, I must give an account of you to my superiors; I have you in charge, and can't part you till you are safe."

" God, of his mercy, direct us for the best !" said Peggy; " for," she continued, turning to him, while tears ran down her cheeks, " we are quite strangers in Dublin; come up after our father, who is ill—dying, I believe—at the

Brazen Head; so, Heaven be your reward, and bring us to him."

"Never fear me," he answered, "you shall soon see your father;" and again he softly drew Peggy's arm within his, and would have done the same by Anty, but, although she entirely committed herself to Peggy's arrangement, the sensitive girl shrank, trembling, from him, and took her way and kept her place by her sister's side.

"I'm a duoul's fool, to be sure, again soliloquized "the boy from the bogs," as he again cautiously followed in their wake: "they say so, in the counthry, any how; an' God help me, when the dance cums on me, I believe I'm as like a fool as any one I ever seen; but that makes no maxim. I'd lay a bet, fool as I am, the sodger doesn't mane what's right; and if *I* have a raison for spakin', at the present time, wid a voice that's not the same God ga' me, it's not so by him, barrin' he wasn't upon a bad schame; so here goes to keep him within the lenth o' th' poor stick, wid a little run to help it."

A good distance from the Barracks, the soldier led the girls up a street to the right, and stopped with them before a mean-looking house, into which, as was evident to the persevering spy, the sisters were unwilling to enter. Yielding to the soldier's arguments, they at last did so, however.

"Murther," continued their guardian without, "bud that's a place I don't much like, one way or other; I'll step in, an' see wid my own eyes:—stop"—and at his own word of command, he did stop in his advance. "That's like the noise iv a scrimmage within— mostha, nothin' else it is;" and he gave a yell and a jump sideways to the half-open door. The girls met him on the threshold, as they rushed out, screaming, and wild with terror. He returned their cry, in a compassionate key, but nothing subdued for its good feeling; they shrank from him too, and——

"Have mercy on us, honest man!" appealed Peggy, while Anty clung to her—"take pity on the young crature—do not force her to go in—it's a wicked house, I'm sure of it—an' they wanted to take her from me!"

"Then, may the duoul his own self, or else the duoul's mad bull, toss me on his horns, widin an inch o' the shky, if I do any sich thing, a-lanna!" answered the champion, flourishing his cudgel, as he grasped it at the proper point for battle.—We felt some disinclination to record his oath; it seemed to us (adopting a phrase that has not at all grown into cant) verging on "bad taste;" and we pondered and sought for neater words to express the speaker's energy; but, with a due recollection of our trust as faithful delineators of character, our caution and our search were vain; so that we even wrote down the very terms he used, and we beg of the reader not to mistake us, or be shocked with us for our veracity.

"If you are in arnest, save us then from this strange, deceitful man," continued Peggy, as the soldier re-appeared in the street—"save my little sister, at least: I fear most on her account, from what I heard and saw."

"Come here, my darlins—jest stand for yoursefs at the back o' me: and now let us see him fornent us:—sarvent, misther sodger;" with great coolness erecting his person in somewhat of the same way any heroic champion of the fair sex might be supposed to do it, if conscious that he stood as a bulwark between one or

more of them, and their deadly foe, man or
dragon.

" Why do you interrupt the young women,
fellow ?" demanded the soldier angrily ; " get
out of the way, they are nothing to you."

" Arn't they ? why then divil take the liars
in his big paw ; maybe you 'd say they 're not
sisther's childer o' my own, that I have as good
a right to, to fight for, as if they war Lanigans
all over ?"

" Come, Jack ; none of your Irish gibberish ;
fall back, and let me speak to my cousins."

" Not a one step, then, to plase you ; an' we
calls that plain English in Munster, my chap
iv a sodger."

" You won't, won't you ?"

" By the stick in my hand I won't ; an' that's
as good as if I tuck an oath on the head of id."

" Then you must—that 's all."

He quickly approached, with intent to dis-
lodge his opponent, who, as if in sport, made
one or two agile movements round him, and the
soldier came to the ground, heels uppermost,
merely by the dexterity of the toe, without aid
of bludgeon : and " Take care, now, or you 'll be

fallin'," said his antagonist, dancing back to his charge.

"Scoundrel!" cried the soldier, losing all temper, as he sprang up and drew his bayonet; "I know you, now! and must I, a second time, meet such treatment at your hands?"

"If it's a thing you don't like," answered the other, his face settling in determination, say 'God be wid you, boy!' an' jest run while you have the use o' the two legs. Whoo, bother," as his armed foe still advanced, "here we are agin, then, like a May-boy."

He resolutely darted forward, flourishing his cudgel about his head and before his person, with such dexterous rapidity as to make its circular motion resemble that of a chariot-wheel, in full speed. The bayonet flew some yards from the soldier's hand.

"Down on your cursed marrow bones, now," pursued the victor, collaring him, "what you didn't do these thousand years—down on your hunkers, I say! or, by the soul o' man, I'll whip the head o' your showldhers as clane as ever I cut a hanful o' barly: kneel down, I bid you!" forcing him to his knees, "put up your two hands, and ax their pardon : spake !" drawing the hooked blade of a large country *couteau*, within a hair's breadth of his throat.

" Well, I do ask their pardon."

" An' God's pardon ?" making another movement of the blade.

" Yes ;" grumbled the half-choked man.

" An' mine ?"

" And yours."

" Very well : get up, now ;" giving him a shove that set him sprawling—" get up, now, an' go practice at your tar-gate."

" Just let me have my bayonet ;" walking towards it.

" Call to-morrow, a-vich," snatching it up :—" make off wid yoursef—go to the duoul, where you 're thravellin' day an' night—run out of the one road wid me—cut your stick—manin' to say, take yoursef out o' my sighth !" During these separate exhortations, the conqueror, holding the bayonet in his left hand, and incessantly flourishing the good cudgel with his right, gradually worked himself into a mad caper round and round the soldier ; and—" whoo ;" he continued, intently watching the wonders of his own feet—" whoo ! you say you

have a knowledge o' me—an' so you have—
(duoul thank you)—to your cost—whoo ! here's
the boy that 's not ashamed o' what they christen-
ed him—" and thereupon he yielded his usual
stave, only varying one word, by way of present compliment—

" My name it 's Conolly the rake,
    I don't care a sthraw for any man ;
  I dhrinks good whishkey an' ale,
    An' I'd bate out the brains of a sodger-man—
                                        Whoo !"

The battle between Peery and his antagonist
had continued but a very short period, during
which the sisters looked on in trembling anxiety,
fearful to risk further peril, by a flight they knew
not whither; now, their recognition of Peery,
as he threw off his feigned voice and character,
and most convincingly proclaimed his own name,
gave them, in the first instance, great relief ;
and with a " Thank God !" they pressed each
other's hands, and awaited his leisure to return
to them.

" Scoundrel, I 'll reckon with you for all
this," muttered the soldier, about to withdraw.

" Aha !" cried Peery, suddenly stopping his
buffoonery, and changing into a wild yet stern

vigour, as he again darted at the man's throat—
" an' I a'most forgot to make my eye-sighth sure
o' *you*—show us your face, a-bouchal—" in a
voice sufficiently low to be lost to the sisters—
" yes—it 's your ownsef—but I won't be the
man to hould you here :—we know where you 're
to be had for the axin'. I 'll jest lave you to
them that gets their bread by ketchin' rogues o'
your sort—only be off, I say, out o' sighth an'
hearin' of her that one look from you 'ud kill an'
murther !—there—go your ways—" And the
soldier ran down a lane, and disappeared.

" An' come now, my poor sowls o' girls ;
come wid me ; an' let us go the wide world,
wherever we like, our ownsefs."

" Are you hurt, Peery, my poor boy ?"
asked Peggy, kindly.

" Sorrow as much as a scratch, Miss Peggy,
an', for a rason I know, that you won't tell any
body that 'ud be axin you—maybe it 's not the
first time we made a fool o' the bagnet. Wait
abit, an' let us put it up ; there, now ;" slinging it with a piece of cord at his back, in the
way his compatriots sling their sickles, or, as they
call them, " rapiin'-hooks," when they issue
forth, over land and sea, in quest of harvest,

work—" that 's snug ; an' when a handy smith
bates it out a little, an' makes it crooked, an'
puts teeth into its head, it 'ill save the price iv
a hook for the next sason, I 'm thinkin' ;—so,
come : sure I know where you want to go,
my pets."

" Then you know the way to the Brazen-
Head ?" asked Peggy.

" Know the way ? to be sure I——stop ; now
that I think of it, bad manners to me if I do.
But sure I know what you want there ; poor
Daniel, the father, is sick, an' ye can't make
him off ; so here 's to set out on the road,
any how : though, what way," in a low tone to
himself, " Peery Conolly no more knows, nor
if he war a gorçoon o' two months ould."

While he thus half soliloquized, (a habit to
which he was much addicted, and which gave
one of the reasons why he was regarded, " in
his own part o' the counthry," as " not right in
his mind," it being a prevalent opinion that all
deranged persons talked as much to themselves
as to others)—while thus employed, he was, in
turn, closely observed by an individual, who, if
dress and personal conformation did not deceive, might have been half masculine, half femi-

nine. She, however, laid claim to the honour
of being one of the softer sex. She was broad
built as a Dublin coal-heaver : she wore a man's
coat, buttoned close to the chin, a man's hat,
pressed flat in the crown, and forced over a
mob-cap, for she would assert female attire ; and
from the knees downward, a clumsily gathered
linsey-woolsey petticoat more decidedly intimated her pretensions. Under the hat and cap
appeared a red, weather-beaten, rough-featured
face. A flat, shallow basket was tucked under
her arm ; and about an inch of a black pipe
was held between her teeth.

" Whisht," said this questionable person to
herself, as she came to a dead stop ; " isn't that
Peery Conolly from Tipperary ? My sowl to
glory but it 's very like him in the back."

" Then you do not know the way, Peery ?" resumed Peggy, in evident distress, and perhaps
giving some scope to a dread even of her de-
fender, as old recollections came to her mind, and
she found herself completely in his power.

" I jist know as much about it, as if we dhrop-
ped from the clouds, out, this moment : but if
we could come on the road to Molly Houlli-
han, that stops wid a Misthress Taffy, a snug

woman, in Pill Lane, she'd bring us to it, no doubt."

" It's his ownsef," resumed the person al-luded to, now much nearer ˙to him than he thought of; " an' he's talkin' o' me, the poor boy."

" But never mind id, Miss Peggy an' Miss Anty, a-lanna; the' mornin' 'ill soon be shinin' out, as well as it can, in this place, an' for the time o' the year that's in id; an' sure we have tongues in our heads: don't be a bit afeard; there's neither hurt nor harum, shame nor shkandle, 'ill come next or near ye, while Peery's four bones hould together."

" Wait now," continued Molly, " until I take a shtart out iv him."

She hastily put up her black pipe-stump; wiped her mouth with the sleeve of her man's coat; caught her flat basket with both hands; raised it aloft; and having stept softly after Peery, as he turned his back and talked on, complimented his shoulders with such a crash of the wickerwork as made him shout aloud— thus greeting him, during her salute—" Musha, bad end to you, for one Peery Conolly; an' is id there you are, this mornin'?"

" Where 's the sprong ?" cried Peery, un-
slinging the bayonet, and wheeling round ; but
looking closer, he soon changed his manner ;
and contenting himself with an open-handed,
long drawn " dowce," across the side of her
head, affectionately piped out — " Arragh,
Molly, how 's every inch o' you ?"

" Brave an' hearty, gossip ;—an' so, here I
find you ?"

" My mother's son ;" and the minor love-
salutes took place.

" Who 's them by the side o' you, Peery ?"
glancing suspiciously, with the air of a woman
of untainted virtue, at the two girls, who shrank
back from her in some terror.

" Whisht, it 's a shame for you, Molly, so it
is; I 'll tell you who they are ; an' you 're jist in
time to lend a helpin' hand."

" Why, what concarn would I have wid sich
as them, why ?"

" Bother, Molly, I 'll show you the ups an'
downs iv id."

Every thing now created suspicion in the
breasts of the two poor girls. It appeared to
Anty that some further mischief was intended,
she became again ill, and sank suddenly in
Peggy's arms.

" Is that id ?' resumed Molly, interrupting
and breaking away from Peery's story, and gal-
loping to them; " musha, musha, my poor
childher—och, murther, here's one o' them, all
as one as stone-dead !"

" Molly, a sthore," whined Peery, " jist put
an arum round her, I'm shy to do id."

" Oh, if you have Christian hearts, help us !"
cried Peggy, " we are strangers here, without
money or friends; our father is dying or dead,
in Dublin, we don't know where, and we can't
find him ; give my little sister a help, and God
will reward you."

" I 'll tell you what, a-vourneen," answered
Molly, " I lives hard by in a dacent cellar ; jist
come home wid us, you an' your darlin' little
sisther, stop till the broad day wid poor Molly
Houlihan, an' if she war to pop the last o' the
duds on her back" (no great promise, however)
" ye must have the good bed an' somethin' to rise
your hearts, an' all wid the cead mille phaltea,
as we used to say among the poor hills—"

" Yes, a-graw," urged Peery, " an' sorrow's the sowl but Molly 'ill come fornent you—"

" Yes, an' whin the christhens are all up an'
kickin', an' when the little girl is as well as

ever, sure we'll make off the ould daddy for
you, dead or alive, if he's to be had in Dublin
town; come, *a-chorra-ma-chree;*" seizing Anty.

"Well," said Peggy, still hesitating, "I'll
take your kind offer, but, for the love of God,
do not deceive us! If you are not a proper
woman, if you do not mean us well—listen to
me: there's no wish in my heart to vex you,
I'm sorry if I have; but 'tis all the terror!
We have already suffered so much and by such
people! Good, blessed woman, take pity on
us! do not bring us to harm! on my two bare
knees I pray to you—let us lie down here in the
streets, any where, any thing, sooner than that
—for we are honest people's children, and we
abhor a sin."

"The short an' the long is, a-vourneen, I
see somebody very like the sodger comin' back,
wid his faction to help him, so make the best
o' your way at once wid Molly," said Peery,
as, looking down the street, he fastened the
bayonet on the stick.

Peggy started up from her knees and called
to Molly to come away: "I trust you, I do
indeed," she added, "I put Anty into your
hands; come, I'll help you to bear her off."

" Come then, my darlins ; decaive you ?"

" Whisht, Molly, that's all bother, you know," remonstrated Peery ; " if there's a human crature can look on *them*, an' mane them wrong at the same time, my curse, an' the curse o' Saint Pathrick, an' their own mother's curse on their heads, that's all. Run, my darlins, they see us !"

" Quick, quick !" cried Peggy ; but she stopped an instant to say—" Woman ! God so do to you and yours, as you do to us !"

" Wid all my heart !" answered Molly, and between them they hurried away with Anty, leaving Peery to brave the rallied anger of the person he had treated so unceremoniously a few minutes before, and who now came back, indeed, as he suspected, attended by a group of ruffianly fellows in ordinary costume.

CHAPTER XI.

EARLY upon the morning after Anty's sudden
departure from home, David Shearman, having
returned to his father's sooner than he expected,
walked over to visit Peggy. He found Cauth
Flannigan in a state of the greatest terror and
consternation. Her story was that the house
had been broken into during the night, and robbed of all the money in it, and of her "young
misthress, Miss Anty," too; for, unaware of
the previous presence of the guest whom Anty
had secreted, the poor girl could suppose nothing else, when, getting up at her usual hour,
she found the desk open, and Anty gone.
To his repeated questions, David Shearman
then, for the first time, learned that Peggy was
also from home, and Daniel Nowlan before her;
and the young man stood stupified with horror
and alarm, not knowing what to do, when Mr.

Long's confidential steward entered the house, and stunned him by telling another strange story.

Some days before, the man said, his master had received, from a person who formed one of the gang, private information that Long Hall was to be plundered on a particular night, and its proprietor deprived of life. The informer wrote his letter first in the hopes of reward, next with a clause for self-preservation. He stipulated that, if Mr. Long would pledge his honour to give him a thousand pounds and a promise of pardon, he would enable him to save property and life, and to detect the plotters. Mr. Long acceded by letter to his terms, and the man, no longer disguising his name, which was Studs, wrote back another line, appointing a meeting with Mr. Long, in Dublin, from the neighbourhood of which city, he said, the gang were to go down to the country.

Mr. Long accordingly went to Dublin in great privacy, arranging to write back to his steward the necessary advices; and that confidential servant soon got from him a notice of the night when the house was to be attacked, with other particulars. The gang were to consist of four; one a woman of the name of Maggy Nowlan, whom Mr. Long and the steward knew; two men from Dublin, whom Studs also named; and a fourth man, a soldier, whom he would not further describe, but, he added, whom Mr. Long would recognize when they met face to face. After the receipt of this letter, the steward set about taking the measures previously agreed on between him and the writer, and which it again enforced. With the utmost secrecy, a party of military were obtained from Nenagh, and concealed in the house; and a man who, before Mr. Long left the country, had, the steward believed; intimated some further knowledge of the plot, and particularly of the identity of the soldier whom Studs declined to name, went off to join Mr. Long in Dublin. This person young Mr. Shearman well knew; Peery Conolly. And now came the end of the story. The appointed night arrived. Some of the soldiers were stationed in the house; some out of sight, around it. The lights were extinguished; and when every thing gave signs of repose, the robbers were punctually heard making way through a lower window. Having been allowed to gain the inside of the house, and to commence their plundering, little exertion was necessary in apprehending them. But the woman and the two Dublin thieves alone appeared. The mysterious soldier had not at all come in view. When closely questioned about him, the prisoners would give no answer, except that he had spent part of the night in Daniel Nowlan's house; and it was this hint that sent over the steward the night before, when he met Anty on the road, and that also caused the present meeting between him and David Shearman.

When applied to on the subject, then and now, poor Cauth warmly resisted, of course, such a base insinuation; and the sole new information she could supply only served farther to perplex the zealous steward. What was best to be done none of them could conjecture; what steps the steward was to take for securing this unknown person, or David to discover his Peggy and her sister, or Cauth to get every body back, and to keep the life in " her poor ould misthress of all," who lay at death's door, stunned and terrified by what she heard, and only able to scream aloud or scold her attendant.

At length, guided by Cauth's mentioning

the Brazen Head, in Dublin, as the place to
which, no doubt, Peggy had gone after her
father, David formed his resolution. He ran
home for his best horse. As he got into the saddle, his father's information, previously supplied
to Peggy, but which he had not before received, made him sure that all would be right;
and hastily shaking hands with his amazed parent, he galloped off along the Dublin road,
determined to take fresh horses whenever he
could find them, and not stop, night or day,
until he should reach the metropolis. And
accordingly, some hours before the sisters entered Dublin, David had gained it. He knew
the old Brazen Head in Bridge-street very well;
it was a great resort for honest country-folk,
from every part of Ireland: and he had once or
twice before experienced its quiet, old-fashioned
accommodation. In a short time, therefore, he
was thundering at its massive door; nor had he
to thunder long. "Boots" was up, as in duty
bound, to welcome such travellers as might
arrive by the six o'clock coaches from country
parts, and who, at such an hour, in the depths
of winter, could scarce expect the homage of
a more sprightly attendant of the other sex.

" Was there a Mr. Nowlan in the house ?"
David asked, as soon as the half-alive, pallid
creature appeared, with an inch of candle in his
hand. " Yes, there was." " An old gentleman ?" " Yes." " From the country ?" " Yes,
indeed." " Had he been ill ?" " He had, but
was better, and walking about now." " Was
there a young lady with him—his daughter ?"
" No." " No ?" " No, in troth ; not a living
soul belonging to him, man, woman, or child."
David wrung his hands and stamped about.
Peggy ought to have been in Dublin since that
hour the previous morning. What had become
of her ? He asked the number of Daniel Nowlan's room ; rushed up stairs ; awoke the old
man ; and, with little precaution, told him of
Peggy's departure to seek him, two nights before, and of the sudden and unaccountable
disappearance of Anty on the night following.

Daniel Nowlan, weak and exhausted as he
was, fainted at the tidings. When restored
to his senses, his grief was so childish, that
it reminded David of the necessity to master
his own passion, and summon up his strength
of mind. He feared the old man's relapse
into the sickness from which he had just

recovered ; and to send for medical assistance was his first proceeding. But when the physician arrived, his fears became removed ; and after Daniel Nowlan took some quieting medicine, his young friend prevailed on him to have hope, and bend his thoughts to consider what was best to be attempted.

Before they proceeded to the urgent matter in hand, however, David ascertained that all attempts to find out the sailor who had called himself John Nowlan, had hitherto proved abortive. Then they partook of a hasty and scarce needful breakfast ; and when it was broad daylight, got into a hackney coach, and drove to the office of the Limerick mail, in Dawson-street.

Immediate, though still torturing information here awaited them. They learned that the coach in which Peggy had come up, had broken down near Dublin ; that she had been overlooked in the confusion, and not since heard of ; and the guard of the other coach, which had conveyed Anty from the country, further supplied an account of the meeting between the sisters, near Richmond Barracks, and of their having been left, seemingly under the protection of a soldier, before the gate. To Richmond Barracks David and Daniel next repaired. The sentinel who had been on duty at the time in question, confirmed the account of the guard, adding that they had walked on into town with the soldier spoken of, and whose name was Tims.

Upon this, David proposed that he and the old man should part, and go separately into every public house on their way towards town, and afterwards meet at a police office, of which he inquired the situation and address, and gave both to Daniel. His advice seemed good; it was acceded to by the father, and they parted.

With a flushed cheek, parched lips, streaming eyes, and his white hair flying neglected from under his broad-brimmed, country-farmer hat, Daniel Nowlan went into many public houses, asking vague and abrupt questions about his children, which some answered with concern, some with indifference, some with ridicule, and all without satisfaction to him. Wherever he met a soldier in the street, to him he particularly and most earnestly directed his enquiries; still uselessly, however: until, after walking a good way down Thomas street, two others, whom, as they stood talking on the flag-way, he suddenly addressed, seemed peculiarly moved by his questions.

But as we now turn upon the pivot of our history, it will be needful, with the reader's indulgence, to preface the interview between Daniel Nowlan and these two soldiers, with some conversation that passed between themselves before he came up.

They had accidentally met, in mutual agitation, though of different kinds. One, who was unarmed, almost ran along the street, his face inflamed by half-suppressed rage, and his eyes often cast behind, as if to note whether or no he was pursued. The other also moved, in an opposite direction, at a very quick pace, and his features were also disturbed, but it would seem rather with anxiety and terror than with anger. So much were both absorbed, and so rapid their motion, that they had nearly jostled against each other ere a recognition took place. Then they stared for some seconds in silence, like old friends met to enter upon a business that must break their friendship for ever.

" I was looking for you, Frank," began the

soldier whose feelings appeared to be those of great anxiety.

" Hush !" he was answered in a whisper, " how often have you promised to sink that name ?"

" Tell me in one word," continued his comrade, gasping—" what have you done with the young woman given into your care at the Barrack-gate this morning ? That you are the man I have been informed, by the sentinel in whose charge I left her."

" Brought her where she wanted to go, to be sure ; you 'll find her at the Brazen Head : good-b'ye. I have some business in hand."

" Stop, Sir ; I don't believe your story."

" Indeed ? and why so ?" recovering his habitual self-possession.

" Did you know who she was ?" demanded the other slowly, as he fixed a look on Frank.

" No ; how the devil could I ?—'twas pitch-dark, and her head so muffled up ; and I in no humour for a frolic ; I know nothing at all about her."

" I don't believe you again, Sir."

" You don't, don't you ? let me pass, I say."

" A word first, listen well to me. When, after nearly two years of suffering and sorrow, I met you in the Indies, the very day you took the king's bounty and entered the same regiment with me, you told me *this* of home. You said your uncle had turned you out for marrying Peggy Nowlan; that your father would not receive you; that Peggy herself was unkind and ungrateful to you; that you had no means of earning a shilling for her or yourself; that, in fact, you were starving ; that, forced to the last resource, you embarked for the chances of the patriotic struggle in South America; and failing in that, worked your way to where I met you, and were then glad to enlist as a private soldier."

" Ay; well ?"

" Listen, I say. After leaving the young woman at the Barrack-gate this morning, only a few hours ago, do you know where I went, and on what kind of duty ?"

" No; I had but just walked up to the gate, returning from furlough,—was not in the barracks when you were first called out, and, until I went into town with the girl, heard nothing of the matter."

" Well ; so far I trust you. Did you see your uncle on furlough, Frank, and throw yourself on your knees to him, as you said you would ? But, no matter for your answer. Hear me on. Hear on what duty I went out of Dublin, with the serjeant's guard, this morning. We went, led by a peace-officer, and that very uncle, Frank."

" Damnation ! " interrupted the hearer, thrown off his guard, and starting back.

" By that very uncle, to take into custody two old friends of yours, in the lone house, about fifteen miles from town."

" Whom do you mean ? *Did* you take them ?"

" They are now in Kilmainham jail, charged as accomplices before the fact in a robbery at Long Hall, the night before the last ; so that, while Maggy lies in Nenagh prison, along with her two companions, on the spot, we have here secured her wretched mother and brother—"

" I thought as much, by —— ! I knew when that scoundrel turned back, almost at the first stage, it was to peach !—it 's all out now ! no use of bamming you any longer—help me to cut off, that's all; I'm in your hands. Tell me—has Studs blabbed of me to my uncle?"

" No. He declined at first to mention your name, and this morning it was out of his power to do so. Carey and her son had murdered him."

" Say you so? the best of their good deeds, by ——! They found out the villain's treachery of course. Where did it happen?"

" We found the body in a coal-hole in their house."

" Well, good-b'ye, there's but a run for it: will my uncle prosecute me?"

" Stop, I charge you again, but not on that account. In the horror and revulsion of my heart I leave you to your God for that: and fear nothing from your uncle, he does not yet know who the soldier is that Studs refused to name. I alone, Frank, exclusive of your infernal accomplices, guess you to be the man, because I know you went on furlough to the country. And that brings me to my own point—"

" How did you hear all about the swag at Long-Hall?"

" From your uncle himself. When I went back to my party, a few hours ago, I knew him the moment I looked upon him ; and, having taken an opportunity to say who I was, he told me all the facts I have told you. He told me more, Frank. He told me the real causes of your sudden flight from Ireland, and about the deceptive and shocking letter too, yet unexplained to him, which you wrote from London."

" There was no deception in that letter. I wrote it a few days before the appointed day when, according to the black-cap, I was to swing ; and, without my expecting it,—indeed, without my caring,—a change of the sentence into transportation for life, which they called a merciful pardon, came to hand."

" And—heavenly Judge of hearts !" exclaimed his companion, much agitated, " from that eventual sentence, which was indeed merciful, you escaped, I suppose, to the place where I met you abroad ?"

" The good preacher is shocked," sneered Frank ; " why, Sir, having a wit to do it, would you have me remain the wretch I was ?"

" Horrible !" clasping his hands, as he stepped back, " all this is more dreadful even than

I had heard or thought. I had hoped that letter was only a falsehood. I had hoped the husband of Peggy Nowlan—"

" Pshaw, Sir, let me pass on, I say, or keep me here if you like or dare ; for her sake, keep me here : you see I have not a moment to lose ; between Maggy, her mother, and brother, and the two other bunglers, my name and identity cannot remain unknown from my uncle and the world, and, considering this, act as you please."

" Even supposing your accomplices to be silent, there is one man, who, the moment he sees your uncle, from whom he is now separated by chance, will make the discovery : he saw you lurking about Long Hall for some days before the attempted robbery."

" I guess the man ; his name is Conolly."

" It is. But I wish not, for all we have talked about, to be the person to ensure your fate to you. I bid you stay only to satisfy me on the first question I asked, and out of which our talk has grown. When I told you I did not believe your assertion of the young woman you had in charge being unknown to you, I was bound to show you why, by showing you that your uncle's account of your flight from Ireland was different from your own, and that, by your deliberate falsehoods you had forfeited all claims to my belief: additional reasons now appear why I should doubt you. Yes, Frank; *you* knew who she was, although *I* sat by her side in the post-chaise for an hour without guessing the fact. You are not the man, supposing the very halter round your neck, to walk side by side with an innocent country girl, and not gloat your vicious curiosity by a view of her features, at the least. I believe, that while nature or habit has cursed you with a heart fit for any act of crime, your loose love of women is, perhaps, your master-passion. You knew her, I say; what have you done with her? Recollecting all the past, and my newly acquired knowledge of the things you can do, there is room, Frank, for dreadful suspicions of the way in which you may have disposed of her. Come with me to the place where you say you left her."

" That I cannot do."

" You had better. The only, or the strongest reason why I do not hold you here till the civil officers come up, is on her account; but on her account also,—and, oh God ! perhaps in a more serious sense! I *must* detain you until—Eternal Providence!"—the speaker interrupted himself, and catching Frank's arm, stared up the street, as if a spectre approached him.

"What's the matter now? why do you turn white and shake so? Let go my arm."

"Look look, Frank Adams—my father!"

Daniel Nowlan, indeed, at that moment came up.

"Let us pass him, or turn off—come—I was not prepared for this, so soon—I cannot face the old man now; turn back with me."

But the afflicted father did not allow them time to walk away.

"I ask pardon, gentlemen," he said, in a hoarse, exhausted voice, "a thousand pardons," getting before them and confronting them, "but I am looking for my child."

"Sir?" interrupted John Nowlan, meaning to affect a tone of indifference, while his pale features, and particularly his mouth, worked with a choking emotion.

"I meant no offence, gentlemen, and I'm sorry——," pulling off, in the weakness of his mind and body, his broad-brimmed hat.

"Put it on, Sir! put it on! it is not to us,

or such as us, your grey hairs should be exposed," again interrupted John.

"Thanks, Sir," bowing repeatedly, "many,
many thanks: I see you pity me, and, God
knows, I want it; for the ould heart in my
body within is a'most broke, at last;—oh, gentlemen, you're sodgers, and you ought to have
a mind to help the wake an' the disthressed: an'
indeed, indeed, I'm wake an' disthressed."

"How's that, Sir? Is it poverty? you do
not seem a poor man."

"Of this world's wealth I have enough; of
its joys, too, God blessed me with an arly store;
but as arly—welcome be the will o' the Lord—
began to take from it. I had a son, Sir, an
only son——but no matther, that's not it; an'
I'm botherin' you, as I see by your looks. My
present business in Dublin is this:—I came here
to look afther that son, now not seen this many
a long day: I tuck the sickness; it a'most
brought me to death's dour: my family knew
nothing of it till a few days agone; then, Sir,
my daughther Peggy left home to see afther
me, but is now in Dublin, an' never came next
or near me, an' we can't make her off. It's said
she was last seen wid a sodger, Sir, an' that's

why I make bould to come fornent you; an'
more, agin——"

"Has she not yet called at the place you
stopped, Sir?" interrupted John.

"Avoch, Sir, no; never a call."

"You see, Frank," speaking aside to him,
"here is proof of my suspicion; so now, at
least, account to me for my sister."

"Don't, gentlemen, don't lave me yet,"
resumed the old man, following them; "I was
a-goin' to tell you more o' my thrials;—an' here
they are.   The night after Peggy left the poor
cabin, sure it was robbed an' spoiled of all the
money in it; an'—och, sad is my heart to say
it!—robbed of my other poor child, at the
same time——"

"God of heaven!—what's that you say,
Sir?"

"Kind gentleman," continued Daniel Nowlan,
while he clasped his hands, cried like a child,
and shook all over—"it's the thruth I'm tellin'
you—the man that took my goold took my
darlin' Anty, too: an' some that are as bad as
he, an' that went down to the poor counthry
wid him on another robbery, it seems,—why,
them people say that he was dhressed like one

o' ye, gentlemen, a sodger like—but I mane no offence again—an' I ax pardon again ; for it 's sure I am he was no sodger, nor no thrue man neither to do what he done."

After a moment's pause, during which he made a great effort to keep in his rising passion, John Nowlan again took Frank aside. " I always hoped, Frank," he began, in a conciliating tone, " and I try to hope still, that you were and are a fair fellow on some points: I think, at least, that you will not continue the misery you see before you, and of which you have been the cause:—where are my sisters ? where, in particular, is poor little Anty ?"

" By Heaven, I know nothing of either."

" Don't outface me, Frank. This is a desperate case. Don't make me as desperate."

" Gentlemen," resumed Daniel Nowlan, a second time breaking in on their private discourse, " maybe, it 's talkin' about it to thry an' help me ye are; an' so I ought to tell ye a word more. Afther Anty left home, she was seen along wid Peggy, however they came together, near the gate of Richmond barracks, an' they say the two girls went off, arm in arm, wid the sodger I first spoke to ye about."

" Well," resumed John, in a whisper, " I do not pretend to understand all your ways, or all that has happened, Frank ; but, by this last account, both my sisters are traced into your hands : what have you done with them ? Come, man, I do not believe you are so bad as to turn the deaf ear to my question : we have been comrades, Frank, in toil and danger—we have been friends, brothers—" wringing his hand hard, while his voice failed and the tears flowed—" where are they ?"

" I will answer you truly, on my life and soul. When I brought them into a house—"

" *A house !*—but go on."

" A ruffianly country fellow forced them from me, and I have not heard of them since."

" Take care, Frank, I say again. In this matter you see, if shame or ruin in any shape has come upon them, I am a party to it. So come, where are they ?"

" I have already answered."

" Monster ! where are they ?" collaring him, and speaking in the loudest tone, while old Daniel Nowlan now began to look on John in some misgiving : " where is your first victim, poor Peggy ? and where is the other innocent girl? where are my sisters? tell me now, man! the truth in one word!"

"Who calls them his sisters?" asked Daniel, as he stood trembling with clasped hands, and gazing, through tears, into John's face; "the Lord be praised for all his wondhers and blessins'! praise be to God! Is it their brother and my poor lost boy, John Nowlan?"

"Father, it is!" turning to him, as he still held Frank—"the wretched outcast, John Nowlan, who is at last punished in a ten-fold curse for all his doings! I dare not kneel down to you yet, father,—though I will,—I dare not yet ask you to forgive me; something is to go before that—"

The old man, rendered almost insensible by his weakness and many sudden emotions, took off his hat, dropped, half stupified, on his knees in the street, and with extended arms and pallid lips, continued to mutter, "Praise be to God! the Lord be praised for all things!" A crowd began to stop and gather round.

"Deceitful, treacherous, and lying villain!" pursued John to Frank, "keep me no longer in this doubt! give me up this old man's daughters! Do they yet live for his grey hairs,

or live worthy of them? Answer me! Dare not
repeat a word of your lying story! this moment
lead me to them! this moment! or if you do
not, or if they are not forthcoming, or if there
has fallen upon that innocent child one spot,
one stain, though no more than the touch of
one vile finger, by Him that is to judge between
us, I will wrench you limb from limb, joint
from joint!"

"Let me go! I say, I have answered you."

"Liar and ruffian!" drawing his bayonet.

"John! John Nowlan, a-vich!" here cried
his father, moving on his knees, and encircling
those of his son with his arms: "John, ma-
bouchal, never mind him a-while, but turn to
the poor father; give me your two hands, and
let me kiss your lips, John Nowlan, my son,
my own an' only boy!"

He clasped John's knees close. The sinner
uttered a heart-rending cry, and only pausing
to dart his bayonet into its sheath, and to say
to the by-standers "Secure him! he is a robber! a murderer! all that is bad!" disengaged
his father's arms, lifted him up, received his
embrace, and then flung himself lowly and in
great agony at his feet.

In turn, the old man instantly strove to raise him; some of the spectators assisted him, for he was badly able himself; and again they were locked in each other's arms.

"Don't cry, a-cuishla, don't, don't, it 'll all pass by, an' we 'll live to see it; we 'll buy you out from among the sodgers, an' the Father in heaven 'ill forgive you as I do, for my sake an' my prayers, an' for all our sakes; an' when Peggy an' Anty is found, an' brought home again—"

John's attention was here diverted by Frank's voice, and his struggles to escape. He darted upon him like a tiger.

"Keep him fast!" he cried.

"You needn't tell us to do that," said a man in a strong English accent; "he is now my prisoner; I have been looking him up some time, and have just arrested him on a warrant from a London office, for getting tired of Van's Land before his time; but, whatever is your concern with the youth, you can attend him to the next of your own police-offices at hand."

"Yes, that is the only way left; and now the loss of a second's time is a sin against Heaven. Come, man, no resisting! one struggle,

one word, and I'll stab you to the heart! come
and show me that, through you, I have not
shamed, hideously shamed, or murdered my
own sisters, the children of my own mother!
and that the curse of father, mother, and sisters
—of man and nature—is not, along with every
thing else, fallen upon my head!—Come, Sir,"
turning to his father, while he held Frank hard;
and Daniel Nowlan, and a commiserating or
wondering crowd, accordingly followed him,
Frank, and the London officer.

CHAPTER XII.

In the kind of place to which they hastened, we are induced to anticipate their probable arrival, by raising the curtain of our
last act upon other individuals of our history,
about whom, we respectfully hope, our kind
readers are, conjointly with them and us, much
interested.

The scene is, indeed, a police-office, to be
found on a certain quay of that city of quays,
Dublin. Upon the bench, or rather behind the
counter, is seated, or rather stands, a learned,
amiable, but somewhat deaf old gentleman,
whose early profession of barrister was not so
all-engrossing as to hinder him, about the me-
ridian of life, from accepting the at least certain and most useful appointment of police
magistrate. By his side are his clerk, and
occasionally one or two confidential officers.

Before him a crowd of watchmen, " constables of the watch," and the jumbled and curious street-sweepings of the last night, all awaiting either to make charges or to meet them as they can ; but immediately at the side of the counter, fronting the worthy magistrate, we recognize two acquaintances, Peery Conolly and Molly Houlihan, and by their sides, Anty Nowlan, sitting in a very weak state upon a chair kindly provided for her, and Peggy Nowlan, standing over her and holding her hand.

At the moment when we look in, Peery and Molly are, with great energy, alternately addressing the bench.

" Yes, your reverance," says Peery.

" Whisht, Peery, he's no reverance ; he axes pardon, my lard ; he 's a gawk from the counthry ; yes, my lard."

" Yes, to what?" demanded the magistrate, who, by holding his hand scoop-wise to his ear, required no interpreter to hear the loud tones in which he was addressed : " yes, to what, good people ? Pray listen a moment."

" Oh, by all manes, your honour," assented Peery.

" Spake your mind out, my lard," added
Molly, both in a patronizing tone.

" Thank you. I wish, then, to see if I comprehend you. You were at last conveying the
young woman to your lodgings, you say,
and—"

" Yes, plase your lardship," taking up
Molly's version of the title, " an' that's what riz
the whole o' the last scrimmage on us," interrupted Peery.

" The what ?"

" He 's only a simple-tongued gorçoon, just
cum up, my lard; he manes the 'ruction, like.''

" And what does the 'ruction mean ?"

" Lard save us, sure every christhen-sowl on
Ireland's ground knows that—the fight, my
lard."

" Yes—that's it ;—yes, your honour," pleaded
Peery ; " Molly was jist for gittin' 'em down the
steps o' the cellar, when, up comes Misther
Sodger again wid his faction,—' An' now, you
baste,' says he to myself, ' I 'll have your Irish
life, so I will.'—' Will you ?' says I—an' I up
to him wid the sprong to the end o' the stick."

" What do you call the sprong ?"

" Hould your whisht, I tell you, Peery, an'
let me discoorse his lardship ;—jist on the
turn o' the stairs, my lard—"

" No, Molly, you're wrong all over ; you war
on the flure, when it happened—"

" Musha, Peery, no—; see, my lard—"

" I hear a great many strange words, but I
can see nothing : stand back ; and you, my
good girl—the elder girl, I mean—pray relate
this last part of the case, as briefly as possible."

" I will tell you, Sir, if I am able."

" Take time ; do not distress yourself."

" Thank 'ee, Sir. Before we got to this good
woman's place, we saw Peery Conolly running
towards us, and the soldier and his friends
following him. Hurrying down the cellar, she
and me, with my little sister between us, I
heard angry words above, where Peery stood to
bear the brunt, and a noise of such things as
that," pointing to Peery's bayonet, which,
mounted upon his cudgel, he stoutly shoulder-
ed—" I knew they were pressing him too hard ;
I screamed and ran up ; other good people came
by, and the soldier and his faction ran away."

" Every word of id, jist as id turned out,"
said the hero of the tale.

"As pat as A. B. C." assented Molly, slapping one palm upon the other.

"Silence!" cried the magistrate, who, though deaf, was inconvenienced by the smack:—"did you then remain in her lodging?"

"May all good be multiplied ten-fold to her and hers, Sir!—I did; at first, to tell the truth, in doubts of her, the place was so poor and mean; but she undeceived me well, by the comfort she afforded to my sister and me."

"An' Peery, over head, in the sthreet, wid the bagnet on his shouldher, your lardship," added Molly.

"Your business here, then, is to prosecute the persons who have insulted you?"

"No, Sir; we forgive them, and hope they may be forgiven."

"No, my lard," said Peery; "the *meeroch'* 'ill come on 'em soon enough, widout our helpin' id; maybe we 'd do a thing to 'em wid our sticks," throwing himself into position, gently flourishing the cudgel, and smiling confidently on the magistrate—"when thrashin' 'ud be good for 'em; but that 's no raison we 'd turn informers; they shan't have that to throw in our teeth, when we get home to Tipperary." And

Peery drew up, full of indignation that it should be supposed he would put his greatest foe into the fangs of the law.

"It has been mentioned to me that you came. to Dublin to seek your father—perhaps you wish this office to assist you?"

"Oh, Sir!"—Peggy could get no farther.

"Avoch, no, Sir; too late for that," said Peery.

"Then what do you all want?"

"I ask your pardon, Sir," resumed Peggy, trying to check her tears;—"I'll try to tell you about it. This poor faithful boy went at my request to seek my father at the place where we knew he slept, and came back with word that a few moments before he had gone away in a carriage with another person, we didn't know where; home, we think and hope; and so, Sir, as I lost all my money on the road, and my sister lost all her's in that wicked house—and as we are quite strangers in Dublin, we came. here—indeed this charitable woman brought us here—to ask—oh, Anty, Anty!"—interrupting herself, and overcome by a sense of her forlorn situation, she fell on her sister's neck.

"Arrah, look at 'em," blubbered Peery, "an' your lardship sees how it is wid the cratures;

that's the up an' down iv id; they have nothin'
more to do in Dublin town; an' we want to
send 'em home again, safe an' sound. The little
Molly an' I had was at their sarvice, only they
wouldn't hear of that; and there's a great gin-
tleman, a friend o' my own, in the town, or
nigh-hand to it, that 'ud give them or me a
help, only myself doesn't know where to face
to look for him, now that we 're onct asundher;
so here we up and we come to beg a bit for 'em;
an' if your reverance 'ud jist bid the dhriver
give 'em a lift on the sate, for nothing but out
iv love or pity, like————"

"Do, my lard, an' may you have a long life,
a good death, an' a favourable judgment!" interrupted Molly, while tears ran down her harsh
man's face.

"'Tis a sad story enough; yet there are so
many impositions—in fact, if the young women
can get any one to give them a character ————"

"Och, I 'll go bail for 'em," cried Molly.

"And who are you, pray?"

"I 'm a basket, my lard," dropping a curtsey.

"A basket!"

"Yes, my lard; to a Misthess Taffey."

"She manes that she stops wid a Misthess

Taffey, your lardship, a snug woman, in Pill-
lane; and Molly is a gossip o' my own; an'
I 'll go bail for *her,* and for them too, along wid
her."

" And who are you, too?"

" Peery Conolly, my lard," judiciously interrupted Molly, as Peery's stick, bayonet and all,
began to describe some flourishes round his head,
and his nether limbs to shuffle; both movements
ominous of the usual rhyming answer, in his
usual way—" Peery Conolly, a dacent father's
and mother's child, though I say it."

" Deserted from Captain Rock, I presume."

" No, in throth, then, your honour," replied
Peery, at once changing into a dry, simple sub-
tlety of voice, face and manner;—" I 'll never
deny there was a thrifle o' that same goin' on in
the place; but myself never loved nor liked
their night-walkin', from a boy up; and sure
they war for swarin' me; an' when I wouldn't,
an' for fear they'd be angry, faith I cums away
from them all to where's there's pace an' quiet-
ness; so there's the holy and blessed thruth,
your honour, since your honour put us on
sayin' id."

" Well, we shall not question your loyalty,

though we may take that freedom with your simplicity ; and, on reflection, your respectable bail will do. Here," to an officer, " hold this money, and see the poor girls safe out of town."

" Glory to you !" screamed Molly.

" Long may you reign !" chimed Peery ; "an' come now, a-vourneens ; we 'll have you safe back, any how—Murther !—an interruption," as he glanced to the door, "murther in Irish ! stand out o' the way, there ! hurroo !"

With one of his hop-step-and-jumps, Peery hurled himself through the people between him and the door, and instantly re-entered, prancing and capering round Daniel Nowlan, and making the peaceful office ring to his egotistical song, which the officers in vain tried to quell.

" Do you know who brought you a bit of the road in the shay, this morning, Peggy, a corrama-chree ?" asked the old man, smiling through his tears, after long embraces had been interchanged between him and his daughters.

She was about to answer, when another bound and another cry from Peery, and the question of—" What brings any thievin' sodger here ?" again diverted her attention to the door ; and, looking up, John Nowlan appeared leaning against the jamb, pale, trembling, and, his eyes fixed on his sisters, gasping with smothered emotion. At first they did not know him; and there was a pause, during which Peery added, "Where's the sprong?" and approached the supposed intruder.

" Softly, man, softly," whispered John, beckoning him; " come here, let me hold you; I can hardly stand; I am their brother, John Nowlan."

" Och, mille murthers! here, lane your best on me, poor boy! poor priest John!"

" They will not know me—do you think they will ?"

Peggy had been slowly advancing, her eyes distended and fixed on him; her face set; he breathed hard; his surprise and agony were declared in broken and wheezing sounds that " stuck i' the throat:" she came nearer; he extended his arms; she fell in them with a joyful scream.

" That's your brother John, Anty," resumed old Daniel, as Anty looked and wondered.

"That man, Sir! oh, it must be true, for Peggy clings close to him, and you know him too, Sir; but, dear father, you do not know the great re-

lief this gives me ; another time you shall. Now
must not I, also, embrace my poor brother ?"

The father led her to his arms. Another
yell burst from Peery : " Where 's the sprong
now, in arnest ?" he cried out. In wonder, terror, and, from different reasons, common abhor-
rence, the two sisters clung to their brother, as
the miserable Frank passed to the counter, his
face haggard, his eyes staring, and his step
uneven.

John Nowlan, with permission of the magistrate, removed his father and sisters to a private
room, by which precaution they were saved from
witnessing the horrors that ensued.

The officer, in whose custody Frank had entered, was about to lay his charges before the
magistrate, when the appearance of a third
party interrupted him; namely, Mr. Long,
and his civil authorities, with Maggy Nowlan's
mother, Mrs. Carey, and her son Phil. When
Mr. Long beheld his nephew, horror seemed
to fix him to the spot; nor did the poor
wretch himself remain unmoved. Peery Conolly had sidled towards him, and addressed him
in a confidential whisper.

" Why thin, tunder-an'-turf! what sort iv an ownshuck was you, at-all-at-all, to walk in here, of all places in the world wide? I didn't let out the laste word about you; an' if you have as much gumption in your head as a suckin' calf, you 'll bid good-b'ye to 'em all round, or not wait for that same, but run for your life—The Lord o' Heaven save us!"—suddenly interrupting himself, and stepping back, terrified at the expression of face with which his advice was received.

The culprit first fixed his eyes on those of the speaker with a deep, steady despair: his manacled hands slightly moved under his watch-coat; and then his eye contracted; every muscle of his face and body winced, and he drew in and bit his under lip, as if from a sudden sensitiveness of acute pain. The next moment, his features again relaxed; his eye began to grow fixed and glassy; he swayed from side to side, and would have fallen, but for the support of those near him.

As all looked on aghast, something dropped at his feet. The officer stooped, and took it up. It was a large clasp-knife, smeared with blood; and blood also trickled to the floor, as his person bent forward. Disguising his motions, beneath the loose watch-coat, he had, while staring into Peery Conolly's face, stabbed himself to the core of the heart.

After a moment, he raised his drooping head, and glared vacantly around, until his dulled eye rested on his trembling uncle : " All I could do for you, Sir," he gasped out, smiling hideously, " was this—it saves me from the hangman's hands."

He again fell forward. He was borne out : but, before he reached a neighbouring hospital, was a corpse.

When the confusion occasioned by this sudden catastrophe had somewhat subsided, Mr. Long, though shaken in his very soul, was obliged to proceed in his charges against Mrs. Carey and her son. The young murderer shivered with despair under the anticipation of his fate ; but his mother showed no emotion. Her clothes torn, and her hair dishevelled, she stood, with folded arms, upright and passive as a statue ; and her large and once beautiful black eye, full of the hyena character, that for many years had belonged to it, was fixed, unwinkingly, now on her accusers, now on the magistrate. She did not frown, but her calm, savage glare was appalling

" Wretched woman," said the magistrate, " do you not tremble ?"

" Find that out by your larnin'," folding her arms harder ; " or, here"—suddenly catching the hand of a near officer, and pressing his fingers upon her pulse ; " does yours bate fuller or evener ?" And when the man turned away in disgust, he related that the throb was steady and regular as that of innocence at rest.

Mr. Long, his sad and stern task over, sought the room whither John Nowlan had conveyed the old man and his sisters. David Shearman was now added to their circle. All left Dublin together.

———

" Dear Barnes,

" It was about a month after this day that, in my wanderings among the black Tipperary hills, I became acquainted with the Nowlans, and learned their history. John Nowlan was then suffering under the relapse of a fever, which, accompanied by racking pains in his bones, had seized him the day he crossed his father's threshold. When, about nine months after, I paid the family another visit, I found him restored to health, and, in a degree, to his peace of mind; once more engaged in studious pursuits, and once more habited in black. His misfortunes and experience had thrown a quiet sadness over him: and the humility of sin acknowledged and repented, stamped every feature of his face, and characterized his every look, tone, and motion. He told me he entertained hopes that he would soon be able to soothe his recollections of early crime and sorrow by the discharge of the duties of that sacred profession, to which, under the direction of Mr. Kennedy and his bishop, he was again permitted to look forward.

" Before I left Daniel Nowlan's truly hospitable roof, on this, my second visit, I had the pleasure of being bridesman to David Shearman, upon the auspicious night of his marriage with my gentle favourite, Peggy. She was married by Mr. Kennedy: Friar Shanaghan, after an excellent day's ' quest,' handing round the bridecake for his secular brother; and Mr. Long, at his own anxious request, gave her away. It was as merry a night as ever I passed. What with good cheer, dancing, and unlimited mirth on every hand, I was in such riotous spirits, that I whispered at Anty's ear

my hope of a speedy opportunity of dancing
at her wedding, also. The little rogue told
me, archly enough, ' it was a great shame,
so it was, to be putting such quare things into
a child's head :' but, when, by some pleasant
reasoning, I had led her to believe the contrary,
she engaged me at once to look out for her ;
adding, ' that if I didn't bring her one that
was too little, or one that was too big, or one
that was too old, or one that was too ugly, I
would not find her very hard to be pleased.'
We proceeded in much question and answer,
as to the precise kind of man she might really
prefer, and I found her, as yet, undetermined.
She did, indeed, with more of archness than I
suspected her for, give myself some hard knocks,
by way of jocular hints : in fact, Barnes, I will
talk with you upon this subject, as I consider
you a person of more experience in such matters than I am.

" A. O'H."

LONDON :
PRINTED BY S. AND R. BENTLEY, DORSET-STREET.